Second Chance Serenity

A COASTAL HOPE NOVEL

JESSICA ASHLEY

B.A.D.
PUBLISHING

B.A.D. PUBLISHING CO
believing in the power of reading

SECOND CHANCE SERENITY
Coastal Hope, book 3
By Jessica Ashley

Edited by HEA Author Services
Proofread by Dawn
Proofread by Tasha
Cover Design by Covers by Christian
Photographer: Wander Aguiar
Model: Kyle

Second Chance Serenity

He broke her heart. She needs protection. Can the two of them stay alive long enough to find their way back to each other?

The day Michael Anderson walked out on me was the day part of me died.

I loved him with everything I was, an eighteen-year-old girl ready to spend the rest of her life with the star of the football team. I'd had to learn to live without him. And I did. Sort of.

Unfortunately, just like my feelings for him, he didn't stay gone.

When someone tries to kill me outside the school where I work, it's Michael who comes to my rescue. The former Army Ranger turned bodyguard-for-hire is no longer the boy I'd loved but a man who has seen war.

A Note from the Author

""Then Peter came to him and asked, "Lord, how often should I forgive someone who sins against me? Seven times?" "No, not seven times," Jesus replied, "but seventy times seven"."
Matthew 18:21-22

Forgiveness is something that does not come easy to me.

It's not that I'm a grudge holder, or that I can't accept an apology, but when someone does something that I perceive to be against me—especially if it's not acknowledged—I struggle to let it go and move on.

And how foolish is it that I struggle with forgiving, yet I ask for it from our Savior? When I sin on a daily basis, sometimes not even being aware enough to know that I am doing something that goes against God?

The parable about the master and the servant is one I try to keep at the front of my mind **(it can be found in Matthew 18:23-35)** in moments where I am fighting against those intrusive thoughts telling me that I don't have to forgive. That the transgressions carried out against me are far greater than a 'simple' apology, or that forgiveness makes me 'weak' when in reality the ability to forgive is a great strength.

We are all sinners. Each and every one of us. And if we expect to be forgiven for our transgressions, we have to be willing to forgive others. Even when it feels impossible.

So I will continue bowing my head and asking for help letting go.

In Second Chance Serenity, I wanted to really capture the theme of forgiveness with a swoony second chance romance, where Michael struggles with the things he has done, and Reyna battles with her ability to let it go and move forward.

I believe it's a beautiful testament to what it means to truly forgive and be forgiven, and I hope you enjoy every word of their story.

Also, be sure to read the parable about the master and the servant if you're not familiar with it! It's a great one.

Thank you for reading!

-Jessica

To those struggling with forgiveness.
And those willing to forgive seventy times seven.

CHAPTER 1
Michael

The thrill of the chase is one of my favorite parts of this job.

Boots hammering against the pavement, I sprint through a back alley in downtown L.A. My body is coated in a thin layer of sweat thanks to the humidity clinging to the air, and my muscles are warm. I pay little attention to the trash littering the ground or the stench of dirty wet pavement as I run.

The guy I'm after, a would-be stalker who stole some photographs my client would rather not get out, glances over his shoulder. His beady eyes widen, and he pumps his arms harder, as though that's going to speed him up. Truth is, I could have caught him nearly as soon as I started chasing him, but he deserves to worry awhile. And from the looks of it, that's exactly what he's doing.

His face is beet-red, his expression one of fear as he glances back again. *Good.* I grin. A man who would target a woman who'd just had a baby simply so he could make some spare change off "never-before-seen photographs" should be afraid of what's going to happen when I catch him.

I may be a man of God, willing to let justice be served by appropriate channels, but he doesn't have to know that.

The man trips, his foot catching on a piece of broken pavement, and he tumbles forward, face sliding against the concrete. He cries out in pain and tries to roll over, but I'm faster. I slide to his side, then slam my knee down into the middle of his back. With him pinned to the ground, I search his pockets, finding the phone he'd used within seconds.

"I'm sorry, man! I didn't do anything," he yells as I rip the cell free from his possession.

"I'm confused," I reply. "Are you sorry or did you not do anything?" I ask as I quickly check his phone for the photographs. As soon as I've double-checked he didn't delete them, I shove the phone into my pocket and withdraw zip ties from my back pocket.

His wrists bound, I haul him up so he's sitting, then pull out my own phone. Jaxson, one of our newest partners, had given me an officer to contact.

"Diaz." He sounds distracted, but answers on the third ring.

"It's Michael Anderson. I've got some scum for you to pick up."

Interest piqued, his tone changes. "Send your location. I'll get uniforms over there."

"Great. Thanks." I end the call and share my location with the officer. As soon as that's done, I take a deep breath and stretch, rolling my neck and enjoying every pop from the aches.

I survey the man sitting on the ground. He's short, probably at least a foot below my six-foot-six inches, and his face is red and bloodied thanks to the pavement rash. All in all, dude looks rough. I pop a piece of gum into my mouth. Chewing gum has become a habit of mine ever since I got back from overseas. Being deployed in war zones, shot at, blown up, and nearly killed a time or two has left me with more than just physical scars. And for some reason, the monotony of simply chewing gum helps lower my anxiety.

Not that I'm having any right now. No, right now I'm dealing with the desire to scare this guy so badly he'll never consider doing this ever again. "Long day?" I ask, leaning against the wall and firing off a text to my client, letting her know the images will soon be in the hands of the police.

He glares up at me. "They were just pics, man."

"They were an invasion of privacy," I tell him. "Surely you can understand someone's desire for discretion after they just had a baby."

"Someone's going to get them, might as well be me. They won't get me on anything."

"Maybe not on the pictures," I admit. "Those will

likely be a slap on the wrist." I snap my fingers, then push off the wall. "Except for the fact that my team got footage of you trying to rip the baby from her arms when she wouldn't let you photograph him. That makes it attempted kidnapping."

His eyes go so wide it's nearly comical. "I was going to give him back! I just wanted a picture!"

"Take it up with your lawyers. But I can guarantee they'll be no match for hers. Deep pockets and all." Sirens echo down the street moments before red and blue lights bathe us in color. "Let's go." I haul him up to his feet then march him forward as two uniformed officers climb out of the squad car.

"Michael Anderson?" the one closest to me asks.

"That's me." I open my jacket so he can see the Knight Security badge strapped just inside my leather jacket. "The images on his cell phone are of a sensitive nature, so I'll be delivering them myself. But I'd appreciate it if you could get this guy booked for attempted kidnapping." I hand the target over to the police, then start back up the street to get my bike.

"You heading to the station?" one of the officers calls out.

I wave my hand in response, not looking back at them as I climb onto my rented bike, fire up the engine, and take off down the street.

"YOU'RE SURE THE PICTURES ARE SAFE?" SUNNY QUESTIONS as she cradles her newborn son against her chest. As one of the most popular—and private—actresses in show business these days, having the birth of her son protected was enough to make the call to Lance and hire me.

It's not the first time I've worked for her, and over the last year since she'd called and had me work a red-carpet premiere, I've grown close to both her and her producer husband Geoff. He stands behind her now, his hand on her shoulder. They're nearly complete opposites. As her name would suggest, Sunny has a bright smile and platinum hair that glows beneath the rays of sunshine sneaking in through the windows.

Her husband is nearly as tall as I am, and his hair is almost black, his eyes a dark brown. He was a stunt man in his earlier years and ended up losing his right arm in the process.

"The pictures will never see the light of day," I tell them both. "I saw to it that they were permanently deleted as soon as the captain had written up his report. The phone didn't leave my hands from the moment I caught him until the photos were removed."

"You don't believe the man who took them sent them off to anyone before?" Geoff asks.

"He didn't have time," I reply with a satisfied smile. "He was on the run the moment he snapped them, and the phone was in his pocket until I dropped him to the ground."

Sunny smiles up at her husband, relief on her face. "Close call."

"Yes, it was," he replies, then leans down to kiss her on the top of her head. "What can we do to repay you?"

"Pay your invoice," I deadpan.

Sunny laughs. "Obviously. But there has to be something else."

"We've given your name to all of our closest friends," Geoff says. "You are highly recommended in our circle."

Pride warms my chest. When I'd been medically retired from the military after suffering injuries that wouldn't allow me to remain in the service, I'd thought my time of helping others and fighting the good fight was over.

But then Lance opened his security firm, and my new destiny was revealed. One that allowed me to return to my hometown while also seeing the world and helping as God leads me to do.

"I appreciate that." I reach forward and shake his hand. "Let me know if you need anything else. You can always give me a call."

"We will," Sunny replies.

I offer Sunny a wave then head toward the front door of their private house. Geoff walks behind me, following me out. As we reach the door, I turn to face him. "It was good to see you again, Geoff."

"You, too, Michael. And listen, let me know if you

ever want to take me up on that stunt work. I think you'd be good at it."

I grin. "I'd be great at it, but it's not for me. My life is in Hope Springs."

"Life?" He arches a brow. "I didn't take you for a family man."

"Not yet," I reply with a laugh. "But maybe someday. See you around." I step out into the bright Los Angeles sunshine. My bike sits at the front of their circular drive, and since my flight isn't for another five hours, I opt for a ride along the coast before joining the craziness of the airport.

But before I climb on, I pull my cell out and tap on Lance's contact.

"Knight," he answers.

"I'm going to head to the airport," I tell him.

"Everything go okay?"

"Smooth as butter," I reply.

Lance chuckles. "Good to know."

"How are things back home?" I ask.

"She's fine," he tells me. I'm not at all surprised that he can read between the lines. Lance Knight was my Officer-in-Charge when I was in the service, and we've been close friends since the day we nearly died together, alongside our technical lead, Elijah. He knows me better than I know myself most times, and Reyna Acker—the woman whose heart I broke when I was a teenager—is always on my mind.

"Good. Well, I'll get my report to you as soon as I get back to the office."

"Your plane lands late tonight?"

"After ten," I reply. "So it'll be tomorrow before I get to it."

"Not a problem. Looking forward to having you back in town."

I end the call and climb onto the bike. After firing up the engine, I leave their estate through a massive iron gate and hit the highway.

Wind whips past me as I drive, warm air that kisses my skin. As usual, thoughts of Reyna are at the front of my mind. The girl I'd left behind when I joined the military. I'd promised her a future. A ring. Kids. And then I'd left without so much as a simple goodbye.

Now, I can't get her to give me the time of day.

Not that I blame her. I'd been focused on myself and wanted a life other than the one my father had set out for me, and she'd been planning for a future that would never come to pass.

Forgiveness. I'd told Geoff a family could be on the horizon for me someday, but the truth is I know it'll never happen. A family for me doesn't exist without Reyna. But I've been home for almost five years now, and so far, she's barely even acknowledged my return to town.

Does that mean I'll stop trying? Absolutely not.

Even if it means watching her marry someone else.

CHAPTER 2
Reyna

"So anyway, that's the gist of what I do. How about you, Reyna?"

I smile at the handsome man across from me, appreciating that this entire time we've been out to eat, he's been attentive, kind, and charming...so why can't I feel *anything* beyond base attraction? Why can't my stomach fill with butterflies or my legs go weak?

"I'm a principal at the school," I tell him. "We're a K-12, so I oversee kids as young as five and as old as eighteen."

"Sounds exciting."

"It's never dull, that's for sure." I take a bite of the chocolate cake in front of me. Years of dating. Of searching for anything that even mildly resembles the spark I feel for— *No, Reyna.* I shove thoughts of Michael Anderson out of my head.

Liam Hollander is handsome, stable, looking for a

partner, and would probably never leave me the month before we planned to get married so he could go off and start a new life.

"You grew up in Hope Springs, right? Do you have any family here?"

"My parents," I tell him with a smile. "My brother lives in Boston with his wife and kids. He's a prosecutor for the city."

"Nice. Do you see him often?"

"Once a month," I reply. "We get together for dinner. Alternating who makes the weekend trip. Sometimes, they come here, other times, my parents and I go there."

"Your brother is older?"

I nod. "Three years. How about you? Do you have any siblings?"

He shakes his head. "Only child. My parents both live in New Jersey. I see them once every few months."

"What brought you to Hope Springs?" He moved here only a few months ago and runs a remote finance management company from his house. It'd been the buzz of town for a while, so I knew of him before Mrs. McGinley arranged a meeting for us—without either of us realizing it until we both suddenly *had* to get to the library to pick up a book she'd ordered.

The woman is a lovable menace.

"I wanted a fresh start. I'd lived in Jersey my entire childhood, then spent some time in Philly. After that, I knew I wanted a small town. When my mom shoved a book into my hand and told me the author was from here, I decided to come visit. I've been wanting to write one myself."

"Who is the author?"

"Eliza Knight. Do you know her?"

Why does it make my stomach churn? I adore Eliza. We attend a girls' dinner once a month together. But since she's married to Michael's boss and close friends with him, that makes our relationship...well...complicated. "She's really sweet. Married to a guy who runs a security company in town."

"Yes! I've been trying to come up with a way to introduce myself, just to get my copy of her book signed and pick her brain over the route she took with her publishing journey, but I'm not entirely sure how to do it without coming across as creepy."

I smile because it's honestly so ridiculously innocent that it makes my heart melt just a bit for him. Michael wouldn't have hesitated to introduce himself. The man is a bull in a china shop, never fearing anything. "I would be happy to introduce the two of you."

"Really?" His expression lights up like a kid on Christmas morning.

"Sure thing. She's doing a reading at the—"

"Library tomorrow," he interjects with a nod. "I was planning to attend. I'm sorry, this is weird, isn't it? It's weird. I'm a big book nerd and my mom loves her stuff so—"

I reach over the table without thinking and close my hand over his.

He smiles warmly, attraction burning in his gaze. Man, I wish I felt the same. "Not weird," I tell him. "It's kind. And since I was planning to attend the reading too, I'll happily introduce you afterward."

"That would be great. So great. Now that you know I'm a big reader, tell me about your hobbies. What do you do when you're not at school?" Liam asks.

"I like to hike," I tell him. "I bake sourdough and volunteer whenever I can."

"Sourdough? That sounds delicious."

"It is. There's so much you can do with it. Dessert bread, Italian loaves, bagels, sandwiches," I reply, realizing suddenly that I'm more passionate about baking bread than I am about this date. And that realization makes me feel terrible. He's being sweet, and I can't stop comparing him to the man who left me over a decade ago.

"I'd love to try some sometime."

"Sure." I smile, then check the time. "I really should be going though. I have budget reports to finalize before tomorrow."

"Oh, of course. I'm sorry." He reaches into his pocket and sets some bills on top of the check, then stands and offers me his hand.

I slide mine into his, hoping for a zing. A zap. A connection of any kind—but get none. *God, why can't I find someone—anyone—else?*

"Are you okay?" he asks, brow furrowing.

"Yes. Sorry. Mind on work. It happens this time of

year." School starts in just over a month, and I've had to hire three new teachers while also managing to squeeze in a new arts program for our middle grades. The budget will be stretched to the max, but with some strategically placed fundraisers, we should squeeze by just fine.

"No problem." He walks me out of the small Italian restaurant that sits on the water near the edge of town, then leans in to kiss my cheek. "Can I call you tomorrow?"

"Of course. I look forward to it."

After saying our goodbyes, I climb into the car and lean my head on the steering wheel. Liam didn't grow up here, which means that he doesn't have any idea who Michael is. Which means he's practically the last available man in Hope Springs willing to give a relationship with me a try.

The other few that are left grew up with Michael and don't want to do anything that would risk drawing his wrath. Pathetic, really. Though I suppose since Michael was a prodigy boxer and star quarterback, I can understand on some level.

Even if it infuriates me.

Michael. Ugh. Ruining my life without even trying. He's always around. At the school, helping decorate for functions. Volunteering as an assistant football coach during the season. Giving boxing tutorials as extra-curricular after-school events.

Michael.

Michael.

Michael.

I swallow hard and lean back in my seat, taking a deep, steadying breath. Well, I guess that's it. I'm just going to have to settle for minimal connection or die alone. Who knows, maybe not having a blood-searing, soul-deep romance will be better. After all, the last thing I want is to give someone else the power to break me the same way Michael did...right?

By the time dawn rolls around, I've managed to finalize all of my budget reports, set up our first meeting of the school year, and finish planning the annual fundraising ball for the women and children's shelter in Boston.

The sun rises above the water, casting the ocean in glorious shades of orange and gold. Body slick with a thin layer of sweat from the four miles I've run this morning, I stand on the beach, overlooking God's masterpiece as He paints the early morning.

I'm always filled with such hope when dawn rolls around. Like today, anything is possible. Today, I can let go of the ghosts of my past—at least momentarily—and focus only on the dawn of a new day.

"Morning."

His voice washes over me like acid rain. I turn and face Michael Anderson, a former Army Ranger and the man who broke my heart when we were eighteen. He stands a few feet away from me, wearing shorts and a loose tank top.

He's barefoot, as he always is whenever he runs, and his obsidian hair is curly thanks to the humidity and sweat from exercise. Why does he have to be so beautiful?

"Morning." My response is curt, and I don't wait around for him to try to talk to me more as I turn and head back up the shoreline. I need to shower, get to the hospital for my volunteer hours, then get home in time to start baking for the first school board meeting of the year.

Unfortunately, Michael falls into step beside me. "Sleep well?"

"Fine."

"Busy day?"

"Yup." As always, I keep my responses short, but as usual, Michael doesn't seem to care.

"Me, too. Just got back into town, and I've got some paperwork to catch up on."

"Good for you."

"Reyna—"

"What do you want, Michael? I'm busy." Stopping, I turn to face him and cross both arms. It hurts to look at him, like staring into the sun. Because he was that for me for so long. My light. My everything. And he'd thrown it all away without a second glance.

"I just—" He runs a hand over the back of his hair. "I miss talking to you."

"Then you should have thought about that before you left town."

"Are you ever going to not hate me?"

"I don't hate you, Michael. I just want nothing to do with you. Have a good day." I turn away from him and start running down the beach, hoping that my past stays exactly where it belongs—behind me.

As soon as I've made the thirty-minute jog home, I turn on the shower, then check my phone for any messages that might have come in while I was out. Thankfully, there's not anything overly pressing, so I start the oven's preheat, grab a shower, get dressed, and prep my morning cup of coffee.

My sourdough starter is nice and bubbly, so as soon as I've taken my first shots of caffeine, I prep the dough for the loaves of bread I plan to deliver to Pastor Redding for the church's food drive. As those are setting, I pull out the cookie dough I'd made when I got home late last night and start spooning the balls of dough onto prepared baking sheets.

Baking is my therapy. It honestly always has been, at least as long as I can remember. I'd even worked with the Pastor's wife, Kyra, when she'd opened her bakery my junior year of high school.

So as I pop the cookies into the oven, I immediately start mixing the batter for my lemon blueberry loaf. But as I'm pouring the berries in, I'm hit with the memory of when Michael had helped me bake for our school's fundraiser.

Tears burn in the corners of my eyes, and I plant both hands on the countertop as I'm hit with yet another memory that refuses to stay buried.

———

"You can't keep eating the dough or we won't have anything to sell."

Michael comes behind me and cages me in, placing both of his hands on the countertop, then leans in and rests his chin on my shoulder. The closeness of his body warms me, and I lean back into him.

We've been together so long now that touching him is second nature to me. Being near him is my favorite place to be.

"But it's delicious."

"Still. We need these for the senior trip." I turn in his arms and press a quick kiss to his mouth.

"Gross."

Michael laughs and kisses my nose before pulling away and facing his sister Margot, who came over to borrow a sweater. She's two years younger than Michael and I are, but she and I have been best friends for as long as I can remember. "You don't get any of Rey's cookies."

"Reyna is my best friend," Margot replies. "Therefore, I am automatically allowed to have any cookies she is willing to give me."

"There won't be any if your brother doesn't stop eating them."

Michael sticks his tongue out at Margot, then leans back against the countertop. "I could live off of your baking."

I smile and my cheeks heat. "I could live off of your enjoyment of my baking."

Michael's grin spreads. "Forever then?"

I offer him a ball of uncooked cookie dough. "And a day."

THE PAIN FEELS SO FRESH AS IT TIGHTENS IN MY CHEST, a vise around my heart.

How is it still so real? It's been far too long for the grief of losing him to still be eating me alive, right? And if it hasn't been, how much longer will I be subjected to this torture?

My phone rings, so I reach down and press it to my ear. "Hello?" No one responds, though I hear breathing. "Hello?" Still nothing. Unease settles in my stomach. "If this is a student, you should know that starting off the year by pranking the principal is not going to end well."

The call disconnects.

CHAPTER 3
Michael

Hope Diner is packed this morning, which is not unusual for this time of day, especially since we're in the height of tourist season, given that school starts in just a few weeks. Lilly refills the cups of a young couple, smiling happily as she does it, while her husband Alex runs the grill back in the kitchen.

While Alex is a few years older than I am, I know that he and Lilly have lived relatively parallel lives to Reyna and me. He left Lilly behind to join the military as well, but it wasn't until she returned home after working as a travel photographer that he managed to get her to forgive him.

How? Who knows. Maybe Lilly loves him more than Reyna ever cared for me. Maybe ours was puppy love, like everyone else had called it.

Mood sour, I take a seat at the counter. "Morning, Michael," Lilly greets happily.

"Coffee, please."

She arches a brow. "You planning to greet me better than that, or do I need to let your mom know you missed some manners?"

We've known each other our whole lives, so I smile. "Fair enough. Good morning, Lilly. How are you? How's Sarah?"

"Growing. We're all fine. Thanks so much for asking." She sets a ceramic mug on the counter in front of me, then fills it with coffee. "How are you this morning?"

"Fantastic. Can't you tell?"

She laughs and pulls out her notepad. "Your usual?"

"Please. And to go would be great. I need to get into the office."

"You've got it." She slides the ticket to her husband, then turns back to me. "So what did Reyna do to get you in a twist this morning?"

"Is it that obvious?"

"To me, it is. I've known you both forever."

"Why did you forgive him?" I ask, nodding toward Alex.

Lilly glances at her husband and he grins at her, a lopsided smile that is so full of love that it makes my stomach churn. What I wouldn't give to have moments like that with Reyna.

"He gave me a reason to."

"I've given Reyna every reason, haven't I? I volunteer every spare moment of my time, I try to talk to her, to be friends."

"Have you told her why you left?"

"That doesn't matter."

"I bet it would to her."

I swallow hard, then take a drink of coffee. "I doubt it."

"Well, you'll never know until you try. As for Alex, he offered me an explanation, and I decided that taking another risk on him was well worth the heartbreak that could follow."

"And here you are, married with a sweet baby girl."

"And another on the way," she whispers.

My mood instantly perks up. "Really? That's amazing!"

She laughs and presses her finger to her lips. "Shh. We're keeping the news tight-lipped for now." She's beaming, though. Positively glowing with joy, and it eases my own sour mood.

Lilly is one of the kindest people I've ever met, and knowing she and Alex are so happy, even after everything they went through, honestly gives me hope that maybe one day—someday—Reyna will forgive me for what I did.

"Order up!" Alex calls out.

Lilly turns and retrieves the Styrofoam to-go container, then offers it to me as I set a twenty on the counter. "Give her time, okay?"

"Thanks." I take the container and leave, my mind still on Reyna. The trouble is, I've given her time. I've been home for nearly five years. How much longer will it take? Will she ever forgive me? Or am I merely holding onto a ghost?

"HOW'S THIS?" I ASK THEN GLANCE BACK AT MRS. McGinley.

She cocks her head to the side, studying the photograph she asked me to hang on the back wall of the library. "Perfect. Thank you so much."

"You're welcome." I climb down the ladder and smile at the aged woman. She was practically a second grandmother to me growing up, and there's nothing I wouldn't do for her. "What else do you need?"

"Well. If you don't mind, I could use—" She trails off when the bell above the door rings. My breath catches as Reyna walks in wearing a bright yellow sundress, her red hair twisted in a braid that cascades down over her shoulder.

So much beauty.

Her emerald gaze finds mine and hardens.

"You better close your mouth, boy," Mrs. McGinley whispers. "Reyna! Thank you so much for stopping by."

The moment she says it, I know that this was not happenstance. Mrs. McGinley has a habit of playing matchmaker. She and Edna Montgomery—a friend of hers who passed away last year—take great joy in helping others find love.

Surely she doesn't think this one meeting will change things, does she?

"Thank you for calling me. You said you have the box?"

"I do. But it is quite heavy." She turns to me. "Michael, can you be a dear and take Reyna to the back room? There's a large tub of books there that I am donating to the school's library."

"Sure thing."

"I'm sure Michael has other things to do," Reyna replies coolly. "I can find the box."

"It's quite heavy, honey," Mrs. McGinley assures her.

"I can take them out a few at a time." And she would, too. I know that without a doubt. Reyna would spend all day taking each book out individually just to avoid having to let me help with anything.

"I don't mind. I'm on my way out, anyway. I can get it into your car."

Reyna forces a smile at Mrs. McGinley. "Thanks again."

"Anytime, honey. Michael, it's the one with the blue lid."

"On it." I wait for Reyna to walk past me just so I can smell her floral perfume. I'm weak for her. And the fact that I would be willing to fall to my knees and beg her in front of God and everyone for a second chance grates against my pride.

But I don't miss the chance to inhale her scent as she walks past me and into the back room. "It's right there," Reyna says as she points to the tub. "But I really don't need your help."

"You never do." I lift the tub, surprised that it is actually quite heavy. But when I catch Reyna's gaze on my arms as I turn to face her, my mood is instantly lifted.

So she's not immune to me. Not completely anyway.

That's good to know.

Her gaze pins mine. "My car is out front."

"Lead the way," I reply with a grin.

Reyna starts out, walking past Mrs. McGinley, who is on the phone—probably with her other friend Juniper, the third member of the matchmaking trio. She winks at me, and I chuckle, shaking my head.

Honestly, I can't even tell her to stop because I need all the help I can get.

Reyna pops the trunk to her small SUV, and I slide the tub into the back, noting there are quite a few other boxes of books.

"Collecting books?" I question.

"Yes." She closes it and turns to me. "Thank you for your help."

"I can come help you with the unloading if you'd like. I don't have anything going on right now."

"I already have help."

"Oh."

Reyna's expression softens briefly, and I get the

impression being near me is just as hard for her as it is for me to be beside her. "Have a good day, Michael."

"Reyna, wait."

She turns to face me and folds her arms. The cross around her neck catches a ray of sun and shines brightly for a breath of a moment. "What is it?"

"I—can we have lunch sometime?"

"I told you I'm not interested in dating you."

"I'm not trying to date you. I just—" Why is this so hard? I run a hand over the back of my neck. "I want to try to explain."

"There's nothing to explain," she replies. "I told you that. Goodbye, Michael." She pulls her door open, then steps back and trips against the curb.

Lunging forward, I catch her right before she hits the ground. Reyna stares up at me, our gazes holding for a brief moment as desire shoots through my body like lightning. Having her in my arms, for even this brief moment, feels so right that it can't be wrong.

"Thank you." Reyna straightens and climbs into her car, then pulls away from the curb before I've even caught my breath. How am I supposed to move on when she's the very air I breathe?

God, you're the only one who can help me here. Please. Help me be the man who deserves her.

CHAPTER 4

Reyna

"How many stars do you think are in the sky?"

Michael turns his head and smiles at me. I'm struck by his beauty. By the fact that he can be so handsome and so incredibly breathtaking, all at the same time. The ground is hard at my back, and my feet are sore from all the dancing at prom earlier, but there's no place I'd rather be than lying here in my yard beside Michael Anderson, staring up at the sky.

Even if I am wearing a dress I paid nearly three hundred dollars for.

"Far too many to count," he replies. "But if you wanted to know, I'd count them all for you."

"That would take lifetimes." I laugh lightly.

"Then I'd spend lifetimes counting each and every one of them just so I could give you the answer you wanted."

"You don't have lifetimes."

"You make me feel like I do," he replies.

My stomach twists with the love I feel for him. Love I've carried for longer than I can even remember. "You always know all the right things to say, Michael Anderson."

"That's because I love you, Reyna Acker." *He leans in and presses his lips lightly to mine, and butterflies dance in my belly. My skin warms, my heart pounding in my chest.*

"I love you, too," *I say as he pulls away. He takes my hand and threads his fingers through mine.* "What do you think will happen once we graduate next month?"

He looks back up at the sky and falls silent for a moment. My mind is reeling with all the things he could say and all the promises I yearn to make. "The only thing I know is that I want to stay with you," *he replies.*

"What about football? Boxing?"

"I don't need any of that." *His mood shifts, agitation lacing his tone. He rolls over onto his stomach and scooches closer, pulling me in against him.* "Marry me."

"What?" *I choke out the word, a mixture of joy and shock overtaking me.*

"Marry me, Reyna. Let's run away together. Get married then come back here and start our life together."

"Run away together? What's going on?" *I laugh because he has to be joking, right? His entire family is here in Hope Springs, and so is mine. Why would we run away?*

"We can come back. But let's go get married. Somewhere far away from here."

"Michael, when I get married, I want my family there."

He closes his eyes and leans down, pressing his forehead against mine. "Is that a yes to marrying me at least?"

I wind both arms around his neck and pull him down to press my lips to his. "That's a yes to marrying you, but I want to do it right. I want to do it here. On the beach outside the church." I've pictured it at least a hundred times, from my white dress to the seashells dotting the shore and the groom awaiting my arrival at the end of the aisle.

"I will give you whatever you want, Reyna. Because I'm going to love you forever."

"Forever," I agree, not realizing just how short forever can be.

"HEY!" I SLIDE INTO A BOOTH AT THE DINER, SITTING beside Eliza Knight and across from Andie Montgomery and Margot.

"Hey!" Lilly pulls a chair over and sits at the end of the table, off her feet for what is probably the first time today. "You got here just in time."

I smile at her, not at all feeling like my usual self. Both run-ins with Michael this morning have set me on a collision course with feelings I thought I'd buried. With memories that I'd shoved away in a tiny box, never wanting to see again.

Why they're choosing now to try and break through the anger I still carry, I'm not sure, but they are. And every time I see him, I'm reminded of that evening in my backyard, and I have to fight the urge to run into his arms.

It's killing me.

"What's going on with you?" Andie asks. We didn't run in the same circles as teens, but she grew up here in Hope Springs and only recently moved back after her grandmother passed. Now, she's engaged to one of Michael's partners, Elijah Breeth.

"What do you mean?" I make a show of opening my menu and trying to appear casual.

Eliza, who happens to be married to Michael's boss, plucks the menu from my hand. "For one, you always order the same thing."

"Maybe tonight I want something different," I say.

"Doubtful," Margot replies. "What gives?"

"I'm just tired," I argue.

But then, at that exact moment—because *of course* the timing would work out that way—the door to the diner opens, and Michael strolls in, making his way to the counter. My mouth dries, my pulse kicking up.

He's wearing jeans and a black T-shirt. Nothing overly flashy, yet he's so incredibly handsome I find it hard to look anywhere else.

"We'll be touching on this in a minute." Lilly slides out of the chair and bounces over to the counter. "Michael Anderson, your dinner." She hands him a to-go bag that's sitting on the counter.

"Thanks." He turns and sees us in our booth.

"If it isn't my big brother." Margot grins at him as he crosses over to us. "Where is my son? You are supposed to be feeding him."

Why? Why must this happen *now,* when I'm still so hungover from our last interaction?

He holds up the bag. "That's what this is for."

"Vegetables?"

"Yes, Mother," he replies. "Matty is with Lance at the office right now. I'm headed back."

"Fine. Make sure he eats something relatively healthy, please?" Margot asks.

"I wouldn't be the fun uncle if I did."

"You're his *only* uncle."

"Which is all the more reason to keep him liking me."

I keep my head down, gaze trained on the glass of water in front of me. Michael is only inches away, so close that I can smell his cologne. It's the same kind he's always worn, and the memory of it is messing with my brain.

"All right, I'm headed out. See you ladies later." He turns and leaves, but I don't breathe easily again until the bell above the door dings, signaling his exit.

When I finally raise my gaze, every single one of my friends is staring at me. "What?"

"Care to explain?" Margot arches a brow.

"There's nothing to explain."

"There's obviously *something* there," Eliza says.

"That road is closed," I tell them. "I shut it down the moment he left me." And because I feel like a jerk for being so short, I take a deep breath. "Mrs. McGinley orchestrated a face-to-face with us earlier at the library."

The women around me all laugh at the same time. "It would be her." Lilly shakes her head as she retakes her seat.

"The woman is a lovable menace," Andie adds with a smile.

"She just doesn't get it. No one does. Michael and I were supposed to be together forever. It was us against the world, and he just left. It took me years to move past the pain, and I'm unwilling to go through that again." I look at Lilly, knowing full well she went through the same thing and now she and Alex are happy, in love, and have a sweet baby.

She puts her hands up. "You know my stance on it. I am beyond grateful I gave Alex a second chance even though I was terrified to do so."

"It's not the same." Except it is, but thank you, Lilly, for not pointing that out.

Margot taps her hands on the table. "Well. Since he is my brother and I love him, you should know that he's put down some pretty deep roots here. He won't run off again."

"I appreciate that, but I can't go there again. I won't survive it." I take another deep breath, trying to calm some of my nerves. My phone dings, so I pull it out of my purse, grateful for the distraction.

Liam: Hey, Reyna! I was hoping we might be able to get together again soon? I had so much fun at the signing today.

"Is that cute library guy?" Eliza asks.

I look up at her, only to find everyone staring at me

yet again. "Don't you all have anything else to talk about besides my lack of a love life?"

"Who is cute library guy?" Andie asks, leaning on the table.

"His name is Liam, and he came to the reading at the library today with Reyna. He seems sweet."

"He is."

"But that's not enough," Margot says.

I look up at her. "Sweet can go a long way." Annoyance laces my tone, and I almost feel bad about it. Margot has always been at my side. Even when her brother left me, she'd let me vent. Was even angry for me. "But, no. There isn't a connection past that."

"Does he know that?" Eliza asks. "Because he was awfully drooly over you today."

"Over me? He was thrilled to meet you. How did the rest of the signing go, by the way?" I change the subject with absolutely no grace, but thankfully no one calls me on it.

They all turn their attention to Eliza and her signing today, how successful it was, and how her agent has been looking at shopping television rights for her bestseller. As they talk, I let my mind wander back to Michael.

To the past.

To moments where I didn't feel so alone.

And as I do, I seriously wish I could convince myself that Liam is who I want to spend my life with. He'd be honest. Dependable.

Honestly, his only flaw is that he's not the six-foot-six former Army Ranger who will always hold a piece of my still-broken heart.

———

As I make my way down Main Street toward my car, I regret every moment of my decision to leave my car at the school and make the fifteen-minute walk after eating my weight in apple pie. It's late. Dark. And I'm still reeling over my interactions with Michael.

Lightning splits the sky overhead and I groan. *Of course* it would storm tonight. Truthfully, it's fitting, given the one brewing in me. I've managed to avoid facing off with Michael for the last five years, but I have a feeling the final showdown is coming. One final conversation to make him see that he needs to let me go.

That I can move past what he did, but that doesn't mean I will forget the way it made me feel.

I turn the corner and see my car parked clear across the lot, near the front of the school. And then the downpour starts. "Oh, come on!" Rain soaks me nearly instantly as I pick up the pace and sprint across the lot to my car. Water pools on the pavement, and I splash through it as I make my frantic dash toward dry ground.

Of course it would be raining.

Why wouldn't it be raining?

Perfect ending to a perfect day.

Stop, Reyna. You are grateful for the day. And you are grateful for the rain. I re-center myself mentally. Truth is, it could be a whole lot worse.

Thunder booms overhead and the rain really starts pouring. It soaks through my jacket easily and mats my hair to the sides of my face. I sprint toward my car now, running as fast as I can on my heels.

And then I fall.

The pavement comes up fast and hard, and pain radiates up through my chin. "Come on," I groan and start to push myself up. Before I can get completely off the ground, someone rips me to my feet, nearly yanking the hair from my head as they do.

I hit a hard body, and an arm bands around my waist. "Got you, Reyna Acker," a man growls in my ear.

I scream and slam my heel down onto my attacker's foot.

He yells and releases me, shoving me to the ground. I hit it with a hard thud, the pavement biting into my hands and knees. I try to push myself up but fall again, thanks to my slick heels. Kicking them off, I roll over onto my back.

Lightning splits the sky and I get a look at a masked man wearing all black. He stands completely still, a living nightmare. I scream again and scramble to my feet. I try to run. To sprint toward the school where the security cameras will see...but he hits me with such force that I slam back into the wet pavement, and more pain shoots through my body.

Fight, Reyna.

Fight.

I try to steady my nerves, to call upon the self-defense classes I've taken.

He reaches for me again, so I swing. My fist makes contact with his face, and he mutters something I can't hear over the storm. Gripping the front of my dress, he tugs me forward, then slaps me.

"You're coming with me," he growls. "And if you make it difficult, I'll make it painful."

I try to get my bearings, but he hits me again, and my vision wavers. A coppery tang fills my tongue. Is this how it ends? In the parking lot of the school I grew up in?

Tears spring to my eyes.

Please, God. Please, no.

CHAPTER 5
Michael

Rain hammers my windshield as I head home from dropping Matty off with Margot. It was a fun evening, even if I hadn't been able to get Reyna out of my head. The feel of her as I'd held her up from the ground earlier...the scent of her delicate perfume...she's haunting my every moment.

The school comes up, and like I always do, I turn toward the parking lot. Will she be working tonight? Tucked away in her office prepping for another school year?

Lightning shoots across the sky as I pass, illuminating the school's parking lot. My heart stops beating and my stomach plummets.

A large figure has a smaller one pinned to the ground.

Right beside Reyna's car.

Without hesitation, I jerk my truck into the lot. As

soon as my headlights shine on the fight and I get a clear view of who is being attacked, all rational thought leaves my mind. The masked attacker hauls Reyna up and tries to drag her toward her car.

I throw my truck into park and grab my gun. Flinging my door open, I jump out and rush forward. Rain slams into me, soaking me instantly, but it doesn't matter.

Nothing matters but *her*.

"Let her go or I'll drop you where you stand," I snarl.

She's drenched in rainwater, eyes barely open, face bloody. It takes every bit of training for me to keep my head level when all I want to do is rip him apart where he stands. Doing so, though, could put Reyna in even more danger.

So I leash my feral temper.

"Let. Her. Go," I repeat. "This is your final warning."

The man pulls her in tighter, and the sleeve of his sweatshirt climbs up, revealing a tattoo that dips down into his glove before climbing up past his sleeve. It's the only mark I see. Everything else is covered.

He leans down closer to her, then shoves her forward. Reyna hits me hard, and I stumble back, though I'm able to remain on my feet. Even as I want to look her over, I shift my attention to the immediate danger—only to find he's gone.

Another flash of lightning. The man is clear across the parking lot, so I grab Reyna and carry her to my truck, setting her in the passenger seat and buckling her in before getting back in. I leave the gun in my lap and assess her injuries.

"Talk to me," I urge. "Where are you hurt?"

Her teeth chatter, eyes half closed.

"God, please. Stay with me, Rey." I crank the heat up and throw the truck in gear.

My tires screech as I burn out, driving in the direction the man ran. I need to get Reyna help, but if I can take this man out on my way... I reach the other side and see nothing.

No sign of her attacker.

I slam both hands onto the steering wheel, then guide my truck back onto the road.

Doc.

We need Doc.

My heart pounds, adrenaline surging through me. "Talk to me, Rey," I tell her. "Please."

She mutters something, but I can't understand it.

"Rey. I need you to stay awake." I reach over and take her hand in mine, clinging to her in hopes that it will keep her alert and keep my heart from beating right out of my chest. With my hand on the steering wheel, I press and hold the Bluetooth button.

"You back in town?" Elijah answers.

"Someone attacked Reyna outside the school."

"When?" he asks, tone morphing into business mode.

"Just now. I'm on my way to Doc."

"I'll get footage pulled up. Is she—"

"She's alive," I tell him. "Have Lance and Jaxson canvas the area. Find him."

"We're on it. Keep us updated."

Doc's house is closer than the hospital, so I park my truck right in front of his place and don't even bother turning it off before I jump out, rushing around to get Reyna from the passenger side. I gather her into my arms and rush up.

I'm not entirely sure he'll be home, but I have to try.

"Doc!" I beat on his door. "Open up, please!" I look down at Reyna who is limp in my arms. "Please, Doc!"

A light comes on inside and seconds later, the door is pulled open by a wild-eyed Doc Harding. "Michael, what—" He sees Reyna and steps aside. "Get her on the couch. I'll grab my bag." He rushes out of the room wearing shorts and a sleep shirt, and I set Reyna on the couch.

My throat constricts, and I can't tell if it's tears or rainwater rolling down my cheeks. "Please, Reyna. You need to stay with me. Who's going to tell me how much they hate me? I'll get a big head about it without you humbling me." I brush her wet hair from her face, noting the bruises already forming.

The rain washed some of the blood off, making it easier to see that it's coming from a scrape on her chin and her split lip.

"Tell me what happened." Doc takes a seat on his

coffee table and reaches into his bag for a small pen light. He checks her pupils.

"I'm not sure. I was driving by the school and saw —" I don't even want to repeat it. "She was being attacked. He was trying to drag her to the car."

"You catch him?"

I shake my head. "He got away."

"What's going on?" Patricia Harding, Doc's wife of thirty years, steps out wearing a long robe. "Oh, Reyna. Is she okay?"

"I think she'll be fine," Doc says. "Can you get Michael a towel? He's dripping all over the rug. And can you grab one for Reyna too? I could use it to wipe some of this blood off."

"Of course." She rushes out of the room, and I run both hands over my face. Every muscle in my body is tense, my heart desperate for vengeance. I should have shot him where he stood. Put a bullet in his leg so he couldn't run.

So I could—

"Here you go, honey," Patricia says as she hands me a green-and-white striped towel. Her interruption thankfully rips me from the darker thoughts trying to take root in my mind.

Vengeance belongs to God. I repeat it, over and over again, trying to ease my barely leashed temper—the side that's urging me to get back into my truck and hunt her attacker down myself.

"Thank you." I run the towel over my hair and body

as best I can, and she uses the other to wipe some of the blood and rainwater from Reyna's face.

My chest constricts, my stomach a gravelly pit of fear as I watch Doc look her over. Shouldn't he be doing more? Shouldn't we be getting her to the hospital? Patricia steps away from Reyna and takes my towel with a tight smile. Someone knocks on the door.

I don't tear my eyes away from Reyna. Is this really happening? Please tell me this isn't happening. This can't be happening.

"Hey," someone touches my arm and I look down to see Eliza standing beside me. She wraps an arm around my waist, so I sling one around her shoulders, holding on to my friend if for no other reason than I need someone to ground me in reality. "She's going to be okay," Lance's wife tells me.

I don't even have the strength to respond.

"Okay," Doc starts, "she probably has a concussion, though I won't know for sure until she's fully awake, and she could use some stitches on her chin." He's bandaged it up for now, and Reyna groans before opening her eyes.

"Reyna, can you hear me?" Doc asks.

She nods. "What is—" And then it must all come rushing back because she tries to shoot up off the couch. She groans, then presses a hand to her stomach as she lays back down. "My head. Why does my head hurt?"

"Easy," he tells her. "Michael is going to help you to

his truck and we're going to take you to the hospital, okay?"

"I—no." She looks at me, and the pain I caused her all those years ago slides over her expression, a protective mask she wears whenever I'm around. It guts me. "I need the police. I need to report what happened."

Eliza smiles at her. "Sheriff Vick is aware. He's over at the school now and can come by the hospital to get your statement."

Reyna relaxes slightly.

"Let's get you to the hospital, okay?" Doc asks again. "You need some tests run to make sure there's no other damage."

She takes a deep breath and nods. "I want to ride with you and Patricia," Reyna says. "Please?"

Doc looks back at me, a sympathetic smile on his face. I nod, even as it's a dagger twisting in my heart. "That's fine, honey. Let's get you up." He tries to help her to her feet, but she falls.

Without waiting for an invitation, I step forward and lift her into my arms.

"I can walk," she says, but leans against my shoulder anyway.

"I know you can," I say. "But with me here, you don't need to."

"ANYTHING?" I ask as LANCE and ELIJAH cross through the waiting room to where Eliza and I have been sitting for the past few hours.

Doc had a full workup run on Reyna, but so far I haven't gotten any news. Not that I will. I'm not technically family, and God knows she won't talk to me. My only hope is her parents, who thankfully don't seem to hate me. They may not like me much, but that's a far cry from hate.

Elijah shakes his head. "We got her phone, but her purse is gone."

"Mugging?" I ask. Though that seems highly unlikely. The man had been trying to take her, not just her purse.

"It's possible. But based on what you said and what the cameras showed, we're not convinced." Lance wraps an arm around his wife's shoulders as Eliza leans against him.

"Camera footage give you anything?"

"We have the whole attack recorded," Elijah says. "But his face was covered, and he disappeared from view before getting into whatever vehicle he drove."

I recall him trying to drag her to her car. "I believe he was on foot. He'd been planning on taking her in her car."

"But why Reyna?" Elijah asks.

"Hey!" Andie, Elijah's fiancée, comes rushing off the elevator with a tray full of coffees. She hands them out, starting with Elijah and ending with me. "From

Lilly," she says with a tight smile. "How's our girl?" Since Andie grew up here, she's known Reyna for quite some time. Though it wasn't until they started their monthly women's night out dinners with the church that they really started getting to know each other.

"I don't—"

I'm cut off when the doors open and Reyna's father walks out. Henry looks beyond exhausted as he steps into the waiting room, baseball cap in hand. His greying hair is disheveled, and I know it's likely because he's been running his hands through it.

"How is she?" I ask.

"She's okay. Concussion, some scrapes and bruises, but—" His bottom lip quivers. "It could have been so much worse. I—" His expression falls and his shoulders shake.

Eliza wraps her arms around him, and he hugs her back, holding on as he cries over the daughter he'd nearly lost tonight. "She's okay," she tells him.

"I know. Thank God, I know that." After a few minutes, he straightens and crosses toward me. He holds out his hand, and I take it. "You saved my baby tonight, Anderson. You saved my little girl. And regardless of what's happened in the past, you have my endless respect and gratitude."

I don't even get the chance to respond before the elevator doors open again. Reyna's brother, a man who has made his dislike of me no secret, looks beyond stressed—and then he sees me and his expression turns murderous.

"What are you doing here?" he demands, charging toward me. He's ready to knock my teeth in, has been since the day he tracked me down at an Army base in Georgia three months after I got out of basic training.

A buddy of mine had been the one who'd kept him from doing it then, and I'd been such a hothead that I would have fought back—and probably won. But now, I prepare for a fight, more than willing to take a few hits if that's what will help him move on from his current view of me.

"Check your anger, Carter," Henry tells him. "Michael is the only reason your little sister is alive."

Carter stops in his tracks. "What's that supposed to mean?"

"Michael saw her being attacked in the parking lot. He rescued her," Lance tells him.

"You did?" His angry glare is pinned to me.

"I did."

Carter nods, but his expression toward me doesn't soften. "Is she okay?" he asks his father.

"She's okay. Banged up. Scared. Sheriff Vick just left the room a few minutes ago. He's talking to Doc now." Henry turns to me. "Said he's coming out to talk to you next."

I cross my arms. "I'll be here."

"Can I see her?" Carter asks. "Is she awake?"

"Yes, of course. Come on." Henry leads Carter out of the waiting area.

As soon as they're through the doors, I take a seat in a chair and do my best to steady my breathing. I've loved Reyna Acker my entire life. From the moment I saw her in the fourth grade, I'd known she was someone special.

I hadn't understood it then, but my life without Reyna just doesn't make sense. While I don't expect her to ever give me a second chance to be the man she loves, I would settle for being an acquaintance. Someone who gets to see her in passing.

But tonight, she'd nearly been ripped from this life.

From me.

God has a reason for everything, but why this? Why her?

"Are you okay?" Lance asks.

I nod. "Fine. I'm not the one in a hospital bed."

"No, but you've taken some hits," Elijah says, and I know he doesn't mean physically.

The doors open yet again, and Sheriff Vick steps out, his expression angry. "Hey, boys," he greets. Creeping up on sixty, he's getting close to retirement, and lately things have been far more stressful here in Hope Springs than in the years before.

In the last three years, we've had a dangerous stalker, murder, kidnapping, vandalism…and now this. A violent attack at a school with an otherwise impeccable safety rating.

"Sheriff," Elijah greets, shaking his hand.

Lance does the same, and then the sheriff turns to me. "How are you holding up?" he asks.

"Why does everyone keep asking me that? I'm not the one who was attacked tonight." My throat is tight, emotions raw.

"You care about that girl," he says. "And you're the only reason she's alive."

I swallow hard. "I was in the right place at the right time." I consider the fact that I had nearly stayed to play *Halo* with Matty but had the feeling I needed to get home before the storm hit.

If I had stayed, I wouldn't have been anywhere near the school when Reyna was attacked. She would have been gone.

Thank you, God, for getting me there at the right time.

"Can you tell me what happened tonight?" the sheriff asks, reaching into his pocket.

"I was driving home from Margot's. As I was passing by the school, some lightning flashed, and I saw her being attacked."

"Build of the guy?"

"Tall. She was wearing heels, but he seemed to be quite a bit taller than she was. He was masked, though, so I didn't see much." But then I remember the tattoo. "He had a tattoo on his right arm. I didn't see much of it, but it went down into his glove, and climbed up beneath the sleeve of his shirt."

"That's something." The sheriff writes it down on his notepad. "Anything else?"

"He leaned in like he was whispering something to her, but I didn't hear what it was and I couldn't ask."

The sheriff's expression says it all.

"What did he say?" I demand, pushing to my feet.

"I'm only telling you this because I'm hoping you can help me find him." He sighs.

"What did he say?"

His expression darkens, turning angry. "He said, 'I'm coming back for you.'"

CHAPTER 6

Reyna

I've just finished getting dressed when someone knocks on the door.

"I'll grab that, honey," my mom says, smiling tightly as she heads over to open the door. I hear her say something, but the curtain is still closed, blocking my view of who it is. And since their voices are muted, I can't quite hear what anyone is saying.

"Who is it?" I ask.

A few seconds pass by before she opens the curtain. Michael stands beside her, his expression twisted in a mixture of fear and relief. My heart jumps at the sight of him, my stomach swimming with nerves.

His hair is dry now, though it's mussed like he's been running his hands through it. The obsidian strands have always been a bit wavy, but they're even wavier after the rain. His strong jaw is set, his brows furrowed over dark almond-shaped eyes.

Why do I still feel this? After everything? All the years we were apart? How is he still the only man I want? Even more so now because out of everyone, he's the only person on this planet who makes me feel safe. My eyes fill, so I rapidly blink the tears away.

His gaze darts around the room, and I know he's just as uncomfortable as I am.

"I haven't had the chance to thank you," my mother starts.

I glare at her like she's a traitor even though I also owe the former Army Ranger a ton of gratitude.

"You don't need to thank me, Mrs. Acker," he tells her.

She reaches up and cups his face, a feat given he towers over her. "I do need to thank you. You saved my baby tonight. Without you, there's no telling what would have happened."

"I will always protect Reyna," he says.

"Thank you." She smiles and releases him, then turns to me. "I'm going to check in with your father. I'll be right outside if you need me." She shuts the door softly behind her, and the room seems to close in on Michael and me.

"If you want me to go, I can."

He saved me. So even though I know I *should* send him away, I don't. "Thank you for tonight," I tell him as I stand. I ache, but I do my best not to show it on my face. The last thing I need is him seeing me as even more of a damsel.

"Why does everyone keep thanking me?" he asks angrily.

"Because you saved my life."

"I did what anyone would have done."

I doubt he meant the words the way they came out, but all I heard was that I am not special to him. Never have been, never will be.

"Fair enough. But it was you who pulled into the parking lot. You who saved me. So you get the thanks."

"I didn't mean it that way—" He closes his eyes and takes a deep breath. I've *never* seen this man rattled before. He's one of those people who always has a smile on his face, even as the world burns to ash around him. Nothing ever gets him down.

So to see him so broken up, it tugs at the strings still attached to my heart.

"Are you—" He takes a step forward, then stops. "Are you okay?"

"Physically, I'm fine," I say.

"The rest of you?"

"Not great," I admit. "Being nearly kidnapped doesn't necessarily leave a lot of room for feeling okay."

"Of course not." He runs a hand through his hair. His clothes are still a bit damp, and the shirt clings to him like a second skin, defining every muscled ridge of his toned torso. The jagged scar along the side of his face looks even more apparent now, and I don't know if it's because of the way he's tightening his jaw or if I'm imagining that it's changed because I'm seeing him differently now.

When I look at Michael now, I'm not seeing the teenager who broke my heart but the man who screeched into a parking lot and jumped out like a warrior, his gun raised and ready to fire.

"Listen, I appreciate what you did. And I want you to know that." I shrug into the cardigan my mother brought for me, needing even more space between us and hoping the fabric will do the trick.

My heart still beats for him, even as the broken pieces struggle to fit together.

"Is this how it's going to be between us forever?" he asks.

"What?" I turn back toward him, and Michael moves in closer. I can see the flecks of copper in his dark gaze. Eyes I used to stare into for hours.

"We're strangers."

"What else are we supposed to be?"

"Friends?" he nearly whispers it.

"I don't need any more friends, Michael."

"Rey—"

"No. You don't get to call me that anymore," I snap as emotion sears my throat. I want so badly to run to him. To bury my face in his chest while he holds me and tells me everything is going to be all right.

But doing so won't fix the past.

It won't erase the years of heartache, or the constant

question of why I wasn't good enough to make him stay.

"I'm sorry. I don't—"

The door opens and Liam rushes in, eyes wide, face flushed. "Reyna! Thank God you're okay!" Before I can fully process what's happening, he wraps his arms around me. "I was so terrified when I heard what happened." He pulls back. "Are you okay? What did they say? Did they catch him?"

My gaze lifts to Michael, who looks about ready to throttle Liam for the interruption.

Liam seems to notice that we're not the only ones in the room, and he turns to offer Michael his hand. "You must be Michael Anderson. I heard what you did for Reyna."

Michael takes his hand and shakes it.

"Thank you so much for saving her. You are truly a hero."

"Yeah, that's me." Michael meets my gaze as Liam wraps me in a hug again.

One date. We had one date, and one partial date, and the man is behaving as though we're betrothed. Should I be grateful he cares? Or just as annoyed as Michael is that he interrupted us?

"I'll see you around, Miss Acker." Michael turns and leaves just as I'd wanted him to.

So why do I feel so alone the moment he walks out the door?

"I REALLY AM OKAY," I TELL CARTER FOR THE HUNDREDTH time as he carries in yet another bowl of soup. It's the third one he's made me eat since I woke after sleeping nearly all day yesterday and nearly half of today. Honestly, if he keeps feeding me like this, I am going to be sick.

"I don't know what else to do." He plops down on the couch beside me.

"You don't need to do anything," I tell him as I clasp my hand on his knee. "I promise I'm okay."

"You could have died."

"And I didn't."

"Because of Michael."

Just the mere mention of his name brings up a thousand feelings I'd rather leave buried. Especially when the image of his furious expression as he stood, drenched in rain, gun pointed directly at the man, floods into my mind all over again.

I'd been out of it, dazed, but that is one sight I will never forget.

Michael coming to my rescue.

"Because God made sure I wasn't alone in that parking lot."

"And He chose Michael to save you."

"What are you getting at?"

"I don't like the guy," Carter says. I don't point out that they'd been best friends before Michael took off.

Just like Margot and I were. Only we're still close. He and Michael had a massive falling out that led to Carter tracking him down at Fort Benning.

As far as I know, last night at the hospital was the first time they'd seen each other since.

"But he's always had a torch for you."

"Good for him. Mine burned out when he left town." I take a bite of soup.

"I know, but maybe—" He stops talking and takes a deep breath.

"Just spit it out, Carter."

"Maybe see if he can hang around a bit more. Just until they catch this guy."

"Absolutely not."

"Reyna—"

"No, Carter." Setting my soup aside, I stand. "You have no idea what it felt like," I tell him. My brother and I have always been close, so being vulnerable with him is as familiar as breathing. "He *left* me. Walked out without so much as a goodbye."

"I know that." Carter stands and crosses over to rest his hands on my shoulders. "But you need someone watching out for you now."

"I have you. Dad. Mom."

"You do. And we'll do anything we need to do to keep you safe."

"But?" I ask, sensing one coming.

"We're not trained bodyguards, Reyna. Michael is."

"So are the others who work at the security firm."

"Then go to one of them. I'll pay the bill. You can send it straight to me and I'll take care of it. But please—"

"Carter. It was probably just a mugging. I doubt the guy is coming back."

"None of your cards have been used."

"So? It's been less than twenty-four hours. Maybe he's—"

"He told you he was coming back."

I can still feel the heat of his breath against my neck, the way his arm banded around my chest. My heart rate kicks up as panic sets in. It's been years since I struggled with anxiety the way I have in the past few hours. And having someone to watch my back until we know for sure what the motive was might ease it. "Fine. I'll talk to them. But I think it's unnecessary."

"Thank you." He pulls me in for a hug. "Let's go. Get your shoes."

"Go where?"

"I made an appointment with Knight Security for this afternoon."

"You did what?" I stare at him, trying to process how this went from a, *fine, I'll talk to them*, to a, *let's go, it's time for your appointment.*

"It's in thirty. We better hurry."

"How did you? When did you—?"

"I had a hunch I could talk you into it. Besides, if you hadn't caved for me, I had Dad on the back burner. Then Mom after him."

At that exact time, my father walks out of the kitchen. It's his lunch break, so he's covered in grease from the automotive shop he runs. A half sandwich in hand, he looks at me and shrugs. "We love you, Reyna."

"You guys are turds." I lightly punch Carter in the arm, and he wraps his around me.

"We know. But we love you. Now, shoes."

With a light laugh, I head down the hall and step into the room I've lived in most of my life. Should I have gone to my house after I got out of the hospital? Probably, but the idea of being alone right now terrifies me.

Tomorrow. Tomorrow, I can go home. Until then, I'm going to stay here with my parents.

After sitting on my bed and putting on my tennis shoes, I get down on the floor and withdraw an aged cardboard box. I stare down at the lid for a while. Every memory I have with Michael. Everything he gave me fits in this box. It's how I've coped with the loss of what we'd shared. I put it in here, shut the lid, and refused to let myself think about it.

Shoving it back under the bed, I stand and grab my sweatshirt.

If only I could leave my still-broken heart inside that box, too.

CHAPTER 7
Michael

Reyna's attacker stands frozen on my computer screen. I've watched the footage more times than I can count, searching for anything that might help us ID him. I traced his steps from off-camera through the parking lot, until he hid behind her car.

It's not until she was distracted by the rain that the coward risked jumping out.

And she fought back.

I pop a fresh piece of gum into my mouth, barely noting the minty flavor as I refocus again on the scene that took place in that parking lot.

"Dude, you're going to drive yourself insane staring at it," Jaxson comments.

I look up at the former LAPD detective, who'd moved out here nearly a year ago to work with us full-time. "There has to be something here."

"There's not. Elijah's run him through recognition software, but nothing has popped. There were no prints, he dropped nothing. Right now, Reyna is the only link we have to the guy."

I lean back in my chair. "We have to find him."

"We will. Sometimes it just takes a little time."

The front door of our office opens and Lance strolls in, Elijah beside him.

"Full house today?" I ask, trying to get my mind off of the one woman I shouldn't be thinking about.

"Did you not tell him?" Elijah asks, looking at Jaxson.

"Tell me what?"

Elijah looks back at me. "Reyna is on her way in with her brother."

"I'm sorry, what?" I practically shoot up out of my chair.

"That's why I didn't tell him," Jaxson says. "Because I knew he was going to go out of his mind the entire time we're waiting for them to arrive."

"Why are they coming?"

"They want to hire us for protection," Lance says. His expression alludes to there being more, but he hesitates.

"What is it?"

"She didn't want you here. I insisted on it, given that we're partners, but I wouldn't expect her to be willing to hire you."

The stabbing pain is back. Straight to my heart. I

shove it back down, reminding my foolish pride that her safety is all that matters. I'd trust any of the men here with my life—and hers. "That's to be expected. When are they coming?"

"Should be here—"

The door opens again, and Carter comes in first. We used to be best friends, despite him being two years older than me. But after what happened with Reyna, he wanted nothing to do with me. Until the hospital, I hadn't seen him since that stifling day in Georgia.

Reyna comes in behind him, and a vise closes around my heart. Her beautiful face is bruised. Battered. Her chin is covered in a bandage. Just seeing her infuriates me all over again, and I have to bite back the surge of rage that pummels me.

"Thank you for coming," Lance greets Carter. "Lance Knight."

"Carter Acker. Reyna says she knows you."

Lance nods. "We've met a few times." He offers her a friendly smile. "This is Elijah Breeth, Jaxson Payne, and —you know Michael."

"I know Michael," Carter says, his tone clipped, his glare pinning me where I stand.

"Thank you for seeing us," Reyna says as she purposely avoids eye contact with me.

Probably a smart move, since I imagine my face likely still reflects the anger I felt watching that man put his hands on her yesterday at the hospital.

Liam Hollander. A new-to-town finance manager.

Thirty-seven. Never married. Elijah ran a background on him, and it came back clean, but I still don't trust him.

I knew she'd date again. That she would find someone else. So why it caught me so off guard, I'm not sure.

"Please, sit." Lance gestures to the couch.

They do, with Reyna keeping her gaze down and Carter shooting me a glare every chance he gets.

"Can you tell us what happened?" Jaxson asks as he flips open his notepad.

"She already went through this with Sheriff Vick," Carter insists.

"We need her to go through it again," Jaxson replies. "I'm sorry, Reyna. I know it's hard, but we need to run back through it so we can ensure we're covering all of our bases."

"It's fine." She smiles and pats her brother's knee, then takes a deep breath. "I was headed back to my car from the diner, and it was raining, so I was rushing. I slipped and fell. Or I think I slipped and fell. I'm not entirely sure now if I did trip or was pushed."

"Pushed," I tell her. "It was on the camera footage."

Carter's glare turns murderous.

"I guess it's nice to know I'm not that clumsy." She puts her hands in her lap and clenches them together. She's nervous. Scared. And I want to chase all the monsters away. Except this time, I think *I* am what she's afraid of. "Anyway, I was getting up when he grabbed me." She reaches back and touches the back of her head. "It was all a blur."

"Did he say anything to you during the attack?"

Her bottom lip quivers. "When he first grabbed me, he said, 'I got you, Reyna Acker.' Then when I fought back, he told me, 'You're coming with me and if you make it difficult, I'll make it painful.'" She closes her gorgeous eyes and takes a deep breath. "I'm sorry. I'm—"

"Don't apologize. Please, take your time," Lance tells her. "What happened to you was traumatic, Reyna. It's completely normal to feel spun out of control."

She nods and attempts to regain her bearings. It's all I can do to remain seated. To not reach out for her. "He told me that he was coming back for me," she says. "After Michael arrived, right before he shoved me toward—" Now, her gaze finds mine and I hold it, wishing I could say more without actually speaking.

Does she know I still love her?

That I would do anything for her?

That I would sacrifice everything for her?

"Did he give you any idea as to why he was after you?" Jaxson jots some notes down on the notepad he almost always has.

She shakes her head. "He took my purse though. So I told Carter it could have just been a mugging. Maybe he was saying that to scare me."

"That's not a risk you can take," I tell her. "He has your driver's license. Which means he knows where you live. Given that he knew your name when he attacked, makes it highly unlikely it was a mugging. This was a targeted attack at your place of employment."

"Targeted attack?" Carter questions. "You think this guy was after her specifically?"

"I do. Otherwise, how would he know her name?"

"It's a small town." Her voice is barely above a growl now. "It's possible he was mugging me and knew me from around here."

"Unlikely," I reply. My cool tone is a direct contrast with her anger.

Ice to her fire.

"I still think a bodyguard might be overkill."

"Has anything strange happened over the past few weeks? Anything that seemed unusual?" Elijah asks.

"I did get a weird phone call. But I brushed it off. It's likely a prank."

"When?" I demand.

"Um, I guess the morning before the attack? It was after I ran into you at the beach." Her tone changes, turning annoyed.

"What did they say?"

"Nothing," she replies. "They just breathed into the line."

Stalker. It's a common first step toward communicating with their target. They start with something small. A phone call. A note.

"Can you tell us what you did earlier in the evening?" Jaxson asks.

"I was out running errands between meetings at the school. Then, I worked for a few hours before having dinner with friends at the diner."

"We'll check with Alex and Lilly. See if anyone they didn't recognize came into the diner today or if any of the regulars happened to follow you out." Lance makes a note.

"Did Liam know you were going to be alone in the parking lot?" It's a low blow, but I can't keep the accusation from spilling out of my mouth.

"As a matter of fact, no." She sneers.

"You don't tell your boyfriend where you're going to be?"

"Michael," Lance warns.

"No, it's okay." Reyna turns her full attention to me, her glare furious. "As a matter of fact, he is not my boyfriend. We've had one date, which—in case you were wondering—has nothing to do with this case and therefore is none of your business."

My thoughts travel back to the way he'd hugged her. To the fear in his expression and the way he'd wrapped his arms around her without hesitation. "You only had one date?"

"Yes," she snaps the word.

"He seemed awfully familiar with you for one date."

"That's how emotionally healthy men are." She glares at me. "They're not afraid of their feelings."

"If that's—"

"I'll pay for it," Carter says, interrupting me. Which is probably for the best given I have a habit of putting my foot in my mouth when it comes to her. "Whatever it costs."

I take a deep breath, knowing a tangent is the last thing I need to go off on. Especially when it comes to her dating life.

"Do you already have a security system through another company on your house?"

Reyna shakes her head. "You guys monitor the school, but I don't have one at home. I've never needed one."

"You do now," Carter says. "You can install one of those as well?"

"We can."

"How soon?" he asks Elijah.

"As soon as this afternoon," he says. "We've got a lean day."

"As far as protection goes, we will monitor the house at night from here and have someone shadow you during the day."

"Not Michael," she says.

It's another hit. A blow to my already tattered soul.

"I can't do it, anyway," I reply. It's not entirely true. I could—and would—drop anything and everything for her. But my plate is full as it is. With my trip to L.A., I've got things here to catch up on. "And since it doesn't seem like I'm needed here, I'll be going." I push up from my chair and head outside to suck in a breath. Everything hurts. The walls are closing in. I'm eighteen again, signing over my life as I leave behind the woman I love because I didn't feel good enough.

I still don't feel good enough.

"Michael."

I turn, surprised that Carter follows me outside. "What? Come to take another swing?"

His jaw tightens, and he walks down from the porch. "I hate you for what you did to Reyna. But I know you still love her."

He's got me there, so I don't argue.

"She won't give you another chance," he says.

"I gathered that," I snap, turning away from him. The ocean is stormy today, a direct reflection of what's happening inside of me, too.

"But I'm asking you to not turn your back on my sister."

I face him again. "Why would you think I'd do that?"

"You messed up, Michael. We were friends. I was thrilled for you and my sister, and for whatever reason —I don't need excuses—you turned your back on all of us. I'm begging you not to do that again. I'm asking you, as someone who used to love you like a brother, to watch over my sister."

"Doesn't sound like she wants me to."

"She may not. But I do," Carter replies. "Because even though you broke her heart, you're still the only other person I trust with her life."

CHAPTER 8
Reyna

Day three is far worse than days one or two. Everything hurts. My head, my neck, my arms…there's not an inch of my body that doesn't ache as though I was thrown from a moving vehicle. I lie back on my bed, a heating pad on my back, a warm washcloth over my eyes.

Elijah and Lance are out in the living room installing a state-of-the-art security system that, personally, I think might be just a bit excessive. Carter and my mother are out grocery shopping for me before he heads back to Boston.

He'd wanted to stay, insisting on sleeping on my couch, but with Knight Security and my parents watching my every move, I don't see much of a point. He has his own life, two small children, a wife, and a business to run. The last thing he needs to do is stick around and babysit me.

Babysit. Is that what I agreed to by allowing Knight Security to assign me a bodyguard? Michael's handsome face fills my mind, and my belly churns as I relive what I'd said. *"Not Michael."* Does he even realize the only reason I can't be around him is because I don't trust myself not to fall in love with him all over again?

My phone buzzes, the vibration like nails on a chalkboard to my sensitive ears. I reach over and retrieve it, but it falls from my nightstand, and I hit the ground with a heavy thud after it.

I groan, shooting pain firing straight up my back.

My door is thrown open, and the light from outside is nearly blinding. I have to narrow my eyes to see the bulky man framed in my door.

Michael.

Of course it would be Michael.

Why is he even here?

"Did you forget how to knock?" I groan as I start to get to my feet.

He rushes in and lifts me as though I weigh nothing, depositing me back on my bed. I look up into his dark almond gaze and hate the way my stomach twists at the sight of him. So handsome. So masculine.

So strong.

Why did he have to break my heart?

"I heard you fall."

"And your first thought was 'Hey, I'm going to bust into her room without asking?' I could have been changing, you know."

"Do you often fall when you change?" he asks, the corners of his lips lifting in a quirky smile.

I glare at him. Michael has always had this innate ability to diffuse my anger. No matter what was wrong, Michael could always make me feel better. Maybe that's why it hurt so bad when he went away? Because there was no one to help me pick up the pieces he'd left behind. After all, how do you keep your head above water when the only person capable of settling your storm is the one who caused it in the first place? "Why are you even here? I told your company I didn't want you here."

"Elijah needed a few extra cameras," he says. "I brought them from the office and was going to help finish the install since he's running behind on an update that's due."

"Good. Then go do that." Lying back on the bed, I place the washcloth over my eyes, then reach for the covers. But I don't have to reach far because Michael is tugging them up for me, basically tucking me into bed.

I swallow hard, tears stinging the corners of my eyes.

He'd done this once before. When I'd had the flu and my parents were both working. Carter had a job interview, so Michael and his mother came over to sit with me. He'd tucked me in while she made soup.

The memory assaults me like a battering ram.

"I'm sorry, Reyna. I didn't mean to bother you."

I hate that I want him to touch my face. Just a trace of his finger over my jaw like he used to do. So even though I don't actually want him to leave, I say nothing as silent tears begin to fall. I've cried so much over Michael Anderson. The day he left. The weeks that followed. Whenever I think about him, there's this gut-wrenching pain that follows.

Why can't I get over him?

IT'S DARK.

Rain hammers down on me. The parking lot is empty, except for a single truck. It's a deep olive-green, large, and I'm drawn toward it because I know that he's waiting for me inside.

Lightning flashes and I jump back as a masked man lunges toward me. I scream, falling back on the pavement, but he jumps on top of me, pinning me to the ground.

I scream again but no sound comes out.

I fight, but my fists do nothing.

He laughs at me.

"Keep fighting," he tells me. "I enjoy the struggle. I'm coming for you, Reyna Acker."

"Reyna!"

I'm ripped from sleep, but I keep fighting as hands grip my shoulders. "No! Let me go."

"Okay!" He releases me and steps back. As I fully come out of sleep, I stare up at Michael and Elijah. Both men look utterly terrified, their faces pale, eyes wide.

I crumble, sobbing. Michael crosses over and reaches

for me, but I slap his hands away. "No! Leave me alone! You're making everything worse!" I rush into the bathroom, doing my best to breathe through the panic. It claws at me though, suffocating me.

The door opens, and my brother rushes in.

"I can't breathe," I tell him. "I can't breathe." I cry, suffocating beneath the weight of my panic.

"Easy, little sister, you can breathe," he tells me calmly as he sits beside me and pulls me toward him. "Five things," he says. "Five things you can see."

I don't speak.

"Five things, Reyna."

"You."

"Good. What else?"

I scan the room, focusing on the things around me that are tangible. The things that are real. "The blue and white towels."

"Good. Give me another."

"The black tile outline," I say, focusing on the one tile that ended up twisted before it dried. We go through the motions, and I give him four things I can feel and three things I can hear.

By the time we've finished going through the list, I'm grounded in reality once more. I know that there is no man in my room. I'm not in the parking lot of the school. And I've got full control over my surroundings.

Still, Carter and I sit on the floor of the bathroom while he wraps an arm around my shoulders. "God, please be with Reyna. Please strengthen and protect her. Amen."

"Amen," I whisper and lean against him.

When I was young, I started having night terrors. Horrifying nightmares that would have me screaming for help in the middle of the night. They started from nothing and came out of nowhere. But it's been a long, long time since I had one.

I think the last one I had was when I was eleven, maybe?

"I'm sorry," I whisper.

"Why?"

"I probably scared Michael and Elijah half to death."

"The whole neighborhood," he replies with a nudge of my shoulder. "Besides, Michael deserves a few scares."

"Fair enough. But Elijah?"

"Collateral damage," he replies with a grin. "Are you okay?"

"I am. Better now."

"Want to talk about it?"

"Just a nightmare," I tell him. "About the parking lot." I leave out the olive-green truck I'd been walking toward, as I try to understand just what Michael's truck being there means. Probably nothing, possibly everything.

I take a deep breath, and Carter gets to his feet before pulling me to mine.

"Hey, I have an idea." He brushes some hair behind my ear.

"What?"

"Come back to Boston with me. Kleo and I have a spare room, and the kids would love to hang out with Auntie Reyna for a little while."

"School is starting soon," I say. "I can't leave. But I really appreciate the offer."

"Reyna, a change of scenery might be good."

"I'm okay, Carter. It was a nightmare, that's all. I just —I need some time to get back to where I was, okay? Normalcy will do me good. I'm afraid if I start running, I'll never stop."

He clenches his jaw. "I just want you safe."

"I know you do. Thank you." I squeeze his arm gently, then step out of the bathroom and into the hall. Elijah is standing at a panel near the front door, but Michael is nowhere to be seen. And for the first time, I'm looking for him.

"He's outside," Elijah tells me without turning around. "Felt it was better to be out of the way."

I look back at Carter.

"Go, I'll make us some food," he says.

"Just not soup."

"Not soup," he replies with a chuckle, and crosses into the kitchen.

After slipping my sandals on and grabbing a long cardigan from my closet, I head outside onto the front porch.

My house is situated on a cul-de-sac, three doors down from my parents' house. With large trees lining everyone's yards, it's a beautiful place to be whenever the seasons change because it feels like you're in a snow globe for spring, summer, fall, or winter.

This place has been my haven for as long as I can remember, and the fact that Michael's parents still live directly across the street from my parents' house only adds to my feeling of comfort. They were there for me when Michael left.

His mother was apologetic, offering to help however she could, but my relationship with his father changed forever. He'd once been like a second dad to me, but after Michael left, he grew distant. I always wondered if it wasn't because he thought I drove his son away.

Michael sits on the porch steps, his back to me. My stomach in knots, I make my way over and take a seat beside him. "We used to sit out on your parents' porch a lot," he says.

"Drinking lemonade," I add. "I remember."

"I can't forget," he says. "I've tried so hard to forget everything. To move on, but I—"

"You need to, though. I have." The moment the words are out of my mouth, I want to kick myself for the blatant lie. Michael may not see it as one, but God certainly knows my heart. And He knows I'm still madly in love with the man beside me. Even if I struggle to admit it to myself most days.

"With Liam?"

"We had one date," I tell him.

"He has a clean background," he tells me. "If you were curious."

"You ran him?" I don't know why I'm surprised. Michael's dad is retired police. Michael works with a former detective, and he, Elijah, and Lance all served as Rangers in the Army. Of course he looked into Liam.

"We've run everyone in your life. Past. Present. Future."

"You include yourself on that list?"

He snorts. "I know my transgressions," he replies. "And I'm still paying for them." His gaze finds mine, and the air between us charges with tension.

I could have spent my forever with him.

But now I can't trust him.

"The nightmares something new?"

"I had them—"

"As a kid. I remember," he interrupts. "But now. After—"

"Yeah. That was the first one I've had in a long time." My throat burns as I try to swallow back the emotion. "I know I survived. That could have been so much worse. But I just can't get the feeling of helplessness out of my head."

Michael stares straight ahead. "Helplessness is something I understand quite well," he says. "I wish I had gotten there sooner."

"I'm just glad you got there at all."

We fall into silence, something rather unusual for the

man sitting next to me. A man who always seems to know the right thing to say. "I want you to know that even though you don't want me as your bodyguard, I will never let anything happen to you."

"I know."

He turns to me. "Do you?"

Something in the question catches me off guard. A deeper meaning behind those two words that feeds the pieces of me unwilling to let him go. "Yes. And thanks again." I reach out and offer my hand.

Michael studies it, and for a minute, I wonder if he's going to refuse the handshake. But then his large hand closes around mine and I see the simple gesture for what it is: a mistake.

Because the feel of his hand against mine soothes a need I've carried since the moment he walked out of the door.

CHAPTER 9
Michael

"Michael." My father stands in my doorway, his arms crossed. He's in uniform, about to leave for the night shift, and based on his expression, he's not thrilled with me.

Closing the book I was reading, I glance up at him.

"Margot, I need to speak with your brother."

My sister sits up and takes her book with her, giving me an apologetic glance as she goes because we both know what this is about. As soon as she's out of the room, he moves all the way in and closes the door.

Then, in typical-of-my-dad fashion, he stands there like a statue, letting the tension between us simmer. I know from experience that he doesn't want me to talk. No, he wants to let the silence draw out because he thinks it makes me sweat.

It doesn't. Because I'm used to his typical brand of lecturing.

"Your mother said you haven't applied to any colleges. Is that true?"

"Yes."

"I'm a bit confused about that, seeing as how you've received multiple scholarship offers."

"I don't see how you're confused," I reply. "I told you exactly what I want to do after I graduate."

My father's eyes, so like mine, flash with anger. "And I told you that you will do better than working as a grease monkey for the rest of your life."

The fact that he just insulted Reyna's father and the business he built from the ground up infuriates me. I push to my feet. "You don't get to make that decision for me."

"Actually, I can."

"No. I have enough credits to graduate, I'm eighteen, you don't get to control my life. Not anymore."

My father takes a step closer. I'm already half a foot taller than he is, but he still tries to intimidate me. He may have never put hands on me, but he's certainly threatened a time or two. "You still live in my house. You are my son."

"I'm eighteen," I snap back.

"Do you really think Reyna is going to want a life of struggle? Do you really think she'll be happy with your mediocre life? And if she's so intent on you staying here and becoming a nobody, then you shouldn't be with her."

Fury radiates through me, and I clench my hands into fists at my sides. "Are you telling me to break up with her?"

"I'm telling you that you need to think long and hard

about the decisions you're making. You have a chance at being somebody. At making a lot of money."

"Not everything is about money." I practically spit the words at him because it's the same old argument.

Be a pro ball player, Michael, you'll make lots of money.

Be a pro boxer, Michael, you'll make lots of money.

Go to college and be a doctor, Michael, you'll make lots of money.

Over and over again.

Money. Money. Money.

"You aren't going to live in my house," he snaps. "Not when you refuse to make something of yourself."

"I'm not going to college," I yell. "I have my life planned out, and just because you weren't good enough to go pro doesn't mean I have to. You don't get to live your life through me!" I scream at him until my throat burns.

And by the time I'm done, I know nothing will be the same.

"Get out of my house. You have until I get back from my shift or I'll throw you out myself." He turns and leaves, slamming the door behind him. I stare at it, half expecting it to open again, but when it doesn't, I slowly sit back on my bed.

My mom won't fight him on it. She never does.

But where am I supposed to go?

What am I supposed to do?

Reyna. Emotion claws at my throat and my eyes burn with unshed tears. *What do I have to offer her if I'm homeless?*

"MA, YOU IN HERE?"

"Back here!" Her voice echoes toward me from somewhere in the back of my dad's shop, so I move carefully through tall towers of boxes, tubs, and other various items he's collected over the years.

She's at the top of a ladder, trying desperately to pull down a box with a blue lid. "Want some help?" I ask, brow arched.

Delilah Anderson looks down at me and grins. "If you'd shown up sooner, perhaps I could've used it."

I laugh. "Sorry, Ma, I was busy. Come on and let me get it for you so you don't break your neck."

With a roll of her eyes, she climbs back down the ladder and gives me a big hug. Since I get all my height from her, she's only about six inches shorter than me, and three inches taller than my dad. "You showed up right in time."

"I usually do." I wink at her and climb up the ladder, then bring the box back down with me. It's heavy, though not obscenely. Still would have given her a massive struggle trying to get down the ladder. "What is in here?"

"Old pictures. I told your grandmother I'd mail some to her."

"You know I can get all that scanned for you and you can just email them."

"Your grandmother will lose her mind if I email

anything, you know that. I don't think she even knows how to turn on that computer we bought her."

"Fair enough." I laugh. "Dad inside?"

"He is."

I don't have to ask to know what kind of day it is. The dark circles beneath her eyes tell me everything. Shortly after I'd left for the Army, my dad was in an accident that nearly took him from us altogether and robbed him of his ability to walk.

Ever since, he's struggled with depression, anxiety, and thanks to the head injury that had him in a coma for three weeks, he has moments where he forgets that he can't walk and then gets furious all over again.

He's struggled with his temper his entire life, and although he's never been physical with any of us, the man can make you feel two inches tall with his sharp tongue.

"I'll head in, then. This going too?"

"Yes, please." She falls into step beside me. "How is Reyna doing?"

I swallow hard. My mother adores Reyna. She'd considered her another daughter and had honestly been just as furious at me as Carter was for leaving Reyna behind. If only she'd known that the man she's married to is the real reason I left. "She hired a bodyguard."

"One of you boys?" she asks.

"Jaxson."

"But not you." She narrows her gaze.

"You know how she feels about me, Ma, and I can't

exactly blame her." We walk through my mother's colorful garden and up the back steps onto their porch. The soft music from handmade wind chimes fills the silence as we move into the house.

I can hear the television going, a football game my dad has recorded and rewatches almost daily, since he refuses to do anything else. I cannot even imagine how hard it was for a man like him, who'd spent his entire adult life as a police officer, to go to no longer being able to care for himself, though I wish he'd realize that he didn't die in that accident.

Sometimes, it seems, he forgets.

"Hey, Dad," I greet as I step into the living room. He's seated in his recliner, the wheelchair he uses to get around right beside him. There's a harness dangling from the ceiling that I installed a few years ago so that he could sit more comfortably whenever he didn't need to be mobile.

"Michael," he greets, turning toward me. His eyes are sunken in, his expression hollow.

"How's it going?" I take a seat on the couch and stare at the game. My heart sinks. It's a home video of one of my old high school games. He's standing at the edge of the field, having stepped in to be an assistant coach when Coach Miller was ill.

"Fine, son, you?"

"Going okay. Did you hear about Reyna?" I hate even asking him about her, hate even mentioning her name in his presence, given the final fight we had before

I left for the Army, but I know he used to love her like another daughter.

A long, long time ago.

"Yes. It's good you were there when you were."

"Yeah. Agreed." I glance to my right, not at all surprised to see my mother hovering, her expression tormented. Years of watching the man you love all but give up on life has eaten away at the joy she'd once exuded. "How are you feeling? Up for some fishing later? I can take you out on the dock."

"No. I don't think so. Maybe next time." It used to be his favorite thing to do, and now whenever I invite him, it's the same exact answer. *No, I don't think so. Maybe next time.*

"You sure about that?"

"Yes," he replies, a bit more sternly now.

"Okay." It's so hard for me to see the man who'd raised me beneath the shell of what he's allowed himself to become. The accident was hard, sure, I won't take that away from him. But God kept him here. He let my father remain on this earth with my mother, my sister, his grandson, me—why can't we be enough? "Well, I'm going to head over to Margot's and pick up Matty. I can take you with me if you'd like? Get you out of the house?"

"I've already told you, no."

"All right. See you later, Dad." I stand up and head over toward my mom. After planting a kiss on her forehead, she walks me out the front door. "Why don't you come with me? We can get you out for a bit."

"You know I can't leave your father," she replies. I can see the sadness in her gaze, the brokenness. My mother used to be incredibly active in the church. She'd had friends, a life, and now she barely leaves the house. Margot does most of the shopping, and I take care of all maintenance around the place.

"I told you, I can hire a nurse to come in and take care of him."

"No. He's my husband. It's my gift to be able to care for him when he needs me."

"Ma—"

"Michael, I'm okay. I promise. Please. I love your father, with everything that I am, and even if he has a hard time remembering who he is, I never will." He'd been a caring husband, a loving and supportive father to Margot, and—well—an active father to me. I know that's what she's holding onto. Honestly, it's what Margot clings to on hard days, too.

"Okay. Just think about it, please? You can take care of him and still have a life."

"Thank you." She smiles and stretches up to kiss my cheek. "Let me know if Reyna needs anything, okay?"

"I will." As I climb into my truck, I look up the street to Reyna's house. Jaxson's car is parked right out in front, and just seeing it there—even as I know there's nothing romantic between them—is like sandpaper to my soul. It should be me in there. Protecting her. Loving her. I should be her husband, her partner, and I allowed myself to be chased out of town.

Forcing myself to look away, I climb in and make the fifteen-minute drive to the Hope Springs Bed and Breakfast across town. My sister has been running the place ever since she and her now ex-husband, Chad O'Connell, bought it from Betsy Lee five years ago.

It had been her dream to own a place like it, so when he left, I'd bought him out so she wouldn't lose the place in the divorce. Now, we're technically co-owners, but I'm a silent partner and have been secretly squirreling away my portion of the proceeds for Matty's college fund. If he ever gets there.

With my nephew's temper, he may just end up in jail first.

Margot is standing behind the counter on the phone. Her dark hair is up in a messy bun, her large-framed glasses slipping down her nose. When she sees me, she holds up a finger and flashes a quick smile. "Fantastic, Mr. Phillips, I have you down for that reservation. Yes, sir, I will take care of it. Absolutely. Okay. Wonderful. See you then." She ends the call and plants both palms on the counter. "You are a sight for sore eyes, big brother."

"Why is that?"

"Two of the lightbulbs in room 2A are out. I don't suppose you could—"

"On it."

She laughs and follows me as I make my way down

the hall to the supply closet for spare lightbulbs. "How is Reyna? I tried to call her earlier, but she didn't answer."

"She's shaken up," I tell her as I retrieve the box and head up the back steps.

"Jaxson told me she hired you guys and that he's protecting her."

Since the former LAPD detective hasn't quite decided where he wants to live yet, he's been renting the maintenance apartment here at the B&B ever since he got to Hope Springs. "Speaking of Jaxson, why isn't he changing these out?"

"Busy protecting Reyna," she replies as she slips past me and unlocks the door to the room. "Which, by the way, you should be doing."

"She doesn't want me to."

"It's a mistake. You have to know it's a mistake."

"I'll let your maintenance guy know that you think he's a mistake."

She rolls her eyes. "You know what I mean."

After unscrewing the broken lightbulbs, I replace them and then turn to face her. "I appreciate it, Margot, but Reyna made her choice and I respect it."

"Well. I love her, but it was a dumb choice."

"I left her behind."

She crosses her arms. "We both know the reason, though. Have you told her yet?"

Margot is the only person in this world who knows why I left. Why I felt like I wasn't good enough for

Reyna and the life I'd planned for us was not what Reyna deserved.

And her knowledge isn't even because I told her, but rather because my sister was eavesdropping from the other room when my father told me that I needed to be better than this town. That if I didn't go off to college and pursue a football scholarship, I was wasting my life.

He'd been insistent on it, and honestly, it was the first time he'd tried to pressure me into anything. Likely because it was the first time I'd gone against what he wanted for me. He was a cop. His entire life was this town. And he'd wanted more for me. Trouble was I'd never wanted anything but Reyna.

Our fight drove me out of Hope Springs, though, and convinced me that I would never be good enough for her.

"The reason doesn't matter," I tell Margot, "because the end result was the same. I left, and Reyna will never forgive me for that."

"It's not fair."

"I messed up."

"And you've apologized."

We head out into the hall and she locks the room up behind her.

"If Chad came back today and apologized for leaving town, would you forgive him?" It's a low blow, but I don't know how else to get her to see it.

"That's different."

"How's that?"

"Chad got me pregnant, married me, then took off and left me with a thirteen-year-old to raise on my own. You joined the military, served your country, and nearly died for it."

I chuckle and wrap my arm around her shoulders. Margot has always been my biggest supporter. Out of everyone, she's who I wrote the most when I was overseas, and she'd always written back. Even when she and Chad started having problems and she'd caught him cheating on her the first time, she'd written to me as though all was right in the world. She's strong, maybe too strong for her own good because she refuses to lean on anyone. "You paint me as a hero, but to Reyna, I—"

"Should be a hero," she interrupts. "Yes, you messed up. Yes, you suck for that. But you're a human and it's in our nature to mess up. And you came back. I just—I love her like a sister, but I wish she'd see."

I want to continue the conversation, to convince Margot to see it from Reyna's perspective, but I know she never will. Because even though Margot can see my many, many faults, she is the first person to offer forgiveness for them. Anyone's faults, really. It's why she stayed with Chad as long as she did.

"Is Matty ready to go?"

"Matthew," an annoyed teenage voice calls out from the kitchen. "And yes." He steps out wearing dark jeans, a black T-shirt, and a black leather cuff bracelet. His dark hair is long and shaggy, and he has to brush it out of his face.

"There's my boy." Margot wraps her arm around his shoulders and kisses his cheek.

He groans. "Stop, Mom."

"Why? Uncle Mikey is the only one here." Margot grins at me.

"Mikey?" I can't hide my grimace.

Matty grins. "Actually, you know what? You call me Matty, so I think Mikey is actually fair," he replies with a grin.

Margot laughs. "Be good, Matt. And get your homework taken care of before you do anything else."

"Yes, Mom. I promise."

"Good. Dinner tonight?" she asks me.

"Sure thing. Tell me what to bring, and I'll be there."

"Just my son." She points to me. "And hopefully all in one piece."

"That was *one* time," I reply. "And it was just a few strands of hair."

"A few strands of hair? He'd used your clippers to shave half his head."

Matthew grins at me, and I roll my eyes.

"Fine. But if you ask me, he could use a haircut right about now."

CHAPTER 10
Reyna

At the soft knock on my office door, I glance up as Jaxson stands and pulls it open. Liam peeks his head in and smiles at me, then moves in all the way and I see the bouquet of red roses in his hand.

Annoyance toys with my already frayed nerves and I have to force my own smile. "Hey, Liam, what are you doing here?"

"I went by the bank today and your mom said you were at work. I wanted to bring you something to brighten your day." He offers me the roses, and I stand to accept them.

"This is sweet, thanks."

He glances back at Jaxson, then turns to me again. "How are you feeling?"

"Sore, but better." The bruises on my face have already begun to turn yellow thanks to the near-week since the attack. And so far, everything has been quiet. I canceled all of my cards, ordered a new ID, and my mother replaced the purse that was stolen as an early birthday gift. Things are getting somewhat back to normal—minus the nightmares that still won't leave me alone.

"I'm so glad to hear it. I've been worried about you."

"I'm doing better. But I will take all the prayers I can get."

"Absolutely." He rubs his hands together. "So, listen, I know you have a lot going on right now, but I wanted to see if you might be up for dinner again. I'd love to take you out a second time, if you're interested." He laughs nervously, and I glance back to see Jaxson trying his best to stifle a grin as he sits down in the chair he's occupied most of the day.

"I appreciate that, but I cannot accept any invitations until I know what my life is going to look like. You know, given everything."

"I completely understand," Liam replies. "And, seriously, please don't mind me, I'm around if you need me." He turns to Jaxson. "Jaxson, nice to see you again."

"You, too, Liam. Have a great day."

"You, too." He smiles again, offers me a wave, and slips from the room.

Jaxson continues grinning from where he's sitting.

"What?" I demand.

"That was uncomfortable."

I can't even deny it, and truth be told, I appreciate

him calling it like it is. Because it *was* awkward. "He's so nice, I just—"

"He's not Michael."

"What? What do you mean?"

Jaxson looks up from the book he'd just picked back up. "You know exactly what I mean."

"There is nothing between Michael and me." Even though I'd been appreciative moments ago that he'd called it like he saw it, now I'm annoyed at the implication.

"Look, it's none of my business, and I don't want to get involved. I just think that if you don't feel for Liam the way he clearly does for you, it would be better for you to tell him sooner rather than later. No decent man wants to be in a one-sided relationship."

The way he says it makes me wonder if he's had experience with heartbreak himself. I know he's not married, relatively quiet, and spends most of his evenings at the diner reading quietly in a booth by himself.

But was there someone else in his life at one point?

"I don't want anything with Michael," I tell him. "But you're right about Liam. There's just nothing there."

"Then be honest. Liam will appreciate it, and you'll feel better." He goes back to reading his book, and I stare at the cursor blinking on my screen.

I'd been in the middle of an email to our school board when Liam walked in, and even though everything I'd wanted to say had been fresh in my mind, now I'm completely blank. *Better start over again.*

I start to look it over again when my cell rings. I don't recognize the number on the screen, which is not unusual this time of year, since I haven't programmed every one of my employees into my contacts. Without thinking, I answer. "Hello?"

"Hello, Reyna Acker."

My blood goes cold. "You."

Jaxson sets his book aside and stands, crossing over toward my desk. He pulls out his phone and taps the screen. After muttering something I can't quite make out, he puts it on speaker and sets it on the desk, then gestures for me to do the same.

Swallowing hard, I hit the speaker button. "What do you want with me?"

"Speaker, huh? That's okay, I don't mind talking to your muscle, too." He sighs into the phone. "You have made things difficult for me, Reyna." The way he says my name churns my stomach.

"I wish I could say I'm sorry," I reply sarcastically. "But I genuinely hope that I continue to do so."

"Gave me a bit of a shiner with that right hook of yours. I have to say, I'm impressed."

"Why did you come after me?"

"You'll find out soon enough. Jaxson Payne, I'm assuming you're listening on the call?"

"You know who I am. Good for you."

"I know who you all are. Lance Knight. Elijah Breeth.

Michael Anderson." When he says Michael's name, my stomach churns again and bile burns the back of my throat. Is this a threat? Is he threatening everyone I care about now? Why? "I know that Reyna's mother works at the bank and her father owns an automotive shop. Then, of course, there's Eliza Knight and Andie Montgomery. They are quite the lookers. Even Anderson's sister, Margot." He whistles. "Now, there's a gorgeous woman."

Jaxson's expression turns murderous. "You'd better start giving me information I can use, or this call is over."

"I merely wanted to reach out and let you know that you and your team have one opportunity to back off before this gets really ugly for all of you. It would be a shame if something happened to someone you care about, Reyna."

Spots invade my vision, and I suck in a breath. He's threatening people I care about, and he won't even tell me why. I'm just a principal. Why is this happening to me?

"If you've truly done that much digging into us you know that we won't back off. Not until you're behind bars."

"This doesn't have to include you. You're doing your job, and I can respect that, but this isn't a battle you can win."

"You clearly have no idea who you're dealing with," Jaxson says.

"Maybe not. But I know that Reyna Acker and I have unfinished business. And I know that if you don't stay out of my way, I won't hesitate to start shortening the branches of your makeshift family tree." He ends the call, and I suck in another breath.

"You got all that?" Jaxson asks.

"Got it," Lance replies through the speaker of Jaxson's phone. He ends the call and crosses around to put both hands on my shoulders. "Breathe, Reyna."

"He's threatening everyone. Why? What did I do?"

"We'll figure it out, but you need to breathe."

I suck in a ragged breath. *God, please help me. Please, please, please don't let this man hurt anyone because of me.*

The door flies open, and Michael rushes in. His gaze is furious, and I know without a doubt he was likely in the office when the call to Lance came in. The lighthouse they work out of is only a few miles away, but he must have left as soon as the man started talking.

"Breathe, Reyna," Jaxson tells me.

I obey. One breath at a time.

"He's not in the parking lot," Michael replies. "I cleared it." His gaze lands on the roses left on my desk, but he doesn't say anything.

"How did he know Jaxson was with me?" I ask, my breathing ragged.

"Probably been keeping tabs on you. We'll sweep your house again, make sure there aren't any bugs or hidden cameras."

"What? Again?"

"We checked it when we installed the system," Michael says. "It's routine." He reaches forward and touches my shoulder. The moment his hand touches me, a sense of calm washes over me. An assurance that he's here.

I know, without a doubt, Michael Anderson would lay his life down for me. Does the man on the other end of the line know that I would do the same?

"I don't understand why this is happening to me." I remain where I am for a moment, even though I know I should pull away. Put distance between us. But the feel of his hand on my shoulder...I force myself to step away and a deep, steadying breath. "What could I have done?"

"I'm not sure," Jaxson replies. "But we'll figure it out."

Michael shoves both hands into his pockets. "You should probably get home. Someplace more secure."

"I'm in a school," I reply. "How much safer could I get?" But even as I think it, I know he's right. I'd feel better at home. Safer. More tucked away.

Every time this man has come after me—the parking lot and now this phone call—I've been here. It's likely coincidence, but I can't deny the fact that this place is feeling a lot less safe these days.

CHAPTER 11
Michael

I drop down and sweep my leg out, knocking Elijah to the ground. But he doesn't stay down long. He flips up, bouncing on the balls of his feet as he does, then swings.

His fist makes contact with the side of my face, and I fall back, pain shooting through my head as the rope surrounding the ring scrapes against my back. I lean against it, sucking in a ragged breath as I spit out my mouth guard.

He does the same. "You could have dodged that last hit," he tells me as he makes his way over to his water bottle.

"You're fast." But we both know he's right. I'm distracted. Head not in the fight because right now, Jaxson is protecting Reyna instead of me.

He's following her into the school, standing by as she preps for the next school year. It's been a week since she hired us. Seven full days of sitting on the sidelines, when I want to be front and center. And yesterday, after seeing the terror on her face as everyone around her was threatened—I'm desperate to do something. Anything.

"I am fast. But not that fast." He climbs through the ropes and drops down off the side of the ring.

Since it's still two hours from officially opening for the day, the gym I started after returning home is empty except for the two of us. This is when I like it the best. Quiet. Controlled.

"What do you want me to say?" I ask him.

"I want you to admit what you're feeling."

"What's that?"

"Anger. Probably some pain."

"Pain." I snort. "My relationship with Reyna ended a long time ago."

"Doesn't mean you've moved on."

"She certainly has." I think of Liam. Of the fact that Jaxson told me it was him who brought her those roses yesterday. I nearly scoff. She prefers tulips. Always has.

Will he ever know that?

Will he ever know that she likes a dash of cinnamon in her coffee?

Or how she hates wearing matching socks?

Honestly, he probably will. And I bet he never would've let his father chase him out of town when he had the love of a woman like Reyna.

Reyna.

Her bruises have begun to fade, though they're

currently in the stage of being a nasty yellow. Every time I see them, it makes me even angrier that I hadn't been able to run her attacker down with my truck.

Would I have felt bad about it?

Probably not.

"You're more pent-up than I've ever seen you," Elijah comments. "Honestly, it's refreshing to not be the grumpy one of the group anymore."

I glare at him. "You're happy and in love. Congratulations. Great for you."

Elijah laughs. "You sound so happy for me. Thrilled, even." He pushes to his feet. "I thought you should know the sheriff called at the end of my shift this morning. He said that they found an abandoned car a few miles out of town. It had been wiped clean of prints and reported stolen two weeks before."

"From where?"

"Boston," he says. "They're having it towed to the station as we speak."

"Boston. So whoever was after her is from Boston?"

"It's a big city," Elijah says. "It's entirely possible whoever came here wasn't even targeting her specifically. But rather looking for a type."

His words make me nauseous. "Serial killer?"

"I don't know," Elijah replies. "But it would be foolish not to consider every possibility. And the way he's toying with her—it has all the markings of a cat and mouse game."

"Why didn't you tell me this earlier?" I demand,

interrupting. If it's a serial killer we're dealing with, things will be a lot more complicated. He'll be harder to track, and there's no telling if he'll move on to someone else before we manage to catch him.

"You would have been even more distracted," Elijah says. "Besides, there wasn't much you could do until now." He stands. "I'm headed back to my apartment to shower and change. See you in an hour at the diner?"

"Yeah. I'll be there." I push up from my chair and head down the hall toward my apartment at the back of the gym. When I'd purchased this place, it had been the shell of an old vehicle sales lot run by Mr. Whitaker, a grumpy old man who never let a deal slip through his fingers. Including my offer to buy him out after I'd returned home.

I've never seen a man grab at three hundred thousand dollars so fast.

It was the only place big enough for my gym, and since I invested every penny I had into it, I'd needed somewhere I could live too. Thankfully, the gym does well enough that I've made back everything I invested and then some. Which made it possible for me to help my sister when her husband left her.

Pushing through the door into my apartment, I strip out of my clothes and step directly into the shower, not turning it on until I'm beneath the spray. Cold water hits me, and I remain where I am, letting it run down my sore body.

I've been in the gym every day over the past week.

When I'm not working or with Margot and Matthew or my parents, I'm in the ring or in front of a bag, letting my anger out on whatever willing participant just so happens to be in front of me. It's been years since I felt this helpless. This lost.

This angry.

As soon as I've finished washing, I step out and dress quickly, then drop some flakes into my fish tank before grabbing my wallet, phone, and keys, and heading out of my apartment and into the employee area.

"Morning, boss," Jennifer, one of the trainers I hired last year, offers me a wave as she sets her stuff in her locker.

"Morning. You have a full schedule today?"

She falls into step beside me, walking out into the main room of the gym. "Yeah. Picked up a couple new self-defense clients. I think you might actually know the first one that's coming in."

As soon as she says it, the door opens, and Jaxson walks in, Reyna right behind him. She stops in place. "Reyna?"

"Yeah. She booked with me yesterday."

"Great." So now she's going to be in my gym, too. Protected by my security company, yet I can't be the one at her side. Here in the gym I own, but I can't be the one to train her. Does she enjoy tormenting me?

"Is that okay?"

"Fine. I'm headed out for the day. Call if anything pops up."

"You know I will." She offers me a final wave before crossing over toward where Reyna sits in the waiting area.

"You good with this?" Jaxson asks, stepping out front with me.

"Fine with it."

He crosses his arms. "She asked if I could teach her some self-defense, and I told her she should talk to you."

"I appreciate that, but she won't come to me for anything. Not anymore."

"No, I got that when she refused. I did manage to convince her to give Jennifer a try," Jaxson says.

"You could have taught her," I tell him. Honestly, the former Marine can handle himself better than most. He would've been a great trainer.

"No, I couldn't."

"If she were anyone else, would you have?"

"Sure. But she's not anyone else, is she?"

I watch through the window as Reyna, wearing leggings and a blue T-shirt, climbs into the ring with Jennifer. "No," I admit. "She's not."

"You're here a few days early," Pastor Redding

comments as he crosses over and shakes my hand. "Sunday isn't for another two days."

Standing in the church feels heavier today, as though my faith is being crushed by misplaced anger.

"Better early than not at all," I reply.

He laughs. "Fair enough. How are you doing, Michael? How's your mom?"

"She's good." I pull out a pack of gum and pop a piece into my mouth.

"And you?"

"That's a bit more complicated, I suppose."

"Ahh, isn't it always?" He gestures to the front pew, so I follow him over and take a seat beside him. "Tell me what's on your mind."

Pastor Redding has been a friend of my family since before I was born. He grew up playing baseball with my dad, and even went on a date with my mom when they'd been in high school. Of course, they realized quickly they were better off friends, and my mom ended up introducing him to his now-wife. Confiding in him is as easy as breathing, yet I still choke on the words. "I'm angry."

"At who?"

"Myself. God."

"Care to elaborate?"

I shake my head and bounce my left leg, my need to be on the move stifling. "I left Reyna. I made my choice. And I've been kicking myself ever since."

"You were young, Michael."

"I was foolish."

"Tell me, what was your reason for leaving?"

I stare down at my hands, unsure how to even put this into words he'll understand. "My dad told me that I needed to go pro. That I had a gift and I should use it to better my life. He told me that marrying Reyna right then would be a mistake. That I was throwing away a life better than the one he had."

The pastor is quiet as I talk, processing everything I'm saying.

"I suppose I left because I thought he was right."

"Yet you didn't play football."

"I never wanted to play," I tell him. "I was content working at the shop with Henry. I was happy with Reyna."

"You ran from your father."

"Which is stupid, I suppose. I know that now. But it felt so suffocating back then. Like by marrying Reyna, I would be proving him right. But I had no interest in playing professional ball."

"Oftentimes our parents don't realize that they're trying to force us down a path we don't feel called to take. Did you feel called to the service?"

I sigh. "Honestly? I'm not sure. I got scared, and it was the fastest way out of town."

"Do you regret the time you served?"

I consider his question. "No. I regret leaving Reyna behind, walking away without saying goodbye, but I'm proud of the time I spent in the service. Of the men I served with."

"How has your father been since you've been home?"

"Distant. But that's not unusual given everything he's dealing with. He told me he was glad I didn't die, which for him these days is a declaration of affection."

The pastor chuckles. "Your father has never been great with words."

"Understatement."

We sit in silence for a few minutes, both of us staring straight ahead. "You said you were angry with God."

"Reyna could have died in that parking lot. Or been taken and suffered horribly." Just saying it brings a fresh wave of anger rushing through me.

"But you saved her."

"And had I been even a minute later, she wouldn't be here. It doesn't make sense. Reyna does more for this community than nearly anyone else. She helps, volunteers, works at the school. Why her?"

"Why would anyone suffer such a fate?" Pastor Redding asks.

"Exactly. It's just—I've seen horrible things happen," I tell him. "And Reyna—she deserves better."

The pastor sighs and nods in understanding. "All I can tell you is that sometimes horrible things happen and there seems to be no explanation for it. But God uses our pain, or distress, to bring us closer to Him. You've spent your adult life punishing yourself for walking away from the girl you loved. For all intents and purposes, you shouldn't have been driving by that school at the exact time she needed you, yet you were."

"One minute later," I say again, fear at the mere idea of something happening to Reyna clawing at my throat.

"You weren't one minute later," he says softly. "You arrived right on time because God led you to her in her time of need."

"She never should have been in danger to begin with."

"People do bad things because people are sinful, Michael. There is no escape from that in this world. But turning away from Him in your time of pain is only going to bring you more agony in the end."

"And my anger? How do I handle that? Because I've been struggling with the desire to hunt and kill the man responsible for her pain."

The pastor doesn't look the least bit fazed by my confession. "'Do not take revenge, my dear friends, but leave room for God's wrath, for it is written: 'It is mine to avenge; I will repay,' says the Lord. On the contrary: 'If your enemy is hungry, feed him; if he is thirsty, give him something to drink. In doing this, you will heap burning coals on his head.' Do not be overcome by evil, but overcome evil with good.'"

"Romans," I comment. "It's one I've turned to more than once since she was attacked. But I can tell you now, I'm not near strong enough to offer her attacker something to drink."

Pastor Redding chuckles. "You're a good man, Michael Anderson. Being angry does not change that. And if anyone can overcome the evil she suffered with good, it's you. You just won't be able to do it alone." He points toward the ceiling. "Ask for help. For guidance."

I stare at the cross directly in front of me. Suffering is a part of life. That's something I came to terms with a long time ago. And the truth is, I did get to the school in time to save Reyna. But what if I'm not where I need to be the next time something happens?

What if—next time—I'm too late?

CHAPTER 12
Reyna

I prep another cup of coffee, then head into the bedroom I turned into an office. After taking a seat, I glance out the window at the late afternoon sky. It's a truly beautiful day, with the sun shining brightly. My gaze drops to Jaxson's car. He's seated inside, reading a book. Right there if I need him, but far enough away that I don't feel smothered.

Thankfully. I've certainly been feeling boxed in lately.

My cell rings and I check the readout. Ever since that call at the school, I've been careful not to answer any numbers I don't recognize, so when I see *Emily Reed* flashing on the screen, I breathe a sigh of relief. "Hey, Em," I greet. A social worker out of Boston, she's who I coordinate with for most of my volunteer work.

"Hey, girl! How's it going?" Per usual, her voice is pure sunshine. The woman is a constant ray of light in this world, always there for everyone who needs her. Which is why I don't want to burden her with what's happening with me. Her focus needs to be on the women and children she's dedicated her life to helping, not on me.

I glance again at the bodyguard outside my window. "That's a question that would require far more effort than I can currently give."

She laughs. "I hear that. So listen, I just heard that Pauline is not going to make it to the banquet this year."

Oh no, the banquet. With everything going on, I'd completely forgotten it was coming up. How did I forget? "Why can't she make it?" Pauline Rivers is the in-person organizer for the entire event. She works directly with the caterers, the band, the decorators—all of them. I put the event together and handle the logistics, and Emily coordinates the donations and handles the legal side of things, but without Pauline, the actual setup won't happen. Not unless I make it out there early to take over for her.

"Well, she just found out she's pregnant." She laughs. "And is currently dealing with morning sickness that could take down a horse."

"Oh no. I'm sorry to hear that. Exciting about the pregnancy, but the sickness sounds awful."

Emily laughs. "She was not looking so great when I went to pick up the event binder from her. I figured I would overnight it to you so that you can take a look at everything before the event."

I close my eyes. Is it even possible for me to go? Is it even smart? How can I not, though? This is the largest charity event of the year in Boston. If Pauline was going to be there, she and Emily could easily manage things without me. But if she's not going to make it...there's no way Emily can handle everything alone, and it's too late for me to hire someone else.

"Yeah, send it over. That would be great."

"Awesome. I'll get it out to you today. Are you doing okay? You sound off."

"Just distracted. I had an accident in the parking lot of my school."

"What happened?"

Since she's likely going to see some fading bruises come event time, I figure I might as well get it over with now. "I was mugged." I downplay the danger, hoping it'll make it sound like it's not a big deal.

"Mugged? Are you okay? Why didn't you call me? What do you need?"

"Nothing, I'm fine. Just some scrapes and bruises. Someone was driving by when it happened, so he swept in and saved the day." If I mention Michael's name, that will bring up an entirely new conversation—one that I am in no way, shape, or form ready to have.

Not now. Probably not ever.

"Are you sure you're okay? What did they get?"

"Just my purse. And yes, I'm fine."

"Reyna—"

"I really am," I assure her. "I'm taking care of myself,

and I ordered replacement bank cards and a new ID, so everything will be back to normal soon." *God, I hope so. Please let that be true.*

"Okay. Well. If you need anything, you know I'm here."

"I know. Thank you."

"Anytime. All right, I will get this binder out to you —wait! Are you sure you can take this on? I can try to—"

"Send it over, Em," I tell her with a laugh. "You have enough on your plate."

"Always happy to hold more if I need to. But I am grateful you're taking this on. I'll get it out today so you should have it sometime tomorrow."

"Perfect. Thanks."

"Anytime. Talk soon?"

"Definitely." I glance out the window at where Jaxson sits in his car. The banquet is a week from Friday. Which means I'll need to be there Thursday to help get everything set up. I still don't have a dress picked out, and normally, I'd be putting the final touches on the reminder cards by now.

Cards that I haven't even started.

God, I need strength. Please. I cannot do this without You.

After setting my phone aside, I get to my feet and head back into the kitchen to pour my coffee out and slip into my tennis shoes.

A walk. I need some fresh air, and a quick break. Then, I can come back and focus.

Besides, I may need constant supervision, but does that mean I have to stay inside all the time?

———

A RUN ON THE BEACH WORKS WONDERS FOR MY CLOUDED mind. The fresh air, the sound of the waves crashing into shore, the feel of sun-kissed sand beneath my toes…when I ground myself into the reality of this beautiful world God created, I'm able to find my center again.

My anxiety slips away, tucked back into the corners of my mind, and I can finally focus. Out here, the world doesn't seem so scary. There is no man after me, no gorgeous ex-fiancé to captivate my every waking moment, and no banquet that I normally look forward to and somehow completely forgot.

Wind tugs at my hair, sending the strands dancing around my face. This is my happy place. And everything will be fine.

"I thought that was you."

Turning to look over my shoulder, I smile as Kyra, Pastor Redding's wife, who makes her way down to the oceanside, her feet bare. "Hey, Mrs. Redding, how are you?"

"Doing lovely. It's my day off, and I got to spend it with my gorgeous grandbaby. Kassandra just picked him up."

"Sounds like a wonderful day."

"It certainly was." She wraps an arm around my shoulder and tugs me against her. I relax into the hug, enjoying the closeness of a woman who was practically a second mother to me growing up. "How are you doing?"

"I'm managing," I reply.

"I know you better than that, Reyna Acker."

Chuckling, I take a deep breath. "I'm afraid. Stressed. Upset. I don't even know how to put it all into words."

"I still cannot believe you were attacked outside of the school. This town used to be so safe, but it seems the devil has been sending loads of trouble here lately."

"I keep telling myself that everything is going to be fine. That God has a plan for all of this and it's going to come together in His time, but I'm not entirely sure how I'm supposed to survive in the meantime."

"You keep your faith, honey. Keep your eyes on God, your Bible read, and focus only on the things you can control."

"I'm trying."

She's quiet for a few moments. "How are things between you and Michael?"

"Nonexistent." I glance over my shoulder to where Jaxson sits on the steps leading up to the lighthouse that houses the Knight Security offices. He watches everything around us, but he's far enough away he shouldn't be able to hear my conversation with Kyra.

"Isn't he helping protect you?"

"Jaxson is my main guard," I tell her. "Though Michael does have a habit of popping up here and there."

"And how does that make you feel?"

"Are we in a therapy session right now?" I joke. Kyra was the town's therapist for a while before she opened her bakery. Now, she counsels with sugar—or at least that's what we tell her.

"We can be," she replies with a light squeeze of my shoulders.

I sigh. "He's been asking for forgiveness since he came back. I know we're supposed to forgive others as we have been forgiven, but—"

"It's easier said than done," she says.

"Exactly. I can't forget what he did. Every time I see him, I'm reminded of the night before he left. Of the—" I close my eyes. "He'd promised me forever, and then I woke up the next morning and found out he'd left without so much as a goodbye."

She's the only person who knows why I'm so upset. That Michael and I went well past what we should have done as seventeen-year-olds who snuck away and pledged their forever's. "How am I supposed to get over that?"

"I'm not sure, honey. Have you tried talking to him about it? Explaining why you were so upset, and allowing yourself to hear his reasoning?"

"He wrote me letters," I tell her. "For the first few

years, I'd get one a week. Then, it was once a month, and then they slowed to one a year—on my birthday."

"What did they say?"

"I never read them," I admit. "It seemed pointless to rehash a past I wanted so desperately to forget. I was ashamed of myself, of what I allowed us to do, and what that meant for my future."

"Honey." She pulls me in tighter and runs her hand up and down my arm. "You shouldn't be ashamed of yourself. You were young. In love. Sometimes, things happen."

"I gave in when I'd always told myself I wanted to wait. But I thought he was it. I truly believed I would marry Michael Anderson. Then the next day he was gone. I felt used. Discarded."

"I can completely understand why you would feel that way, Reyna. And you will hear no excuses for that boy from me, even though I love him like a son." She smiles at me. "But he did love you, and I'd be willing to bet he'd grant you an explanation if only you'd ask."

Truthfully, I know he would. He's been begging me to listen since the moment he walked back into Hope Springs with an Army duffel and a new darkness in his eyes. Honestly, probably even before then, if the letters contain what I think they do.

But how can I guard my heart if I open it to listen and forgive?

My cell rings, so I pull it out of my pocket and check the readout.

"I'll leave you to it. Come see me soon." Kyra kisses my forehead, then smiles at Jaxson and heads back up the shoreline as I answer the call.

"Hey, Mom, what's up?"

"Your mom can't come to the phone right now," a familiar deep voice says.

My blood turns to ice as panic claws through my insides, shredding every other thought until all I can feel is fear. "Where is she? What did you do?"

Jaxson is at my side in an instant, his firearm out as he scans the beach.

"You should have believed me when I told you I could get to everyone you love, Reyna. Now you're going to find out exactly what I meant."

CHAPTER 13
Michael

"I'm so sorry, I don't know how this happened." Reyna stands beside her mother, both of them visibly shaken as we scour the bank's security cameras. Sheriff Vick offers her a kind smile. "It's not your fault. He likely walked in with the other patrons, then slipped into the back while no one was paying attention."

"Or he paid an employee." Elijah pauses the video. "Isn't that Sheryl Pierson?" he asks, gesturing to a blonde woman who's reaching into Felicity's locker.

Anger burns me up from the inside.

"Sheryl? Why would she steal my phone? We're not close, but I don't understand why she would take it."

"Did she know your passcode?" Elijah asks. He'd tracked the phone down, and we'd found it discarded in a trash can on the beach only half a mile away from where I'd been talking to Kyra.

Half a mile. That's almost no distance at all.

"No. At least, I don't think so." Her eyes widen. "Actually, yes. This morning she'd asked if she could borrow my phone to make a call. I'd given it to her so she could unlock it since I was watching the front." She covers her mouth with a shaking hand. "I didn't see her again after that. What if she didn't steal it, but whoever took it managed to get her first?"

"Easy, Mom," Reyna says. "We'll find her. I'm sure there's an explanation for it."

But as she speaks the words, Reyna's gaze finds mine, and I see the same anger I'm feeling reflected in her eyes.

Whoever used the phone tossed it so we would find it. His way of toying with us. Of letting us know that he's a step ahead and can gain access at any point in time. Truth be told, Elijah's serial killer theory is looking more and more likely with each passing day. And if that's the case, it's entirely possible Sheryl was simply in the wrong place at the wrong time.

My stomach churns.

"I'll find Sheryl," the sheriff says.

The door to the front of the bank opens and Felicity's husband Henry rushes in. "Are you okay?" he demands. "I saw that the bank was closed. The sheriff's car being outside worried me." His gaze scans over the rest of us. "What's going on?"

"The man who is after Reyna ended up with your wife's phone." Lance points to the monitor.

Henry leans in closer to the monitor. "That's Sheryl."

"It is, and we're going to find her and see if we can get an explanation," Sheriff Vick replies.

"My parents need additional protection." Reyna crosses her arms. "This was a direct threat against my mother."

"I agree."

She glares at me as though she expected me to argue.

"I thought you all were supposed to find whoever is doing this." Henry turns to me. "I trusted you with her." His eyes are wide and afraid, his bottom lip quivering.

I start to respond, but what can I say? We've failed up until this point. This guy is managing to fly under the radar. We've got nothing on him so far.

"We will catch the guy," Jaxson assures him. "Sometimes it just takes time."

"Well, he's come after my daughter and my wife now, so how much more time can we spare?"

"The important thing here is that Felicity is okay. We'll put deputies on your house, and I'll make sure you are both protected," Sheriff Vick says as he fires off a text message. "And as soon as I bring Sheryl in, we'll start getting some answers. If she was hired to grab the phone, maybe we'll get a description of the guy."

But I doubt it. And one look at Lance says he does, too. This guy has been careful. He wouldn't allow anyone to get a look at his face—not unless he was certain they wouldn't be able to talk about it later.

"There will be deputies at your home within a few

minutes," Sheriff Vick says as he shoves his phone into his pocket. "And I'm headed to Sheryl's house. You'll keep me apprised of any new discoveries?" he asks Lance.

"Always."

While we're not technically police, we have an excellent working relationship with Sheriff Vick. He lets us investigate alongside him, and we share intel. It's a system that's worked so far, and one I am beyond grateful for.

The sheriff offers one final wave, then turns and leaves the bank.

"I'm taking Felicity home. Unless you need anything else?" Henry asks.

"No, it's okay." Lance gives him a tight smile. "Jaxson, can you drive them home? Then wait until the deputies get there?"

"Sure thing."

"Reyna, come with us," her father urges.

She shakes her head. "I need to take care of some things, Dad, but I'll be fine."

"Please, honey."

"I'm okay." She smiles and takes his hands in hers, holding them tightly. "I promise."

He purses his lips. "I won't survive if anything happens to you."

Reyna leans in and kisses his cheek. "Dad, I'm going to be just fine."

"IF YOU DON'T HIT WITH THE FIRST TWO KNUCKLES, YOU risk breaking your hand." I grab the other side of the heavy bag, and Reyna glares up at me. Since Jaxson is watching over her parents, she came back here with me and has been trying to blow off steam ever since. "Come on, let's get you some lemonade. I just made some this morning."

I turn, and she follows, stripping off the gloves as she does. By the time we've reached the door to my apartment, her hands are bare again. I take the gloves from her and set them on the table by my door—right beside mine.

Somehow, seeing them there together causes the ache in my chest to grow.

Reyna steps into my apartment, and I watch as she studies the photographs on my wall. Images of me overseas, of my work with the kids over there and the translator I'd befriended. She's in my space. My home. And for some reason, I'm feeling more vulnerable now than I ever have with her.

After pouring two cups of lemonade, I offer her one.

"I like your fish."

"Thanks. Matty helped me pick them out when I got back. He was a lot younger then. Cute and helpful versus the moody teen he is now."

She doesn't smile, just continues surveying my space

with the scrutiny of a drill sergeant in a basic training barracks.

Does she like my apartment? Or does she think it's too small? Does it matter?

"Why did you leave me?"

The question catches me off guard, and I stare at her, mind blank, for a few seconds as I try to process it. "What?"

"You heard me." She sets the lemonade aside and crosses her arms. "Answer the question."

"I—" I swallow hard. How do I explain to the woman I'm protecting that I was afraid of my own father?

"That's what I thought. Couldn't give me an answer then, can't give me one now." She turns to walk away, and I reach out to grip her arm. Reyna freezes, and the skin I'm touching practically burns my palm as the connection that's always been between us snaps through me.

"I was afraid."

She rips her arm free and turns to face me. "Excuse me?"

"I was afraid," I repeat. "My father wanted me to go pro. He was pushing me to leave for college and play ball so I'd get drafted by a big team. He told me that staying and marrying you would be a mistake that we both would regret." I swallow hard, the pain on her face shattering my already tattered pride. "I couldn't be the weight that kept you down. I couldn't give you a life that you wouldn't want."

Her green eyes fill with tears as she stares up at me. "I thought your dad liked me."

"He did. He does." I close my eyes. I'm screwing this up. All of it. How many times have I wanted to have this conversation with her? And here I am, messing the whole thing up. "But he told me that I was walking away from a life that would be better than the one he had. He wouldn't leave me alone. We fought, constantly, until—"

"You left."

"Yes."

Her expression darkens. "Yet you couldn't be bothered to tell me why? To explain to me that it wasn't my fault that you left? That it wasn't what we'd—" She trails off, tears streaming down her cheeks, and seeing them fall is like a thousand daggers to my heart.

"Did you not read any of my letters?"

"It wouldn't have mattered if I did."

"Yes, it would have." I take a step closer, desperate for her to see. For her to understand that walking away from her was the single worst decision I've ever made. "Because if you'd read them, you wouldn't have thought for a second that my leaving had anything to do with you."

"Excuse me for not wanting to read your pathetic words when you could have just told me in person!" she screams. "Do you have any idea how much it hurt?

How hard it is to walk down the street and *know* that everyone is whispering about you? About how sad it is that you got left behind?"

Truthfully, I hadn't considered what it would do to her to remain in the place where everyone knew what she'd gone through.

"People told me that they were sorry for what happened. That it was such a shame. But I was young, and hey, first loves never last anyway, right?" A tear slips down her cheek, and I long to reach forward and brush it away. "But you managed to get away from your dad. From everyone. And couldn't even be bothered to tell me why. I gave you *everything*," she says. "All of me. And you discarded me like none of it mattered." She slams both palms into my chest, shoving me back a few steps.

"Do you have any idea how hard it was for me?" I yell the question, unsure how else to get her to see. To understand. "How much I wished I could take back what we'd done so that—" The moment the words come out of my mouth, I want to ram my own fist into my face.

"Take it back?" She growls the words and takes a step back. "You wish that you could take it back?"

"That's not what I meant."

"No. It's fine, Michael. Because from the moment you left, I've been wishing for the same. That I could erase every kiss, every touch, every second I spent in your presence."

"Reyna." I start toward her, but she slams both hands into my chest and shoves me a second time.

"Do not come any closer to me, Michael Anderson. I'm sorry that you felt backed into a corner. That you couldn't come to me and tell me why you had to leave. That you regret everything that happened between us. But that doesn't mean I want anything to do with you now."

"It killed me to walk away."

She gestures to me. "Obviously not, because here you stand."

"I was young. Hotheaded. Stupid."

"I was young," she snaps back. "And I loved you with everything that I was, and you chose your own pride over what was between us."

It's killing me all over again to see her this way. To see the pain on her face. I step closer. "Reyna—"

"Leave me alone, Michael. We may have to work together for what's happening now, but I don't want anything else from you. Do you understand? I *need* you to leave me alone. I need you to give me space. And honestly? I wish you had never come back to Hope Springs. You should have just stayed gone."

CHAPTER 14
Reyna

I haven't spoken to Michael since our confrontation in the gym three days ago. He's avoided any and all contact with me, and it's not like I've been overly thrilled about seeking him out either. Jaxson is the one who let me know that Sheryl accepted a bribe from someone over the phone who said they wanted to play a prank on my mother and offered her five hundred dollars to steal her phone and leave it in a bucket on the beach.

Apparently she didn't think anything of it and agreed. But after the police showed up at the bank, she'd realized something else was going on and took off to avoid getting questioned.

She got no look at the person who paid her, since the money was sent online. And the number that called her had belonged to a by-the-minute phone and has since been disconnected.

I finish prepping the salad, then glance back to where Jaxson sits in the living room, reading a book. Given everything we've been dealing with, my mom wanted to serve him and the sheriff a delicious dinner. My father has been on the phone with my brother for nearly thirty minutes, updating him on everything that's happening here, and although he's made the offer at least a dozen times, my father continues to turn Carter down about coming to stay in Boston for the time being.

He's been insistent, but so has my father.

The doorbell rings. "I'll grab it." I cross the living room and pull the door open without bothering to check the peephole. I'm expecting the sheriff, so when it's Michael standing on my parents' front porch, I'm momentarily taken aback.

My heart jumps in my chest at the sight of him, which makes me all the more angry. How can I be so in love and so angry with someone at the same time?

"Your mother invited me," he says.

Of course she did. Michael is her hero these days. Never mind he shattered me into a million pieces when he left town all those years ago. "Fine." I step aside so he can move into the living room, then immediately head back into the kitchen so I don't get drawn into conversation with him.

"Who was that?" my mom asks, coming out of the pantry with a bag of noodles.

"Michael."

She beams. "Good. It's so good to have him around again."

"Yeah. Great."

Brow arched, she faces me. "Are you all right? Did something else happen?"

"Nope. I'm fine, just tired." I force myself to smile because admitting to my mother just why I'm so angry at Michael is a conversation I would rather never have.

"I'm so sorry for everything you're going through, sweetie."

"You're going through it, too."

"Not like you are." She smiles tightly at me and the doorbell rings again. Since I'm fairly positive I have no other exes that can show up, I head back into the living room to answer it.

And there stands Liam.

Wrong again. Though I suppose he's not entirely an ex.

"Hi, Liam, I'm sorry, I didn't realize you were coming over." Another bouquet of red roses.

"Your mother invited me for dinner. I hope that's okay?"

I shoot a glare over my shoulder only to catch my mother grinning like the crazy woman she is. Now I understand why she invited Michael over. She's trying to make him jealous. To push him into sweeping me back off my feet, despite the fact that I'd like to keep them firmly planted on the ground.

Maybe having that conversation wouldn't be such a

bad thing. At least then she'd probably stop trying to push me back into his arms.

But seriously, don't I have enough on my plate given the crazy man stalking me and the banquet coming up?

"Of course it's okay." I flash him a smile, then step aside so he can come in.

He leans in and kisses me on the cheek. "Whatever that is smells delicious." He notices the other men on the couch. "Michael, Jaxson, good to see you both again."

"Yeah. You, too," Jaxson replies, shooting a grin at Michael, whose gaze hasn't left me since Liam arrived.

Awkward, party of one.

"Let's get those into some water," I say, gesturing to the roses in his hand. As he follows me through the house roses still in his hand, I feel Michael's burning gaze following me.

"Liam! So glad you can join us," my mother greets him.

He offers her the roses. "These are for you. Thank you for having me."

"You are too sweet." She takes them as I fill a vase with water and set it on the counter.

"Not nearly as sweet as you are for inviting me." Liam turns to me. "Can we talk somewhere a bit more private?"

"Sure." I gesture toward the hallway, and he heads down toward the bedrooms. As soon as we're in my childhood room, I close the door gently. "What is it?"

"I got this for you." He reaches into his pocket and withdraws a velvet box. My stomach churns. *Please no. Jewelry? Really?*

"You didn't need to get me anything."

"I know, but I saw it and thought of you." He offers it to me again, so I take the box and flip the lid, my stomach churning like stormy waves. Inside, on top of more velvet, is a golden apple pin. "Just something fun for the start of the year."

I smile at him, so grateful it's not more romantic jewelry. "This is sweet, thank you."

"Anytime. You don't even have to wear it, obviously. I just thought it was neat, and I know you've had a rough go lately, so I wanted to get you something."

"A rough go is an understatement," I reply with a laugh, closing the box.

"I'm sorry for everything you're dealing with, Reyna. I truly am. You deserve better."

"I appreciate you saying that."

"Dinner!" I hear my father call out, so I reach for the door and pull it open.

Michael is standing just on the other side, a furious glare on his face. "Dinner."

"I heard my dad," I snap.

Liam offers Michael a smile and leaves first, but before I can follow him out, Michael comes in and shuts the door, standing in front of it and crossing his arms so I can't get out. His gaze lands on the box, and his expression darkens.

"Already proposing? That was fast."

He's jealous. Why do I like that he's jealous? "Wouldn't matter if he was, would it? You and I are finished."

"You don't know him very well."

"I thought I knew you better than I knew myself. And look how that turned out."

He lets out his breath and uncrosses his arms. "I'm just worried about you."

"Yeah, well, don't be. My dating life is not your concern anymore." I shove past him and head out into the hall, making my way to the kitchen table. My mother has added the two leaves and additional seating so that she, my dad, myself, Sheriff Vick and his wife Cate, Liam, Michael, and Jaxson can all fit at the table with room to spare.

In the center of the table are multiple containers of serve-yourself food. Spaghetti, a salad, meatballs…it all smells absolutely delicious, but one look at Michael and my appetite is gone.

TO MY SURPRISE, DINNER WAS RELATIVELY CALM DESPITE Michael and Liam sitting across from each other. My ex-boyfriend engaged in friendly conversation with my mother while completely ignoring the guy that I've been on two dates with. Unless the library doesn't technically count as a date—then it's only the one.

I wave goodbye as Liam leaves the house, then turn back to the living room where Jaxson has engaged my dad in a deep conversation about the motor on his '67 Mustang GT.

Michael's in the kitchen with my mother, washing dishes as she dries and putting them away. Seeing them there hurts my heart. She'd adored Michael too, and honestly, I think she'd been just as heartbroken as I was when he bailed.

He just fits. And I hate it.

I make my way into the kitchen and force a smile. "Great dinner, Momma. I can take over the dishes."

"I don't mind," Michael replies.

"Liam make it out okay?"

"He did."

"Good. He's a sweet man."

"He is." I keep my responses short so she won't try to get me to elaborate, then begin putting containers of leftover food in the refrigerator.

"Oh, honey, I finished crocheting fifty baby blankets. Think you can take them to the shelter when you head to Boston?"

Michael freezes mid-plate-washing. "Boston?" he asks, setting it carefully back into the sink.

"I host a charity banquet every year."

"Not this year."

"Excuse me?"

"I'm going to go check on your father." My mother

slips out of the kitchen and leaves me glaring at Michael.

"You are absolutely not going." Michael's expression is furious as he dries his hands and turns to fully face me.

"You don't get to tell me no."

His gaze is piercing. "When it comes to your safety, I do. This is my job. Our job," he corrects quickly. "And taking you into the very city where the car your attacker used was stolen from is in direct conflict with your well-being."

"You don't know that he stole that car. It could have been a coincidence." But even I know better than to truly believe that. "And Boston is a huge city."

"Exactly. A huge city you could be swept away in."

"The event has security. And we can bring on more. I can't miss it, Michael."

"Everything okay in here?" Jaxson questions, stepping into the kitchen. He leans against the doorjamb.

"Tell her she's not going to Boston."

"Boston?"

I pinch the bridge of my nose. "I host a charity banquet. The woman who helps me with most of the in-person arrangements cannot make it, therefore I *cannot* miss it. I won't miss it."

"You're going to have to miss it this year."

"Are you not listening?" I snap. "You don't get to tell me what I will and will not do!"

"This is a mistake." Michael turns away from me.

"You work for me, right? Isn't that how this works?" I ask Jaxson.

Michael whirls on me. "Are you threatening to fire us if we don't let you go risk your life?"

I cross my arms, heels dug in so far there's no going back now. "I'm telling you that I'm going, I'm not asking for your permission."

"You—"

"If you want my opinion," Jaxson interrupts, and Michael turns toward him. "We can get with the security working the event and increase it with some of our own. You can remain glued to her side the entire time. That way, she can attend the event and stay safe doing so."

"Absolutely not," I snap. "Michael will not be coming."

"Why not? Worried I'll embarrass you?"

I glare at him. "Hardly. But you will cause distractions."

"Distractions? Why is that?"

Because you're too beautiful for your own good. Because I can't stand the idea of standing next to you all night and not reaching out to take your hand in mine or wrapping my arms around you. "Because I'll be working, and you can't seem to keep yourself from getting under my skin. The last thing I need is you scaring away people I'm supposed to be talking to."

"You're not going alone."

So we've gone from me not going to me not going

alone. I suppose that's progress. "Fine. But Jaxson can stay with me."

"Afraid I'm best working active security from a vantage point," my bodyguard replies. "I'm not much for crowds. Elijah will likely work monitors while Lance coordinates on the ground. Michael is our group's bodyguard," he says. "We made an exception for you given your past, but at an event like that, he's who will be by your side. I can set my pride aside long enough to admit he's better on the ground than I am."

I look up at Michael, noting that he doesn't appear to have taken any confidence from what Jaxson said. It's merely fact, not arrogance, and I can appreciate that. "Fine. But you're all going to need tuxedos. It's black-tie."

After Michael's gone home and Jaxson is settled into my parent's guest bedroom for the night, I head into my childhood room and take a seat on the edge of my bed. I really should have just gone home, but after thinking I'd lost my mom today, getting to wake up and have coffee with her in the morning is all too inviting.

My gaze drops to my feet. Just behind them, beneath my bed, is the box containing all of my memories of Michael throughout the years. Letters he'd pass me in class, love notes left in my locker, dried flowers from Valentine's Day, the corsage from prom…it's all in there.

As are the letters he wrote me.

Letters I've been avoiding opening for years, even more so since our confrontation in the gym.

"Did you not read any of my letters?"

"It wouldn't have mattered if I did."

"Yes, it would have." He moves in closer, his expression tormented. *"Because if you'd read them, you wouldn't have thought for a second that my leaving had anything to do with you."*

Tears burn in the corners of my eyes, but I angrily wipe them away.

They're just letters.

From years ago.

Paper and ink.

So why am I so afraid of them?

I drop down onto my hands and knees and reach beneath the bed, withdrawing the main box and the smaller one with his letters. With nerves dancing in my stomach, I open the top of the box and stare down at the stuffed envelopes inside.

He'd written to me constantly after he left. I'd been so angry that I'd thrown the first few away, not knowing my mom pulled them out of the trash as soon as I'd left the room. She'd given them to me a few weeks later, along with letters she'd removed directly from the mail, and told me that one day I might be angry at myself for not reading them.

That, while the hurt is so great right now, someday, it might not. Though given how badly I still ache, I can't help but wonder if she were merely trying to put my mind at ease.

Well, I'm still waiting for that day to come, but at this moment, I'm glad she didn't let me toss them out. I choose one at random, then slide my finger beneath the sealed flap and open the envelope.

As I draw the folded pages out, I'm hit with a sense of heaviness I can't explain. Like I'm about to uncover something that will forever change the way I've seen Michael these past few years. And I can't decide whether that's a good thing or if I'm just opening myself up for more heartbreak.

Reyna,

I don't know why I'm still writing these letters. I can only imagine that you're tired of reading them—if you even are. I just don't know who else to talk to. And even if you aren't reading them, it feels good to get everything on the page so that I can at least pretend you are.

How are you? How are things back home?

It's summertime, so I imagine you're spending plenty of time at the beach, hunting seashells for your collection or searching for washed-up messages in a bottle. I know that's one of your favorite things to do, and if I knew it would get to you, I would stuff this letter into a glass bottle just so you could find it.

Things here are bleak. Deployment has been rough on me this time around. I'm not sure if it's the location or simply my outlook on all of it.

A friend of mine died yesterday. He was a good man. Had a wife and toddler back home, and now he's just gone. It's so hard to believe.

His wife will be getting a folded-up flag, and all I can think about is how incredibly sad it's going to be for that kid to grow up without a dad, all because of the ugliness of war.

And then that leads me to thoughts of you.

Of how it could have been you getting the folded flag if we'd gotten married like we planned and I still joined.

Which leads me to be grateful we didn't because I wouldn't want you to remember me that way. As a flag. Red, white, and blue.

How do you remember me now? I doubt you'd recognize me if you saw me again. I barely recognize the man staring back at me in the mirror.

Honestly, there's a part of me—a dark, depressing part—that hopes I don't make it home. Because then I will live forever in your mind as the boy I was before I became a soldier.

I want to tell you that I miss you more and more each day.

And as always, I want to finish it off by telling you how sorry I am. How much I wish I could come home to you, wrap you in my arms, and never let you go.

Love,

Michael

By the time I've finished reading, tears are streaming down my cheeks. I read it a second time. A third. Hating how lonely he must have felt. Did he cry while he wrote it? Does he still wish he'd never come home?

CHAPTER 15

Michael

"Y ou're sure about this, son?"

"I'm eighteen. I can make my own choices." I sit across the desk from a man wearing an Army uniform. We're surrounded by posters about how the Army wants me. How the military needs strong, capable soldiers.

I'm strong—right?

Capable.

"I'm not questioning that." The name Caves adorns his uniform along with a rank I don't know enough about to recognize. "But once you start the process, you have to see it through. And you look like you're running from something."

"Not running. I just need a chance. Time away from my town."

"You could take a vacation."

"I don't want a vacation. I want to do this. I want to be something."

The recruiter studies me, and I can see that he genuinely

cares enough to make sure I understand just what it is I'm signing up for. "Do you know what job you might want to do?"

"Anything."

"The first step is to take the ASVAB. Once we have your scores we can go from there."

I think about Reyna. About how we went and took our SATs together. This is somewhere she won't follow me. Do I really have the strength to leave her behind?

"You will never make anything of yourself if you marry that girl," *my father said.* "You'll end up right where I am. Broken and stuck in this town for the rest of your life."

"Then tell me where to be and I'll be there," I tell him. "When can we go?"

My father wants me to go pro. He wants me to play ball for money. All I want is to marry Reyna. Start a family. Work in the shop and build a life here. But I'll never be allowed to do that. My father will never grant us any peace, so my only option is to leave.

To show him that he doesn't have control, and then maybe...maybe she can forgive me.

Someday.

But even as I listen to the recruiter detail the entrance process, I know that it's unlikely she ever will.

"GIVE ME SOMETHING TO DO." I PLOP DOWN IN THE DESK chair across from Lance. He glances over from his computer and arches a brow.

"Feeling a little pent-up?"

I pop a piece of gum into my mouth. "I need to do something. Anything. I can't get my mind off of Reyna and what a massive mistake her going to Boston is."

"We're all going to Boston," he replies. "And I've already started coordinating with her event security. They seem like a great team."

"Good for them. It's still a mistake."

"Possibly, but it's important to her. And you know how we handle things like this. Our client's needs come first. She needs to go? We make it happen safely."

I shake my head. "I'm going insane. I can't do my job because she insists on Jaxson doing it, I can't convince you all that we need to put our foot down and refuse."

"If we do that, she fires us and goes anyway."

"Carter won't fire us, and he's the one technically paying us."

"Michael."

I know I'm behaving like an angry teenager. That if it were any other client I wouldn't be acting this way. But Reyna changes things. She always has. "Fine. But give me something to do. There has to be a client somewhere who needs something. A kitten stuck in a tree? I can handle it. Just give me *something*."

He chuckles and pulls a neon yellow sticky note off of the bottom of his monitor, then offers it to me. "Mrs.

Redding called and asked if we'd add an additional panel at the back door of her bakery so she's not having to sprint across the store to turn it off. Think you can manage an install?"

"Done." I snatch the sticky note from him and jump to my feet, more than ready for the distraction.

After grabbing an extra panel and a bag of tools, I head out to my truck and make the short drive toward the bakery. I put the truck into park and climb out, taking my bag and the panel with me.

The moment I step inside, Mrs. Redding glances up from the customer she's helping. "Hey, Michael, you here to add the other panel?"

"Yes, ma'am."

"Great. It's just back here."

The man at the counter turns and offers me a hesitant smile. "Michael," he greets.

"Liam." I start toward the back.

"Wait, can I ask you something?"

Taking a deep breath, I turn to face him. "What is it? I'm on a schedule."

"You and I don't know each other."

"No, we don't."

"But I care about Reyna, and I sense you do, too. More than it just being your job, at least."

"You can say that."

"I asked around a bit. I know you two were an item back in school, and I just want to make sure we're not going to have any problems between us since I'm courting her now."

Courting her? Who talks like that? "Reyna is her own person," I tell him. "She can be courted by whomever she wants."

He visibly relaxes. "Good. Glad to hear it. Thanks."

"Yeah. Is that all?"

"It is. See you around."

"See you." Jealousy has no business taking root in my heart, but there it is, thorny and infuriating as it spreads through me.

"You look like you'd rather break the panel," Mrs. Redding jokes.

"I'm fine. Just show me where you want it."

She points to the back door. "Right beside there."

"Great." I drop the bag of tools, then set the panel box down on top of a stainless-steel countertop.

"Michael." She places her hand gently on my arm, and I turn. Her husband may be the pastor, but Kyra Redding is nearly as close to me as my own mother. They were best friends growing up, and not much has changed even though my mom rarely leaves the house. "Talk to me."

"I'm working through it," I tell her. "I just—I've realized that all this time I've been holding on to hope that Reyna might forgive me, and now I'm understanding that she probably won't."

"She'll forgive you someday," she says with a smile.

"It just might not be in the way you're hoping for, and you need to come to terms with that."

BEFORE I CAN CHANGE MY MIND, I LIFT MY FIST AND KNOCK on Reyna's door.

Jaxson is parked just outside, and I'm willing to bet he's counting on her slamming the door in my face. I know I am.

She pulls it open wearing leggings and a baggy shirt that falls down to her mid-thigh. Her red hair is wet and dangling over her shoulders. She's breathtaking.

"What is it?"

"I wanted to say something."

"You can come in." She steps aside, but I remain where I am.

"I don't need to come in, this won't take long."

"Okay." She crosses her arms, and I run a hand through my hair.

"I'm a prideful man. It's something I've always struggled with. And I realized today that I haven't given you a straight apology. I've told you that it was a mistake, and I explained—poorly—why I left, but I want you to know, Reyna, I am truly sorry for what I did to you. I hurt you, beyond repair, and I see that now."

Her eyes fill, but she doesn't say anything.

"I'm going to talk to Lance. As soon as we catch

whoever is after you, I'm going to make the move to Boston. Likely not permanently, since my sister needs me here, but I'll be spending most of my time there, aiding our larger clients and running the field office we've been talking about for quite some time."

"You don't have to do that," she says, uncrossing her arms. Her gaze widens.

"I do. Because you're right. I shouldn't have come back into your life the way I did. You deserve happiness. A family. A life. Even if it can't be with me."

"Thank you."

"Anyway. I just wanted to tell you that. I'm here if you need me, Reyna." I level my gaze on hers. "For forever and a day."

CHAPTER 16

Reyna

Forever and a day.

I haven't been able to get Michael out of my head. Especially since that evening on my porch. And being in Boston with him hasn't been any easier. We've been here for two days now, setting everything up, and he's been more quiet than normal but still stepping up and helping as needed.

All of them have truly been great, but Michael has gone above and beyond in helping me pull this thing off. Which I'm more appreciative of than I can even admit given how hesitant he was to let me come in the first place.

I've been trying to find a way to tell him that I read his letters. That seeing the words on the page did make me connect with the mindset he'd been in when he left. But I'm not sure how to do it without bringing up the pain of our past.

He's in the living room of the hotel suite right now, alongside Elijah, Jaxson, and Lance as they prepare for the banquet. Then, tomorrow morning, we get to go home. There's been no contact from my attacker, no action on my house since I've been gone, and I'm truly starting to wonder if he hasn't simply moved on.

Maybe he left town because he realized he was going to get caught sooner or later. I apply a smooth line of lipstick over my mouth then stand back and study myself in the mirror. I've never been one for makeup, so I opted for a bit of color on my cheeks and some pale lipstick rather than a full face.

The gown I'm wearing fits perfectly, and I'm beyond grateful Margot came over and helped me pick it out before we left Hope Springs. Even if she'd given me trouble over calling this banquet evening a date with her brother.

Especially since I'd had him in mind when I'd chosen this particular color. Green is his favorite.

Someone knocks on the door. "Come in." I don't bother to turn because chances are it's Lance checking in on me once again, letting me know the security team has swept the event area, and ensuring no one is in and out who isn't supposed to be there.

It's the tightest security we've ever run. I can only hope no one else notices and suspects that something is wrong.

"You look—"

I turn now, my heart hammering as I face off with

Michael. He looks absolutely gorgeous in a tuxedo, his dark hair styled. And I suddenly feel very, very vulnerable in my dress. Though based on the way he's looking at me, it was a good choice.

"Are we leaving?" I ask, not letting him finish his sentence.

Boundaries.

That's what we need.

"Yes," he replies. "Lance, Elijah, and Jaxson already headed out. So we'll be a bit behind them. Which Lance felt was better for optics. Given that I'm technically supposed to look like your date tonight." He's uncomfortable, which I can appreciate, because so am I.

Mainly because even though I know it's not good, I want this to *be* an actual date. Not just look like one.

Gathering the skirt of my gown, I head toward the door, then follow him out of the room and down the hall to the elevators. He presses the button and we stand in silence as we wait for the doors to open.

The drive over to the event is short, maybe five minutes, but we do it in complete silence. In fact, it's not until he's opening the door for me at the valet that Michael even begins to look like he's having a good time.

Even though I know it's a mistake, I link my arm through his, smiling widely at everyone as we pass. I wave with my free hand, offer greetings, and head into the ballroom with Michael at my side. Even with my heels on, he towers over me, drawing more than a few curious glances.

Which, of course, sparks irrational jealousy.

"Can you hear me?" he asks carefully. I know he's not talking to me, but rather to the guys via the earbud I'd seen him slip in right as we'd arrived. "Great. Let me know if that changes." His hand goes to my mid-back, and he leans in. I have to fight the urge to lean into him farther as he whispers, "We're all good right now."

Before I can respond, a beautiful woman rushes through the crowd, a wide smile on her face. "You're here!" Emily greets. I barely have enough time to get my arm free of Michael's before she's wrapping me in a hug. "And looking absolutely amazing!" She holds me at arm's length and studies me.

I do the same, appreciating the lavender gown she wears and the way it complements her coloring.

"And who is this tall drink of water?" she asks, looking up at Michael.

"Michael. My—uh—date."

"Wait—Michael from high school, Michael?" she asks, arching a brow at me.

Why? Why did I not warn her ahead of time? "One and the same," I tell her, trying to keep my tone casual.

"Wow. Well, it's nice to meet you, Michael. I'm Emily. Are there more of you?" She offers him her hand, and he takes it.

"More of me?"

"Tall, handsome, muscled men? Because as it

happens, I'm in the market for a long-lasting relationship, and so far, I've had terrible luck."

"Emily!" I half scold, even as I can't keep the grin off
my face. This is one of the reasons I adore her. Straight
to the point. Always.

Michael laughs. "Nice to meet you too. While I do
have a single friend, he's not much in the mood for
dating these days," he replies. "Did you help with this
event?" He looks around the room and I long to ask him
what he thinks. Will he be impressed by what we've
done? Bored?

"Shame. Have him let me know if that changes." She
winks. "As for helping, I did, but our girl here organizes
it. All I do is make sure the pieces are in the right place
since I'm local." She beams at me. "There are quite a few
people who want to meet you." She takes my hand and
tugs me along, but I can't keep myself from looking
back to make sure Michael is with me.

His gaze meets mine, and my stomach flutters.

He's finally agreed to leave me alone, and all I can
think about is kissing him. How does that make sense?

I turn back around as Emily drags me across the
floor, introducing me to people I won't remember,
though I should.

By the time I've done the rounds, I'm already
exhausted.

"Here." Michael offers me a mug of coffee, then
guides me over to our table near the front. After
scooting my chair in once I've sat down, he sits beside

me. "This is amazing, Reyna. How long have you been hosting this?"

"This is the third year," I tell him.

"It's spectacular." He looks around the room, clearly impressed, and it warms my heart to know he's seeing all of the hard work I put into it.

"It does good work," I tell him.

"Michael! There you are!" A woman with golden hair and a white dress that manages to be both form-fitting and modest at the same time rushes toward us. Michael stands, and she wraps her arms around him, then plants a kiss on his cheek.

"Hey, Sunny, I'm so glad you could make it."

Jealousy sears me from the inside. Did he seriously invite a date here? Is that how badly he wants to hurt me?

"Sunny, this is Reyna Acker."

I stand and offer her a smile and my hand when she reaches forward for it. "You organized this?"

"I did," I reply.

"It's amazing. So well run. And I—there he is! Over here, babe!"

A tall man steps through the crowd and offers her a glass of water. "Sorry, I got lost there for a minute."

Sunny laughs. "This is my husband, Geoff. Honey, this is Reyna. The woman who organized this event."

"This is amazing. Better than most of the red-carpet parties we've gone to."

"Red carpet—" And then it clicks. Sunny Rune. "You're an actress," I blurt.

She laughs. "I am. Though apparently not a very good one."

"What? No. Sorry. I don't see many movies. But I know who you are."

"I'm just toying with you," Sunny says with another laugh. "Sorry, this is the first outing we've had since the baby, and I'm both excited and desperate to get home. But when Michael called and told us, we knew that we had to fly out and support such a great cause. Our son is back at the hotel with my mother-in-law."

I look from her to Michael, feeling foolish that I thought he might have invited her as a date. "How do you all know each other?"

Geoff wraps an arm around his wife's shoulders. "He works for us from time to time. Managed to save our son when a paparazzi tried to rip him from Sunny's arms so he could get photographs of him before we were ready for anyone to know about the birth. Michael is our hero."

"It was nothing."

"It was everything," Sunny replies, reaching out to touch his arm gently. "Don't be modest."

"She's right," Geoff adds. "Most bodyguards wouldn't have chased the man through L.A. to get his phone and handle the pictures."

"It was only a few blocks," Michael replies with a laugh.

"Still. We're eternally grateful," Sunny says. "Now, how did you two meet?"

Michael looks at me, then back to her. "We've known each other since we were kids."

"Aww, that's so sweet! High school sweethearts?"

"Something like that," Michael replies.

The music shifts, turning to a slow song, and Geoff takes his wife's hand. "May I have this dance, my love?"

Sunny blushes. "Absolutely. Excuse us."

"No problem. Have fun." As they walk away, I try to keep myself from looking at Michael, but then his hand goes to the middle of my back again and I lose myself in the feeling of comfort.

"Want to dance?"

I look up at him. "I have about an hour before I need to speak. But, wait, are you sure that you still know how?"

Michael grins. A real, unguarded smile that steals my breath once more and turns my legs to jelly. "I'm even better now." He tugs me onto the dance floor, one hand resting on the middle of my back, the other holding mine.

I snake my free arm around his neck and breathe through the nerves as we begin to move on the floor. The world around us fades away, leaving just him and me together, moving to the slow beat.

"Do you remember our senior prom?" Michael asks.

"A bit of it." Truth is, I remember every single moment. From Michael slipping that corsage over my wrist to sharing stolen kisses on the dance floor and hoping the teachers didn't see us.

Stupid teenagers who didn't realize their entire lives were about to change.

"It was a good night."

"It was." A month later, he was gone. Right before the graduation we'd both been so excited for. And in the darkest moments of my pain, I'd recalled the way he'd looked down at me when we were dancing. The way the light cast shadows over his expression.

"You looked so beautiful in that dress. It was nearly the same shade of green as this one."

"You remember what I was wearing?"

"I remember all of it," Michael replies.

Our gazes hold, and the moment that passes between us feels so potent one could cut it with a knife. How did we get here, both of us so broken that it seems impossible we could fit back together? "I read your letters."

Michael continues moving, though his expression darkens. "I thought you would have thrown them away."

"I tried to," I admit. "My mom pulled them out of the trash because she knew I'd want to read them one day. Even if I couldn't admit to myself that I would."

He chuckles. "Is it bad if part of me wishes she had left them in the trash?"

"I don't." My tone is serious, my gaze locked on his

even as he turns me on the dance floor. "Michael, I'm sorry that I didn't read them before. If I had—"

"It's okay, Reyna. I hurt you. I shouldn't have expected you to write me back. Honestly, at some point, I knew you wouldn't. But writing to you helped me feel less alone."

The lump in my throat burns.

"Which, of course, wasn't fair to you. I see that now."

"You said that a part of you hoped you wouldn't come home."

"That part was there. For a long time."

"And now?"

He pulls me in closer and leans down, whispering in my ear, "I am blessed to have come home, Reyna, because if I hadn't, I wouldn't be sharing this moment with you."

My heart hammers, need surging through my veins. Even as I know it's a bad idea, that it will likely lead to more pain, I want him to kiss me. Right here. Right now.

The music suddenly dies, and the room is plunged into darkness. It's a bucket of cold water to my face as adrenaline surges through my system, making my movements jittery. My stomach twists into knots. *Are they here? Did they find us? Or is it something totally explainable?*

Everyone around begins to mutter, and Michael tugs me against him. "What was that?" I hear him ask. "Where?"

Phone lights begin to illuminate the dance floor, and Michael pushes me through the crowd, not bothering to pull his own out.

"Jaxson is guiding us," he whispers to me.

I don't speak, just let Michael lead me away from the dance floor. We reach the back room, and something slams into us. I fall to the side and the lights come back on right as Michael tackles a man wearing all black.

"Get back here!" Michael yells, and I can only hope the others can hear through his earpiece.

Through the doors and on the dance floor, the music comes back on, and people begin dancing again, *unaware* of the danger lurking just outside the doors.

"Reyna Acker."

I turn at the mention of my name and find myself staring at a second masked man mere feet away from me. *There are two of them now? Where did he come from?*

"Get back onto the dance floor!" Michael orders.

I turn and rush forward, but the man is faster. He hits me like a linebacker, and I fall to the side, my head ringing where it impacts with the wall.

Michael slams his fist into the man who'd been going after him and launches himself at the man coming for me. The sickening crunch of bone fills my ears as he slams his fist into my attacker's nose, then lunges for me and pulls me to my feet.

He sprints down the hall, taking me with him.

"They're behind us," he says. "Hurry!" He tugs me down the hall and toward an emergency exit. From their planning, I know Jaxson will have left a truck there just in case, keys inside the gas cap. We push through the door, letting it slam behind us, then close the distance between us and the vehicle.

A gunshot rings out, and Michael stumbles.

"No! Michael!" I scream.

He turns and snarls, a predatory growl leaving his lips as he faces off with a masked man holding a firearm. Michael rushes forward, and the man fires again, but he misses this time, and Michael takes him to the pavement.

My heart hammers as I search for a weapon of my own. For something, anything to protect Michael. He grips the man and lifts him, only to slam him back into the pavement. As soon as the man falls still, Michael gets to his feet and starts toward me. He falls forward, and I catch him before he can hit the ground, taking enough of his body weight that I can keep him on his feet.

"We need to get you to a hospital." I guide him over to the truck. "Michael's been shot!" I yell, hoping the guys can hear through the earpiece wherever they are. I open the passenger side door, and Michael climbs inside.

"Where are you hit?"

"Chest," he chokes out.

"Oh no. Please, God, get us through this." I slam his door then run around the truck and climb behind the wheel. After kicking my heels off, I peel out of the parking lot. Thankfully, at this hour, these streets are desolate.

Michael hisses through clenched teeth as he shrugs out of his tuxedo jacket, and I glance over, my stomach churning when I see the blood staining his white dress shirt. "It's just a flesh wound," he says, though he presses the wadded-up jacket against it and leans back, eyes closed.

"Just a flesh wound? That's a lot of blood!"

"I've had worse."

"Because that makes it better," I snap then pull out onto the street and head toward Boston General.

We make it two stoplights before a truck runs a red light and slams into Michael's side of the vehicle. Metal crunches, and a scream ricochets through the truck. It takes me two seconds before I realize it's coming from me. Pain shoots through me, and I reach up with shaky fingers to feel warm liquid coming from my forehead.

The truck backs up and slams into us again.

The horn is deafening.

"Go," Michael growls when our vehicle comes to a stop. He points to the left, to the tree line just out of reach. "Run."

"I—" I don't even get the chance to tell him I won't leave him before the door is ripped open and a masked man withdraws a gun. He points it at Michael and fires.

"No!" I scream, tugging at my seatbelt and trying to get free.

He turns the weapon on me and fires—and everything goes black.

CHAPTER 17
Michael

"Dude, you can't be serious." Private Adams rolls his eyes.

"He's serious," Elijah says, glancing into the backseat of the Humvee. "He wouldn't shut up about it when we met."

Chuckling, I turn my attention back outside. "You guys have no idea what you're talking about." The heat is stifling, making it difficult to breathe. I reach up and rest my hand on the top of my Kevlar vest, just so I can pull it away from my chest for a moment.

"Then tell us. Explain to us how you could possibly justify saying the later HALO games are better than the original?" Adams demands. "You'd have to be crazy to think they got better!"

"I stand by what I said. The storylines are better than—"

An explosion shakes the windows, and the Humvee in front of

us explodes. My stomach lurches, and adrenaline surges through my system.

"Contact!" Captain Knight yells as Specialist Greyson jerks the wheel. But it's too late. Fire licks the side as our vehicle hits another explosive. We flip over, and I'm thrown from the Humvee. I hit the hot sand, and it sears the exposed skin of my face.

But it's the least of my worries.

Pain shoots through my body, and I struggle to suck in a breath. My chest feels like it's collapsing, making it impossible to breathe. I scan the clearing, looking for my friends. Elijah is to the left of me, lying on his back, his weapon discarded at his side.

The letter. I need to get him my letter. So he can get it to Reyna.

I look to my right and spot Adams, dead, in the dirt. His eyes are wide open as he stares straight at me, blood dripping from a wound in his head. It seems surreal. A nightmare.

We'd just been talking, and now he's gone? How is this happening? My pulse skyrockets, and Captain Knight kneels at my side. He's the only one of us on his feet, though his face has multiple scrapes.

"Look at me, Sergeant," he orders.

I do, trying my best to focus despite the pain and panic currently wreaking havoc on my system. I'm going to die. I'm going to be a flag-draped coffin, and Reyna will never know how sorry I am. She'll never know that I still love her.

"I called for evac. You're going to be fine. I need you to—"

A bullet hits the dirt beside me and Captain Knight

whirls. Staying low, he crouches behind a boulder and holds up his weapon to return fire.

"Michael."

I look to my left, and it's Reyna I see crawling toward me through the rubble, her face streaked with blood, her hair matted to the side of her head.

"This isn't right," I manage. "You aren't supposed to be here."

"But I am here," she says as she crawls closer. "Because you left me. Again."

"No. You aren't here," I say again.

"Look at me!" she screams. "Michael! I need you!"

"THERE HE IS. WELCOME BACK TO THE WORLD, BIG MAN."

I blink rapidly, trying to clear my blurry vision. My arms are bound above my head, my legs dangling down, my toes barely brushing the floor. The pain in my shoulder is substantial, but one look at the white bandage over it tells me they at least don't want me to bleed to death.

My vision is blurry, and I'm weak. Whether that's from blood loss or whatever they dosed me with, I'm not sure. But it's going to make getting out of here near impossible. "Where is she?" I manage, choking on each word. There's a vile taste in my mouth, a side effect of whatever it is they gave me to knock me out.

"She is none of your concern," the man in front of me says.

He's tall, bulky, and packing some massive heat at his hip. His dark hair is cut short, nearly to the scalp. I've never seen him before, but I know the type. He's a mercenary. A gun for hire. Willing to do whatever for a buck.

And he's sporting a massive arm tattoo that spans his hand up beneath the sleeve of his shirt. I glare over at him. "*You.*"

"You know, I didn't appreciate you trying to mow me down with your truck. I'd planned on going back for you after we'd gotten the girl, just to square things off. But then you went and made it super easy for me by not leaving her side." He grins. "Thanks for that."

"I'm happy to let you take another swing at me if you'll unchain me," I manage.

The man laughs. "I don't need you unchained to take a swing at you." He pushes off the table he'd been leaning against and crosses over. After balling up his fist, he slams it into my jaw. Blood fills my mouth, the coppery tang only adding to my nausea. "See, my masculinity isn't tied to needing a fair fight. I know what I'm capable of." He slams his fist into my face again, and pain ricochets through me.

Still, I don't let it show. I spit, splattering the concrete floor with blood. "I don't know why I'm surprised you wouldn't want a fair fight. It takes a coward to go after an unarmed woman in a dark parking lot."

The man growls. "You have no idea who you're talking to. Otherwise, you'd watch your mouth, bodyguard."

"Even if I did know, I imagine I'd still be unimpressed."

He reaches up and digs his thumb into my bandaged wound.

I groan, biting back a cry of agony because I know it will only bring him satisfaction.

The door opens, and he withdraws his hand, his gaze going to someone behind me.

"I trust you've been making our guest feel at home," a man says as he comes into my line of sight. The suit he wears is likely more expensive than the gym I own, and his grey hair is longer on top, shorter on the bottom, his face clean-shaven.

"Absolutely," replies the man who'd looked ready to kill me right here.

"Asher, take it easy. I can't have you killing him yet."

Asher backs away, but the murderous glare he gives me is enough to tell me that we're just getting started. Good. I have plenty to say to him, too.

"Your name is Michael Anderson, correct?" the suited man asks, leaning back against the table. The steely gaze he gives me lacks all empathy. Which means he's not a man to be toyed with.

Asher may be the killer, but this man has blood all over his hands.

"You already know that, otherwise I wouldn't be here." I spit more blood to the side.

He chuckles. "Fair point. Now, Mikey, can I call you Mikey?"

"I'd rather you didn't."

His amusement disappears. "Fair enough. *Michael.* Asher tells me that you and your team have been getting in my way recently."

"Wish I could say I was sorry about it, but I'm not."

His grin is back. "You've got confidence, I'll give you that. Any chance you're looking for a job?" Before I can tell him where to put that offer, he waves a hand in front of his face. "Nah, who am I kidding. You do-gooders don't have the stomach for real work."

"If you mean I don't have the stomach for attacking innocent women in dark parking lots, then yeah, you'd be right." I wheeze, sucking in a pained breath since every single movement is agony right now.

"It seems to me we're in the same line of work. You have someone to protect, and so do I."

"Where is she?" I demand again.

"Which she?" he asks. "I'm afraid I need you to be a bit more specific."

"Reyna," I growl.

"Ah, yes. Gorgeous redhead. Legs a mile long. Principal, right?" When I don't respond, he laughs. "Easy there, killer, she's alive. Which is how she'll stay as long as everyone plays ball."

"I want to see her."

"I'm afraid you're in no position to make demands, Michael Anderson."

"What do you want? Money? I can get it for you. Just let her go."

"I'm not after money," he replies. "As you can see, I've got plenty."

"Then what do you want? Why go after a school principal?"

"Let's just say I needed some collateral," he replies. "While I wouldn't have ordered you being brought in" —he glares at Asher, who continues staring straight at me—"I can admit that having two hostages might prove to be rather beneficial. Especially given your close relationship with the man I'm looking for."

"The best trackers in the world will be looking for us," I say, knowing Lance will have called in the cavalry to find us. "You don't stand a chance."

"I'm not worried. See, I did some digging into you as soon as I found out you were here. Michael Anderson. War hero. Nearly killed in action, but somehow managed to pull through despite doctors saying you wouldn't. Works at Knight Security with Lance Knight, Elijah Andrews, and most recently—Jaxson Payne, a former detective with the LAPD. How am I doing so far?" I don't answer, so he continues, "Both of your parents live in Hope Springs, along with your sister and her son, and you and Reyna were hot and heavy all through high school until you left her behind to join the service."

"All you're telling me is that you're good at research," I say.

"Yes. I am. I'm also not a man who toys around, Mr. Anderson. Which means I won't hesitate to put a bullet in you should you prove to not be useful."

"You still haven't told me what it is you expect from me."

He folds his arms. "I expect you to tell me everything you know about Carter Acker."

My stomach twists. Is this what Reyna's abduction has been about this entire time? Her brother? "Seems to me you should have already figured it all out. Being that you're good at research and all that."

He laughs and shakes his head. "Mouthy, mouthy, mouthy." He nods back to Asher, who steps forward and slams his fist into my face. My head whips back, but when I straighten again, I smile, despite the blood dripping from my mouth and the agonizing pain in my shoulder.

"Now, let's try that again," the man in charge says. "See, Acker keeps his life relatively under wraps. I know that he's married and that he has children, but they have a protective detail on them twenty-four-seven. They have no known routines and are a bit more high profile than I care for."

"You're after his family?"

"I'm after his *everything*," he growls.

"Let me guess." I lean back and stare up at him. "He put someone you care about away? Dismantled your organization? What exactly did Carter do to garner your attention in such detail?"

"Let's just say he and I have a score to settle." He clasps his hands together. "Now. Answer the questions, or I will find a way to make you less comfortable."

"I got nothing. Carter and I had a falling out when—as you said—I left Reyna to join the service. I know nothing about his life, his routine, or anything that will be of any help to you."

"Then why do I leave you alive?"

I shrug. "I guess you have no reason to do so." It's dangerous, calling the bluff of a man like the one across from me, but it's all I've got. I have to bank on the fact that there's a reason he's coming to me with these questions rather than going to Reyna when realistically, she's the one who will have the answers.

"I guess we need to go see your girl," he says. "One way or another, I'm going to find out everything I want to know."

"You certainly seem like the type to try."

"Try." Chuckling, he shakes his head. "You are going to make this difficult, aren't you?"

I smile. "I'm not hired for my sunny demeanor," I reply.

"Well—" He comes forward, tilting his head up since he's at least half a foot shorter than I am. "Let me explain something to you, Mr. Anderson. I am not, in any way, shape, or form, similar to the types you're used to dealing with. I do not fail. I do not give up. And one way or another, I will get Carter Acker's head on a silver platter. Now, it's up to you whether or not your sister and his make for a trio." He straightens and turns to Asher. "Let him sweat it out. I've got things to deal with, but go ahead and see the girl." He looks back at me. "We'll start with her."

CHAPTER 18

Reyna

The interview room I woke up in consists of four concrete walls—one with a door, another with a viewing mirror. A steel table is bolted to the ground, and two metal folding chairs sit on either side of it. The cot I was lying on when I came to has no blankets and is situated on the far wall, opposite the door.

It's a nearly exact replica of any police interview room on any crime show ever, but I know, without a doubt, it's not the police who brought me here. As far as I know, they don't crash into the side of your vehicle... and they don't shoot you with tranquilizer darts.

I run my hand over the back of my neck, rolling it to try to alleviate some of the tension. Every inch of my body aches from the impact, though when I woke up, I discovered my forehead had been bandaged, which means whoever grabbed us wants me alive...right?

Michael. He'd been shot and on the side where the truck hit us. Is he even alive? Tears fill my eyes, but I quickly blink them away. I need to get myself out of here, then I can go for him. Isn't that what they tell you on airplanes? Fix your own oxygen mask first?

God, please let him be alive. Guide me to him. Help us get out of here.

Shoving the fear down, I focus only on the task at hand. Getting out of here has to be my top priority, so I aim to keep my heart rate steady and conserve my energy, and try not to catch someone's attention.

I remain standing, my hands on the back of the chair since it's the only weapon I see. Aim high, swing fast. Just like softball. Kind of. I was good at softball. Thing is, the timing hast to be right because whoever comes in, can't see it coming.

The door opens and my heart hammers as a man wearing a shoulder holster steps in. His firearm is on plain display, and the folder in his hands looks relatively thin.

No badge anywhere in sight.

But his knuckles are bloodied.

Michael. Please be alive.

"Who are you, and why am I here?" I demand.

"My name is Asher," he replies with a smile. He looks to be about my age, his hair cut short—prior military, maybe? He takes a seat at the table and gestures for me to sit. A large tattoo starts on the side of his hand

and snakes up his arm, disappearing into the sleeve of his shirt.

"Why am I here?" I ask again.

"You're here because we need information."

"Who is *we*?"

He smiles. "I work for a very small law enforcement agency branched off of the FBI."

"Then you won't mind showing me ID."

His smile turns savage. All teeth. "Of course not." He reaches into his pocket and withdraws a leather badge holder. After flipping it open, he lays it on the table. I inch closer and take a look.

Given that I don't have a lot of history with fake government IDs, I can't tell if it's real or fake. But my gut tells me it's the latter. Still, I slide it back toward him. "Since when does the FBI crash into people's vehicles and tranquilize them?"

"Since we needed this to be completely off the record." He opens the folder and withdraws a picture. He slides it onto the table, and I find myself staring down at an image of Carter crossing the street, talking on a phone. "Do you know this man?"

"Where is Michael?" I demand.

"In another room having his injuries tended to." He runs a finger over his bloodied knuckles, almost in mocking.

"You expect me to believe that?"

"Why wouldn't you?" he asks.

"Because you're the ones who caused his injuries."

"Miss Acker, I can assure you that we saved your life by getting to you when we did."

I don't believe his lie for a second. "Then let me see Michael."

"After I get some answers, I will take you to him." He taps the photograph of Carter. "Now. Do you know this man?"

"No," I lie. "Am I supposed to?"

Asher smiles again. "I know you're lying. But I can imagine you're nervous, so let me help you out. That is Carter Acker. Your brother, and head prosecutor for the city of Boston, Massachusetts."

I don't say a word.

"We have reason to believe he's wrapped up in something illegal."

He's fishing, so I continue to keep my mouth shut.

"Miss Acker, this will all go a lot smoother if you just answer us."

"I want to see Michael."

"After we're done here."

"No. I want to see him now."

"Not possible until you answer my questions."

"Then get me my lawyer. I'm entitled to one."

Asher leans in closer. "Go ahead and call your brother, then." He slides a cell phone across the table. "I imagine he's who you'd call, correct?"

I swallow hard. It's a trap. I know it's a trap. And yet the urge to phone my brother, to let him know something is wrong, is so strong I have to actively fight against it.

I cross my arms.

He chuckles and puts the phone back into his pocket. "As I said. Your brother is wrapped up in some illegal stuff, Miss Acker. We merely need information on his whereabouts."

"Looks like you've been tracking him. Seems to me you could figure it out yourself."

"One would think so," he says. "But as it turns out, your brother has deep pockets and an even deeper connection network. We can't track him or his family aside from the times he's in his office. He hasn't been staying at his house, and his car has remained parked in the underground garage at his office building."

My stomach twists again. All of this is wrong. Everything he's saying is wrong. "Let me see Michael." I plant both hands on the desk. "Now." Jaxson will have sent out an emergency signal, right? Won't he know we're missing?

"Miss Acker. This can be as easy or as difficult as you make it. Give me the information I want, and I will let you and Mr. Anderson go."

"So we are being held captive here. We have rights."

"Rights that became invalid the moment Homeland Security was threatened."

"Homeland Security?" I ask, brow furrowing. "You're wrong. Whatever it is you think you know, it's wrong."

"I don't think it is."

"I do." I slam both palms on the table. "And I'm not telling you anything until you let me see Michael."

Asher glares up at me, then stands, though he leaves the folder on the table. "Maybe some more time in here alone will help. I tell you what, though, how about I go let Mr. Anderson know you're asking about him. He and I have already had one great conversation this morning." The way he says it makes my skin crawl.

He starts toward the door. I have mere seconds to act, so I quietly lift the chair and sprint over toward him, reaching him right as he turns the doorknob.

"Fine," I say quickly. "Maybe I do know something that can help."

"I thought—" He turns, and I slam the chair into his face. He stumbles back, so I hit him again and again, using every ounce of strength I have to take him to the ground. As soon as he's still, I rip his firearm free, grabbing the cell phone, a set of keys, and his wallet, then I kick off my heels so I can keep my movements quiet, before I slip out the door. After checking to make sure the door is locked behind me, I head down the sterile hallway, firearm cocked and at the ready.

I've not used guns much in my adult life, but Michael and I used to go to the range with his dad nearly every summer, so I keep that training in mind as I creep down the hall, checking every door I pass.

There are no cameras in the hall.

No guards roaming around.

It all feels very—odd.

I reach a door that locks from the outside just like the one to the room I'd been in, so I unlock it and pull it open. A man is practically dangling from the ceiling, his arms chained above his head. His feet barely touch the ground, and his head is hung low. He has no shirt on, and the muscles of his back are strained, his skin coated in a mixture of dirt and dried blood.

Michael.

My heart pounds as I use Asher's wallet to prop the door open and rush forward, moving around to the front of him. His shoulder has been bandaged, though blood has already started staining the white gauze, and his chest is covered in both fresh and dried blood.

It drips down his face from a cut along his strong cheekbone and is splattered on the floor beneath him.

I'm horrified at what must have been done to him, but even as I want to tend to every injury, I know there's no time.

"Michael?" I whisper as I reach out to touch him. He looks up at me, and relief pushes past my fear—momentarily. Both eyes are bloodshot, his lip is bleeding, and there's that cut along his cheekbone.

But he's alive. And if we're together, I know we can make it out of this. *Thank you, God.*

"Reyna. What are you doing here?" He chokes the words out, as if speaking causes him pain.

I set the gun and phone down on the table, then rush

over with the set of keys. "I hit someone named Asher with a chair and stole his keys."

He grins, but it falls quickly. "You are amazing, do you know that?"

"Yeah. I know." I drag one of the folding chairs over and stand on it so I can reach up and get to his locks. Fumbling with the keys, I find one that fits the locks binding his wrists and unlock them. The moment I do, Michael falls to the ground.

He crouches low, catching his breath, and I jump down to help him to his feet.

"You need to go," he tells me. "Get out. Use that cell to call Lance."

"I'm not leaving you," I tell him.

"Reyna, I can barely walk."

"Then you need me to help you." I wrap his good arm over my shoulders and stand, biting back my own pain from my soreness after the accident, as I help him to his feet. Then I retrieve the gun and cell phone from the table and start toward the door.

It takes all of my energy to keep Michael on his feet, as well as ensuring we both keep moving forward.

He's wheezing, each breath strained, and my fear for him grows. *Please, God. Please.* I don't even have the words to continue pleading, so I focus on pushing my fear down once more. We can do this because we have God. He will see us through it.

I know He will.

"Any idea where we are?" I ask.

"Nope. Someone wants information on your brother, though."

"I got that."

"We can talk about it later. First, we need to get out of here."

"I came from that way," I point to the right.

"Then we'll try this way." He gestures to the left, so I bend and retrieve the wallet, letting the door close behind us and shoving the wallet and keys into Michael's pocket. That way, if anyone sees the closed door, they'll hopefully believe Michael is still chained inside.

We slip through another door and find ourselves standing in a large warehouse. Hundreds of crates fill the space, massive ones that are covered in cargo nets, as though they're prepping them for transportation.

What in the world is Carter involved in?

Voices ahead have Michael and me ducking down behind one of the crates.

"Get me Asher," a man demands. "He better have some answers from the woman. We're running out of time. Pull everyone from their assigned locations, and get these crates loaded. It's top priority."

"On it," someone replies.

Michael glances back at me, his worry plain on his face. It's only a matter of time before they discover we're gone. And then they're going to rip this place apart looking for us. But at least they're pulling everyone. That means the guards, too, right?

I continue walking toward the edge of the warehouse, scanning the drive as a suited man climbs into a black town car and drives away, the tires practically spitting up gravel as he does.

There's no fence around the place.

No gate to try to leave through.

One thing is for sure. The humidity gives away the fact that we're not in Boston anymore.

At least the field ahead is relatively open until it hits a line of thick trees.

We have to run—and we have to run fast.

Which, given Michael's current state, is going to be impossible.

"You need to leave me," he whispers.

"I'm not leaving you," I snap. "Stop suggesting it because it's *not* happening." I lean him against the wall, tucking us both back behind a crate. I shove the gun into his hand and open the cell phone.

There's no service. Of course there's no service. I shove the phone inside the bodice of my tattered dress, then focus on what happens next.

"We don't have time to wait for dark," Michael says.

"I'm not leaving." I turn toward him again, feeling beyond frustrated and terrified.

Michael reaches up with his good arm and cups my face, his thumb rubbing over my cheek. My gaze instinctively drops to his mouth.

To full lips I've tasted more times than I can count, lips I'm desperate to feel on mine again.

I swallow hard.

Now is not the time.

But his touch feels good.

So good.

"We can make it to the tree line," he says. "But we need to move as fast as we can, not run in a straight line, and no matter what, we cannot look back."

"Okay."

"If they start shooting, you drop me and go, understand?"

"No. I'm not leaving without you."

"Reyna."

"No." Tears blur my vision once more, and I wipe them away. "We're going to make it to the tree line," I say. "And we're going to make it home."

He smiles, but I see the exhaustion on his face. "We will." Michael's hand snakes around the back of my neck and he pulls me in, resting my forehead against his. "God, please be with us. Please guide us out of here and to safety. Amen."

"Amen," I repeat, the lump in my throat growing. I wrap his arm back around my shoulders and we stand together, remaining hidden behind the crate.

"Get in here!" a man roars somewhere behind us. "They're out!"

"Go," Michael urges, and we rush out into the blistering sun.

CHAPTER 19
Michael

K eeping my eyes focused on the tree line, I try to push through the pain and the fatigue. I've been in combat zones less stressful than this, but I know the only reason I feel that way is because I'm here with Reyna.

Not trained soldiers.

Not my fellow Rangers.

The woman I love.

"Into the trees!" I urge. Thankfully, I don't think they've seen us yet, and with any luck, it'll stay that way. We slip through the trees, nearly losing our footing as we leave dry ground and descend into a swamp.

The water sloshes around us, and I frantically scan for cover, for anywhere we can hide until the immediate threat passes. We need the water to settle before they reach the edge, otherwise, they'll follow us, and I know there will be no escaping.

Thankfully, just to the right, there's a thick cascade of brush. "There," I whisper, gesturing toward it. She nods, sweat beading on her brow as she struggles to move through the water that is up to my waist and well above hers.

We slip behind the brush and stop moving as we both turn our full attention to the tree line. Something brushes past my leg beneath the water, and I close my eyes for a moment, breathing slowly and trying to steady my nerves.

Please do not be an alligator.

Don't let us escape bullets to end up in the belly of a predator.

"Can you see them?" a man calls out. "They in there?"

"Nah, it's too thick. Ugh, smells terrible, too."

I keep my gaze focused ahead, and Reyna remains completely silent in my arms.

"If they are in there, they aren't gonna survive long in that pit," one of the men says. "If the gators don't get 'em, the man will bleed out."

"Boss isn't going to like the uncertainty."

"Then let's go wait on the other side. They'll either make it out or they won't. Personally, I'm betting on them getting eaten by gators. But I'm not going in there. We don't get paid enough for that."

I wait until I see the second man slip back out of the trees before I risk looking over at Reyna. Her face is red and slick with sweat, and she has a wound bandaged on her forehead, but otherwise, she looks okay.

"Are you all right?" she asks.

"I'll survive. We need to get moving."

"First." She reaches into the top of her dress and withdraws the cell phone. "Yes! Signal. What's Lance's number?" I give it to her and she types it in as I barely manage to stay on my feet. My vision is blurred, my body going numb. "Lance. It's Reyna." I can't hear what he says, but she presses the phone to my ear.

"Hey, boss."

"Michael. It is good to hear your voice. Elijah is working to trace the call."

"Good. We don't know where we are. A swamp of some kind. So, maybe in the south?"

"We'll figure it ou—"

The line goes dead. "It's not on anymore."

Reyna pulls it away. "The battery is dead. Come on!" She closes her eyes and takes a deep breath. "Okay. Let's do this. Get out of here first, panic later." She shoves the phone back into her dress then begins walking again.

The air is thick around us, the humidity alone stifling. And that's not even taking into account the mosquitos that are already making a dinner out of my exposed skin. The stench of the swamp is rancid, but we're alive—so there's that.

"Where are we?" she asks.

I doubt Elijah had time to trace the call before the phone died, but I'm holding out hope he managed to ping us on a nearby cell tower. That way, they can send out reinforcements and be here by the time we manage to make it to dry ground.

"I have no clue. But I'm fairly certain we're not in Maine anymore."

"This whole thing is insane."

"We're going to be okay, Reyna." *You're going to be okay.* Because truth be told, with how I'm feeling, I'm not entirely sure I'm going to make it out of this swamp. Images of the desert fill my mind.

The hopelessness I felt when I lay there, bloody, waiting for God to call me home.

"How?" she asks. "How do you know we're going to be okay?" She turns her head to look up at me.

Even with the pain and the less-than-stellar circumstances, I'm taken by how beautiful she is. Delicate features, gorgeous wide eyes...I could fall in love with her for the rest of my life. And it's more than her looks that have always drawn me to her. Reyna is a pure soul. A kindhearted do-gooder who has always deserved a whole lot better than me.

A whole lot better than this.

"We have God," I tell her, nodding toward the sky. "And He is going to carry us through this." *Dear God, please let it be true. Please, God, let us survive.*

"This isn't the first time He's guided me out of a life-or-death situation." I try to joke, but my attempt at lightening the mood falls flat. Likely because my tone betrays the pain every step causes me.

It is true, though. There were many times on the battlefield when I'd taken a hit then had to walk or even carry someone else. More times than I care to count where I shouldn't have made it, but I managed to pull through because God kept me alive.

"Yeah, well, let's hope this is the last time He has to do it," she replies.

"We can hope," I reply.

As we continue walking, I keep my gaze focused on the way the water moves around us, hoping that if there is an alligator nearby, I'll have time to react before it pulls us down.

One good thing about walking through a swamp though? Our footprints will be hidden. So on the off chance someone does try to follow us, it'll make tracking us incredibly difficult.

I HAVE NO IDEA HOW LONG WE WALK, BUT BY NIGHTFALL, I'm barely staying on my feet and Reyna's breathing is ragged. My muscles burn with exertion, and the injury in my shoulder has finally reached the point where the pain is so great that it's nearly numb, but thankfully we've run into none of the typical predators one might find in the swamps.

I've been watching for any sign of alligators, snakes, anything that could cause us more trouble. I haven't seen one yet, though I know that doesn't necessarily mean they aren't there. Especially now that night has fallen.

Reyna grunts as she guides me up onto an embankment, then falls down beside me. I hit the ground with a heavy thud, legs collapsing as I lie back.

"I'm sorry." She groans and turns her head toward me.

"You don't need to be sorry," I reply. My eyes grow heavy, so I close them for just a moment, hoping that in the few seconds of stillness, I can catch my breath. Right now, I'll be absolutely no good in a fight, and I honestly wish Reyna would just leave me behind.

If she goes alone, she stands a much better chance at getting out of here alive.

"I'm going to see if I can see anything." Reyna pushes up from the ground with a groan, then walks away. I turn my head, following her every movement. "There's a light," she whispers. "Straight ahead."

I try to get to my feet, but every muscle burns, every movement impossible. "Is it far?"

"No. It's steady, too, not moving like a flashlight would."

"Could be a ranger station, if we're in a state park somewhere."

"A state swamp park?"

"It happens," I tell her.

"If it's a ranger station, they could help us," she replies.

"No. You can't go." Fear claws at my throat. I'm

useless to her right now. Literally over two hundred pounds of dead weight. "What if the source of the light isn't a friendly? What if it brings us more danger?"

"Michael, we need help. They may have first aid, or a radio—something that could help us." She drops down on the ground and grips the side of her skirt. Using her hands, she tears at the fabric all the way around, shortening the gown, and then tosses the swamp-stained fabric aside.

"Please, Reyna."

All I can see is that image from my nightmare. Reyna, crawling along the sandy ground in that stifling desert, her face bloodied.

She crouches down beside me and grips my face. In the dim glow that casts through the trees from the moon above, I can barely make out her expression as she stares down at me. "I cannot lose you, Michael. And that is exactly what is going to happen if I don't get us help."

"I—"

"You're going to wanna set that gun down real slow, son. Then keep your hands where I can see 'em as you turn."

My stomach twists and I tilt my face to find myself staring down the barrel of a shotgun. The man holding it glares down at me, his gaze serious. Using two fingers, I lift the gun from where it rests against my stomach and set it aside. Reyna remains still, her hands resting on me.

The stranger reaches down and takes it, shoving it in

the waistband of his pants. Then, he shifts his gaze back to us.

He has a scruffy beard that has long since turned grey, and his face is dusted with dirt, his eyes wide and afraid. He holds the shotgun steadily, though, and I wouldn't imagine he'd hesitate to shoot me if he felt the need.

"Why are you here?"

"We're not here to cause you any harm," Reyna says.

"I'll decide that, won't I?" he says. "Answer my question."

"Lower your weapon. I don't want either of us getting shot because you have a happy trigger finger," I tell him as I try to sit up enough to look somewhat like I could be a threat. Because right now, I'm a sitting duck —literally.

The man narrows his gaze a moment but lowers the barrel just slightly. "Now, answer me. Why are you here?"

"We were abducted and escaped," Reyna says. "We've been running ever since, but my friend is hurt."

His gaze narrows on my wrapped shoulder. "That true?"

"Does it look true?" I snap, irritable because my vision swims. It's so hot. Why is it so hot?

He clenches his jaw. "You got a real mouth on you for someone lying on the ground."

"Please," Reyna says. "We need help."

His gaze shifts to her, and nerves wreak havoc on my

system. What if he decides she's an easy target? What if he kills me and takes her? What would a man out in the middle of a swamp—alone—do to her?

But then he surprises me and lowers his weapon all the way.

"All right. You both look rather rough."

"Thank you," she says. "Can you tell us where we are?"

"Florida. Come on in. I got supper cooking, and there will be plenty. I also have a first aid kit so we can take a look at that there wound." In a move that is all trust, he holds the shotgun out to Reyna. "You carry this, and I'll get him. I'm more sprightly than I seem."

She looks to me in surprise, then accepts the weapon and helps the man get me to my feet. He wraps my good arm around his shoulder and guides me toward the cabin.

God, please don't let this be a mistake.

We reach it in minutes, and Reyna rushes ahead to push open the door. I watch as she peeks her head in, then steps inside. For the brief seconds she's not in my line of sight, terror creeps into my mind.

But then I see her, setting the shotgun aside and rushing to shut the door behind us.

The man leads me to a bed, and I hiss through clenched teeth as he sets me down. Something cooking over an open fire in the corner, and my mouth waters, my stomach growling with hunger even as pain makes me nauseous.

On one wall, shelving is full of various types of packaged foods. From the kind you get from a store to some he's probably preserved himself.

There's a small refrigerator, but no TV, no lights aside from lanterns hung throughout the cabin, and only a single twin-sized bed. Just over the bed, multiple war medals hang, as well as a black-and-white photograph of soldiers. *So he's military.*

"Solar panels," he says as he mixes whatever's cooking. "Keeps my food cold." When he smiles, I notice a few missing teeth. Crossing back over to me, he reaches beneath the bed and withdraws a tactical backpack. "This is the medical kit, but I need a look at your wound before I can assess it."

"Okay."

He starts to remove the gauze, and it sticks to the injured flesh. Reyna grips my free hand as I hiss through clenched teeth, groaning when the air hits my wound. "Whoever bandaged this didn't care if you lived or died," he comments as he reaches into his pack. "You—"

"Reyna," she says. "This is Michael." Her tone is pained, and she sniffles. She's crying? For me? Or is she hurting?

"Reyna," he repeats. "My name is Caleb. There's a bucket over there. It has freshly boiled water, should still be somewhat warm. Can you soak some of the rags on the shelf right there and bring them to me?"

"Yes. Of course." She offers me a tight smile, then

leaves my side. I watch her go, my vision wavering yet again.

The man presses his hand to my forehead. "You're feverish. There's infection. I'm going to need to clean this, and it's going to hurt."

"Doctor?" I ask.

He laughs. "Medic. Former military. You're in good hands. I'll do what I can to keep you alive."

"Protect her," I choke out as darkness ebbs my vision. "Please."

"Don't you give up, Michael Anderson," Reyna says. She's back again, but I can't see her.

I can't see anything.

But I can feel the pain.

CHAPTER 20
Reyna

With how late it is, Caleb said traveling to the truck he keeps parked on the other side of the swamp would be far more dangerous than waiting until morning. But he says he'll drive us to the nearest town so we can call for help then.

Knowing that we'll be on our way home soon is more of a relief than I can even put into words. Especially since Michael's fever is getting worse, his complexion far paler than it should be. I gently dab the washcloth on his forehead, and he groans.

I've cleaned the blood from his bare chest, trying my hardest not to focus on all the scarring I hadn't noticed before. Multiple scars from bullet holes mar his muscled torso, and my heart aches for the pain he must have suffered when he'd been deployed.

How many times did he nearly die?

How many nights did he fall asleep and not know if he was going to wake up tomorrow?

And then I remember the letters, and how absolutely hopeless he felt for a good portion of his deployment. My heart aches for him, yearning for the man who felt so unsupported that he ran off to join the service, leaving everything he'd ever known behind.

My gaze rakes over the deep purple bruising all along his ribcage and chest, compliments of the accident, as he tries to suck in breath after breath. He's struggling to breathe.

Is he going to make it?

Please God let him make it.

"Here." Caleb offers me a bowl of stew, and I take it, my stomach growling.

"Thank you."

"I can make a bowl for him if you'd like."

Michael groans.

"I don't know that he should eat anything yet," I reply, then take a bite and nearly groan myself. Though mine is out of pleasure at the delicious food rather than pain. "This is amazing."

"My late wife's recipe," he replies proudly, then takes a seat at the small round table that serves as his dining room.

"How long have you lived out here?" I ask, genuinely curious as to why he's out here in the middle of a swamp.

"Who says I live here?" He grins. "About eight years

now, I suppose. Ever since my wife—" He takes a deep breath. "I'm sorry, it still hurts to talk about it."

"I can understand that."

"When she passed away, I didn't see any reason to stick around. So I quit my job and moved out here. I've been here ever since, aside from the occasional trip to town."

"Why out here?" When he doesn't immediately answer, I add, "I'm sorry. I'm being nosy, and it's rude."

"No." He waves his hand, dismissing me. "Not rude. It's been a long time since I had a pleasant conversation." He eats a bite of stew. "I wanted to be away from people. It was like everywhere I turned, there were memories that gutted me. A scab ripped open every time someone asked me a question that brought her up. So I started driving, then parked and went for a walk out here. After that, I built this place, and I've been here ever since."

"I'm sorry for your loss."

"Thanks." He smiles tightly, but I can see the pain on his face. It breaks my heart. "What led to you two being out here? I know you said you were kidnapped, but from where? You seemed surprised to find yourself in Florida."

"Boston."

He whistles. "That's a long way to go."

"We were in an accident and they drugged us. Brought us out here."

He gestures to the tattered gown I'm still wearing. "Somewhere fancy?"

"We were at a charity banquet," I tell him. "Benefitting a women and children's shelter."

"Any idea who grabbed you? Or why?"

"None that make any sense," I reply truthfully. The idea that they think my brother had anything to do with this—I don't understand it. Carter has *always* followed the rules. I don't think he's ever broken one in his entire life. In fact, he loves the law so much, he'd already known that he wanted to be a lawyer by the time he was ten.

So what did he get wrapped up in?

"Well, I can get you to town tomorrow. We'll make sure he gets seen by a doctor, then find a way to get you the rest of the way back."

"His team will be looking for us," I tell him. "With any luck, they'll already be in Florida."

"Team?"

"He's private security," I say. "I hired him after I was attacked."

"You've had a rough go of it recently."

"Understatement." I start eating again, my gaze leveling on Michael.

I study his face in the dim light cast by the lanterns on the wall. He's so handsome. So ruggedly beautiful that it hurts my heart. He could have died today. He still could die if this fever continues to take root.

What will I do then? How will I survive in a world without Michael Anderson?

The image of him jumping out of his truck as I was being attacked in the school parking lot swims into my memory, and fresh tears spring to my eyes. Why couldn't he have loved me enough not to leave in the first place?

"Coffee?" Caleb pulls me from thoughts of the past, so I refocus on the present. "I imagine you won't be getting much sleep tonight."

"You'd be right," I reply with a laugh. "And that would be great, thanks."

He gets to his feet and starts prepping a pour-over container. Then he scoops some water into a Dutch oven and hangs it over the fire. After adding some wood to it, he takes a seat at the table and opens a book that sits on top.

"What are you reading?" I whisper.

"The Word," he replies with a friendly smile, keeping his hand in the pages as he shows me the front of his Bible. It's aged, worn down by years of use, but it's still one of the most beautiful books I've ever seen. "You a follower?" he asks.

"'I am the way and the truth and the life. No one comes to the Father except through me,'" I tell him with a smile.

"John 4:6." He nods appreciatively.

"Yes, sir." I smile.

"It was hard for me to find meaning in her death

after my Sydney passed. But once I started reading her old Bible, I knew there was a reason. Still haven't figured it out yet, but I believe in God's plan." He smiles up at me as he lovingly strokes the cover. "It's hard, sometimes, to praise Him from the furnace."

I glance down at Michael. I didn't lose him in the way Caleb lost his Sydney, but I still struggled to understand why God let him leave me. Why didn't He stop Michael from walking out the door? Free will is a piece of it, sure, and I always understood that. But it hurt me when he left. And that hurt made it impossible to see it from Michael's—or even God's—perspective. What good could come from Michael becoming a soldier?

My thoughts turn to that moment in the warehouse. To the desire I'd had to pull his face down and kiss his lips one final time. Taste the passion we've always shared once more before we faced what could have very well been our death.

It's good I didn't—or that's what I'm going to continue telling myself. Maybe someday I'll believe it.

"I couldn't agree with you more, Caleb."

He follows my gaze. "You two are something special. I can see it in his eyes. The way he looks at you, and the way you watch him."

"We were something special," I reply. "A long time ago."

"What happened? If you don't mind me asking."

I face him again and offer a half smile. "He made a

choice that took him away from me, and he did it without ever telling me why."

"Sometimes men do stupid stuff," Caleb replies with a chuckle. "I bet he figures it out soon. Just how foolish it was to let you go. Women like you and my Sydney don't come along every day," he replies with a wink.

"Thanks, Caleb," I reply, though I don't tell Caleb that Michael already did figure it out. He's been trying to get me back since he returned home. I'm just not sure my heart could take being broken again, and I'm not sure I'm strong enough to find out.

Not even for him.

AT SOME POINT, I DOZED OFF BECAUSE CALEB SHAKES ME awake and presses his finger to his lips. He points outside and shoves a pistol into my hand. "Someone's out there," he leans in and whispers. "Stay here, shoot anyone but me who comes through that door."

"Caleb—"

"I've got you, girl," he says softly, then pats my shoulder.

I check Michael's breathing, noting that it's more shallow now than it was before I dozed off. *Please, God. This is too much. I can't take any more.*

Tears fill my eyes, but I wipe them away and stand, keeping the gun at the ready as Caleb creeps to the door. He keeps his back against the wall and offers me a nod before reaching for the handle. With a deep breath, he opens it.

Men dressed in black file in. One knocks the shotgun from Caleb's hand and pins him to the wall, while three others fill the cabin. They scan the room, and thankfully, I hesitate to fire long enough to realize that I recognize the man in front, though his face is smeared with black.

"Lance?"

"Reyna."

"Let Caleb go, he's the only reason we're alive."

Jaxson quickly releases him, and Caleb smooths the front of his shirt.

"This the team you were telling me about?"

"It is," I reply.

Lance's gaze drops to Michael, and his expression darkens. "Is he—"

"I got him." The only woman in the group rushes over, her near-black hair tied up on top of her head. She's slender and swings a backpack from her shoulders before kneeling at Michael's side.

Lance grips my shoulder, and I look up at him. "That's Bianca Theodore. She's the best field trauma surgeon there is."

"Thanks, but boosting my ego isn't going to get you out of paying me," Bianca jokes as she continues her exam on Michael. She gently peels back the gauze, then glances back at me. "You do this?"

"He did," I say, pointing to Caleb. If she insults him, I might—

"Great work," she tells Caleb. "I might actually not be the best." She winks at me and my appreciation for her grows at the kindness she showed the older man.

Lance crosses over and offers Caleb his hand. "I'm Lance Knight. This is my team. Elijah Breeth, Jaxson Payne, Bianca Theodore, and Silas Williamson." He points to the fourth man in the room, who has been silently standing beside the door the entire time.

Now, he glances over and offers me a curt nod.

"We need to get him to a hospital," Bianca says. "I can give him some fluids now, but they're not going to do anything without a strong antibiotic."

"The airport is forty minutes once we reach the edge of the swamp," Elijah says. "Then it's three and a half hours of flight time, and another twenty to the hospital back home."

"You have a plane?"

"We do," Bianca replies. "And if we can get him there, I can get an antibiotic administered and hopefully stop this infection from getting any worse."

"How did you even find us?" I ask.

"Managed to ping the location prior to your phone dying. Once we got here, Silas took over. Guy could track a fish through the ocean."

Silas grunts in response, but doesn't say anything.

"We need to get moving," Lance says.

"They said they would be waiting for us on the other side," I tell them. "What if they're there now?"

"Reyna, we will get you home," Lance says softly. "I promise."

"I can lead you out of the swamps," Caleb offers. "I know them like the back of my hand. With all of us, we should be able to get out without too much trouble. I just didn't want to risk moving him by myself."

"Understood. And if you could lead us out, that would be great." Lance reaches into a tactical pocket on his sleeve and withdraws his cell. After firing off a quick text, he sticks it back inside and turns to Bianca. "He good to travel?"

"As good as he'll ever be. The sooner we can get him to the plane, the better."

"Then let's get moving."

Caleb grabs a backpack and sticks his Bible inside, then slings the bag over his shoulders, retrieves a lantern and his shotgun, and stands by the door.

"I can carry you," Silas offers, gesturing to my feet.

I start to refuse, insist that I walk, but then I actually push to my feet and feel the ache shoot straight up through my body. "If it won't be too much trouble?"

He doesn't answer, just scoops me up as Lance and Elijah lift Michael from the bed, keeping him draped between the two of them.

He grunts, but remains unconscious, and my heart sinks. Is he going to make it? What if the moving is too much?

"I've seen him survive much worse," Bianca tells me with a tight smile. "He'll pull through."

Dear God, please let her be right. Don't let us have come this far to fail now.

CHAPTER 21

Michael

The beeping of machines is the first thing I hear as I come awake. Next thing I notice is the dryness of my mouth and the bone-deep ache throughout my body. I feel like I got hit by a truck. And then it backed over me. Oxygen blows into my nose, and as I open my eyes, I have to blink rapidly until my vision clears.

The room is fairly dark, though the light pouring in through a crack in the curtains illuminates Reyna curled up on the couch, a blue blanket draped over her body. Her red hair is splayed over the white pillowcase, and I'm struck at the sight of her.

Alive.

Well.

Sleeping.

I glance around the room, trying to figure out just how I got here, and where here is. Are we still in Florida? Did Caleb get us out of the swamps? How do I not remember? There's a board across from me with the nurse currently assigned to me, and right above it, Doc Harding is scrawled beside the assigned doctor.

Doc? Are we back in Hope Springs?

I scoot up, trying to be quiet about it, but the bed squeaks, and Reyna shoots up, her eyes wide and full of sleep. "I'm sorry," I manage. "I didn't mean to wake you."

"It's fine." She wipes the sleep from her eyes and stretches. "How do you feel?"

"Okay. Are we back in Hope Springs?"

She nods. "We got here last night."

"How?"

Reyna stands and walks toward me, her movements slow and pained, then sits on the edge of the bed. Having her so close soothes my soul. Especially when she reaches out and brushes some hair off of my fore-head. I close my eyes, her touch a salve for my brokenness.

"Your team tracked us down in the swamps. Then Caleb led us out as Lance and Elijah carried you."

"Is Caleb okay?"

"He's fine. We said our goodbyes, and he went home." She smiles softly. "We wouldn't have made it out without him."

"No," I agree. "We wouldn't have." I take a deep breath. "Carried me—I was that bad?"

Her eyes fill with tears. "I thought you were going to

die, Michael. You were so pale. And your fever—" She sniffles. "Because of the accident, you had a concussion, three fractured ribs, a collapsed lung, and then there's the gunshot wound. You almost died."

"But I didn't." I reach out and take her hand. "I'm sorry I failed you. It was my job to keep you safe, and you ended up having to protect me instead. That's now how it's supposed to be."

Her brow furrows. "You did protect me. Because of you, I wasn't grabbed outside the party. Because of you, we made it to the swamps."

"You're the one who pulled me out of that room," he tells me. "You're the one that got us to the swamps."

"Maybe physically, but—no. We're not doing this. We got each other out of there. As a team."

"Fair enough." I lean back against the pillow. "Do they know who took us yet?"

"Yes. My brother's set up a virtual meeting with your team this afternoon. My parents are with him back in some undisclosed location in Boston. They send their well-wishes."

I snort. "Good of them."

"I don't know that I can forgive you for what you put me through before—when you left." Her change of subject is so abrupt that I wonder if I misheard what she'd said. "But I want you to know that I'm trying. Even if I'm not sure—" She closes her eyes. "I can't move on. I've tried. God knows I've tried." She wipes her eyes. "No one is you. And I can't tell if that's me refusing to let go of the shell of what we had, or if it's something more."

I'm afraid to speak. To breathe. Because she's saying all the things I've been desperate to hear since the moment I returned.

Before she can continue, the door opens, and a blast from the past strolls in, her obsidian hair in a tight braid over her shoulder. Wearing black combat boots, dark jeans, and a grey *Army* sweatshirt, she looks almost exactly as she did the last time I saw her. Piercing blue eyes find mine, and she grins. "Look who's back from the brink of death."

"Bianca? What? How—"

"Lance phoned a friend when you were MIA. He said you'd been shot and were missing. I owed him one for saving my life, so it seemed a fair trade to rescue your tail." She smiles at Reyna. "You're looking better."

"Amazing what a few hours of sleep and a shower can do."

Bianca laughs. "Girl, don't I know it. It really is good to see you, Anderson."

Bianca Theodore was the best trauma surgeon I'd ever seen overseas. She handled more than a few injuries of mine and had been first on the scene when I'd nearly died. I hadn't even realized she was out of the service. "You, too," I tell her. "When did you get out?"

"About three years ago. I'm a veterinarian now. I prefer animals to people."

"I'm sorry, I'm just surprised to see you," I say as I

realize I'm staring. Bianca and I had a date. One single date, and we both decided we were better off as friends. Me because I was still in love with Reyna. She never told me why she'd felt that way, but I always assumed it was someone back home.

"It's all good. I was quite shocked to get the call from Captain Knight. And when I heard that it was *the* Reyna that you were with, I knew I couldn't say no." She winks at Reyna, who blushes. Bianca has never had much of a filter, so I'm not sure why I'm surprised that she blurted it out.

"I may have mentioned you a time or two," I tell Reyna.

"A time or two?" Bianca laughs. "He couldn't stop mentioning you. It was quite adorable."

Reyna smiles softly, though I note the heaviness of her expression.

"Well, what's the prognosis? Am I going to live?"

"As far as I know," Bianca replies. "But I'm not your doctor."

The door opens, and Lance walks in, Eliza at his side. "Thank God," Eliza says and rushes forward to wrap her arms around me.

I return her hug with my good arm, grateful to be back home with friends. "It's good to see you," I tell her.

"It's great," she replies as she pulls back, tears falling down her cheeks. "I'm sorry. I can't stop crying. I feel like it's all I do right now." She steps away and leans into Lance, who presses a kiss to the side of her head.

When her hand goes to her belly, joy flashes through me. "Are you—"

She nods. "Just found out a few days ago."

"That's wonderful! And perfect news when I'm laying in a hospital bed."

"You're alive," Eliza says. "And that's what's wonderful."

"I'm going to go grab some coffee. Anyone want some?" Bianca asks as she gets to her feet.

"Please. I can come with you." Reyna stands.

I long to reach for her. To pull her back down and ask everyone else to step out so we can continue our conversation, but I doubt it will go anywhere. Not after the interruption. So instead, I focus on being grateful that I get to see my friends again.

She leaves the room, and my gaze lingers on the door.

"She was a mess, worried about you," Lance says.

I shift my attention to him. "Thank you for coming for us. For getting us out."

"Brother, I would walk through fire for you." He takes a seat on the edge of the bed as Eliza sits on the couch. "How are you feeling?"

"Alive. Sore."

"You were in bad shape when we got to you. According to Bianca, Caleb removing that bullet and sterilizing the wound is likely the only reason you survived. The word blood poisoning was thrown around."

"I've survived worse."

"It's not a competition," he replies.

I chuckle. "Fair enough. What's the update? Reyna said Carter's calling in for a meeting later? I want to be there."

"Not a chance. We'll keep you updated, but it has to be done on the encrypted connection at the office, and you aren't getting out of here for at least another day."

"The warehouse was stocked with crates, Lance. There's no telling what they were shipping out."

"Drugs," he replies. "At least, that's what local authorities said they suspected after we called it in and they raided the place."

"What did they find?"

"Nothing." He shakes his head. "They'd already cleared out before we got there."

Frustration ebbs at my exhaustion, and the desire to get out of bed and do *something* is overwhelming. "Did he give you any idea as to why Reyna is being targeted?"

"Not yet. Though my guess is she's collateral damage. A way to try and control him."

"Which means he's known from the beginning she was in danger."

Lance doesn't respond, but I know he agrees, and it infuriates me. Why wouldn't Carter tell us? How could he keep something like this from us? She's his little sister, and he left her completely unprotected!

"I know that look," Lance says. "You need to keep it

together. Long enough that we can figure out what's going on."

"All you're seeing is my desire to get out of this bed and actually do something."

"You will. Just give yourself time to heal."

"I have."

"You've only been in that bed for eleven hours," Eliza says. "Stop being stubborn."

"She's right." Lance stands and crosses his arms. "I promise that we'll keep you apprised, but right now you need to stay safe. Sheriff Vick has a deputy on your door, and Jaxson will be with Reyna."

"She's not staying here?" I know it's ridiculous, but the idea of her leaving the hospital terrifies me.

"That's up to her. Either way—" The door opens again, and another part of my past walks in, though this one is even more shocking than Bianca.

Silas Williamson, a former Navy SEAL, was injured in the line of duty and ended up in the same VA hospital as the rest of us. He'd been badly traumatized and barely spoke, but Lance has a way of connecting with people that has always astounded me. He managed to get the former SEAL to open up, and through it, helped him find faith in the midst of his pain.

"Good to see you alive, Anderson." He closes the door behind him and moves farther into the room.

"It's good to see you at all, Williamson. How have you been?"

"Managing." Last time we saw him, he was packing

up himself and his four-year-old niece and moving off-grid after the murder of his sister. That was two years ago. We'd flown out for her funeral and spent the week helping him pack up her things and get them moved.

Haven't heard from him since.

"Silas tracked you through the swamp," Lance says, "and has agreed to come on temporarily until we manage to get all of this figured out."

"You're an asset, my friend. How is your niece?"

"Good. She's spending time with Andie and Mrs. McGinley right now." He shoves his hands into his pockets.

"All right. We need to get to the office." Lance takes Eliza's hand as she stands. Then he gently touches my arm with his other hand. "I'm grateful God pulled you through again. Life wouldn't be the same without you."

As they leave, I stare at the door, hating that I can't follow.

CHAPTER 22
Reyna

"How are you holding up?" Bianca takes her cup of coffee and sits at a two-seater table in the hospital cafeteria.

"I'm tired, but otherwise okay." I join her, even though I'm more than ready to be back in the room with Michael. Leaving his side was hard, but after everything we went through, my mind is a mess.

"I can't imagine why you'd be tired," she replies with a grin.

I like Bianca. She seems to call it like it is, and there isn't much of a filter there, but her candid honesty is refreshing. "Thank you for saving him."

"There are very few things I wouldn't do for those guys. They're great men."

"They are. You all served together?" I'd gotten half a story, but there hadn't been a lot of time or energy to give me the rest.

"Briefly. I was stationed overseas at the same time they were. Pulled bullets out of them a time or two."

"You were the one who saved him after the—"

"After the IED? Yeah. It took a team of us."

I think about the scar on the side of his face. Of the way I'd held Margot as she broke down after hearing the news. I'd barely managed to keep myself calm when all I wanted to do was lie down and cry with her.

I don't think I've ever prayed so hard in my life, until now.

"When he came out of the anesthesia, he asked for you."

"What?" My stomach twists.

"He kept saying your name over and over again. 'Reyna. Reyna. I need Reyna.' I hadn't known who you were, but it finally made sense why he never looked at me the way I'd wanted him to." Once again, her candid honesty is unexpected.

"You have feelings for him."

"Had," she corrects. "We're friends now, barely, but I did have a good little crush on him for a while. He is one of the nicest men I've ever met. Someone who's kind straight down to his soul. You don't often meet 'em like that."

"I can't argue."

"Can I ask what happened between you two?" she asks. "I never got the story, and given how much I know he loves you, and how clear it is you love him, I can't quite figure out what went wrong. I'm nosy. Blame my upbringing." She laughs awkwardly but doesn't continue.

"He left without a word," I tell her. "I woke up one morning, and he was gone. I didn't even know he'd joined the military until his mother told me. I remember just standing there, staring at her as though she was going to start laughing and tell me it was one big joke." I take a drink of coffee. "One minute he was there. The next he was gone. And I was furious."

"Men can be really, really stupid."

I laugh. "Isn't that the truth?"

"How do you feel now? About him, I mean. Obviously, there are feelings still there. And for the record, this is just me being nosy, I am not in the least bit interested in him in that way anymore."

"I love him." I say it out loud for the first time in years, and the admission lifts a huge weight from my shoulders.

"I know *that*. I want to know if you're going to do anything about it. My vote? Yes. If you're asking. We did just meet and all, so I'm not entirely sure where you stand on my opinion."

Laughing, I take another drink of coffee. "You know, I like you, Bianca."

"I like you, too, Reyna." She gently taps her coffee cup to mine.

"As far as he and I are concerned, I'm not entirely sure what to do about us yet. But I'm trying to figure it out."

WITH A SECOND CUP OF COFFEE IN HAND, I STEP BACK INTO Michael's room. He's sitting up in bed, staring out the window, though when he hears me enter, he turns his head and smiles at me, but it doesn't reach his eyes. "Hey," he greets softly.

He looks worn out. Stressed.

"Hey. I brought you some coffee. But if they show up and yell at you for having it, you didn't get it from me."

He chuckles as I set the cup on his bedside tray. I take a seat in the chair beside his bed. "I'll keep the secret." Michael takes a drink of the coffee, then leans back and groans. "That's good. But given how long it's been since I had coffee, it could technically be terrible."

Silence settles between us as we drink our coffee. I lean my head back in the chair and close my eyes.

"Lance said that Jaxson can stay at your house. If you wanted to go home."

I open my eyes and stare at him. "You want me to leave?" It hurts to think he doesn't want me to be here.

"No. Not at all. Not even a little bit. When you walked out the door with Bianca to go to the cafeteria, I about lost my mind."

Relief settles over me, and I get up from the chair to sit on the edge of the bed. After setting my coffee beside his, I take his hand in mine. The feeling of his large, calloused palm against my smaller hand takes me back to happier times.

To wearing his letterman jacket and walking through the park, not a care or concern. We'd had our whole lives planned out, and I'd been so certain of our future. It never occurred to me that he was struggling with his present.

"I don't want to leave." I lift my gaze to his.

"I don't want you to go." His gaze drops to my mouth, then darts back up to my eyes. I lean forward, ready to give in to my desire to taste his lips again. To restart what never really seemed to end in the first place.

And then the door opens.

"Michael!" Michael's mother rushes forward, and I stand, getting out of the way just in time for her to throw her arms around him. Delilah cups his face and stares down at him. "You scared us!"

"You really did, son." A man in a wheelchair rolls in, and I immediately recognize Michael's father.

Unexpected anger churns in my stomach as I stare down at the man who drove Michael away from me. Who didn't think I was enough to make his son happy —or whatever his ridiculous reasoning was.

"Reyna, it's good to see you."

"I think I'll go call my mother." I need distance from him. From all of this. "Mrs. Anderson, it's good to see you." I walk out the door, breathing easily as soon as I'm not sharing space with Michael's father anymore.

"Reyna?"

Why? Forcing a neutral expression on my face, I turn

toward Michael's father, who has wheeled out into the hallway. "Yes?"

"I'm glad you're all right."

"Are you?" The words are out of my mouth before I can stop them.

His brow furrows. "Of course I am. Just because you and Michael didn't work out doesn't mean I ever stopped caring for you. You were at my house practically every summer, hanging with Margot and Michael."

"And why didn't Michael and I work out?" I snap, stepping toward him. The fury is blazing in my veins now, and even though I know I should stop, that he's here to check on his son who nearly died, I can't. Because the hurt is right there, cheering the anger on.

"I'm not entirely sure," he replies. "Though I sense you believe I had something to do with it." The man was a cop before his injury. I would even go to the range with him and Michael on the weekends. He taught me to shoot, taught me some self-defense right alongside Margot... I loved Michael's entire family.

Which is why this betrayal might sting even more than Michael leaving.

"Did you tell him that he shouldn't marry me?" My bottom lip quivers.

He runs a hand over his face. "I said a lot of things I regret. Things I didn't realize I regretted until—" He glances back at the hospital room. "I'm sorry, Reyna. Truly, I am. I have always wanted what was best for both of my kids. I wanted them to have more than I ever did, and I believed—at the time—that Michael was throwing away a future because of—"

"Me. You can say it. We're both thinking it."

"Yes," he replies. "If I'm being completely honest, that is what I believed. I never imagined he would run off and join the military though. I never thought he'd nearly die just to get away from me." His father chokes on his words, and a tear slips from his eyes.

His genuine emotion chips away at my anger. "You made him leave me."

"I— I am so sorry, Reyna. I wronged you both by what I did, and what's worse is I hadn't even realized until now that I was the reason you two split. Truth be told, I didn't talk to my son until a year after my accident. And I never asked about anything in his life because I was too prideful." He wheels a bit closer, and I stand my ground.

"I loved your son. He loved me. We could've had a happy life together. He was enough for me as he was. If he'd wanted to go play professionally, I would have supported him. But he only ever played football for you." I wipe tears away from my face. "How could you not see that?"

His father's eyes widen briefly, and I see that it's complete news to him that Michael never even wanted to play ball. "I didn't know."

"Of course you didn't. Because you never asked."

CHAPTER 23
Michael

"How are you feeling?" My mother adjusts the pillow behind me for what must have been the dozenth time since arriving here a few minutes ago. She keeps fidgeting with stuff, checking to make sure the temperature in the room is good, whether I have enough blankets.

"Ma, I'm fine."

Her eyes fill and she takes a seat on the edge of the bed. "You almost died—again. When Lance called me and said you were missing—" She chokes up, tears streaming down her cheeks. "Michael, I thought you were gone. That we were never going to see you again."

"I'm tougher than that." My attempt at a joke falls flat though.

My mother simply stifles a sob. "One of these days you're going to pick a fight you can't win."

"No," I reply. "Because I'm not picking these fights, Ma. They're finding me."

My father wheels back into the room, his eyes red.

"What is it?" my mother asks. "Are you hurt?"

"No. I'm fine." He sniffles and rolls closer to the bed. I'm completely caught off guard, unsure how to navigate the emotion on my father's face. "Reyna said to let you know she was having Jaxson take her home after all."

I hate that she's gone. That I have to spend any time away from her. But I imagine her absence has something to do with the man in front of me, especially since he is visibly upset. "What did you say to her?" I snap, rage pushing through every other emotion. Did he yell at her? Claim this was her fault? Did he—

"I apologized."

"Did you—what?"

"I apologized to her. It was long overdue, especially since I hadn't realized that I'd hurt her."

"Honey, what are you talking about?" my mother asks.

"I'm the reason Michael and Reyna didn't work out. Not her. Not him. It was me." He wheels closer. "Why didn't you tell me?"

"Would you have listened?" I ask honestly. "Dad, I'm in my thirties, and you still refuse to see me as a man. How would you have reacted if I'd told you that you were the reason my fiancée and I broke up?"

"Fiancée?" My mother looks completely shocked.

"I'd proposed to Reyna after prom. We planned to get married the month after graduation so we could start our life together."

"Michael—" My mother presses a hand to her heart. "I didn't know."

"Not many did. Because I left town before I got to officially graduate." Thankfully, the extra credit classes I'd taken over the four years of high school gave me the chance to graduate early. I'd been able to request my transcripts and leave before I even had the chance to make the walk and get my diploma.

"When you left us and joined the service, I wasn't sure how to handle it. I wanted to drive to wherever you were and drag you home myself." My father wipes tears from his face. "I'd wanted to scream at you for throwing a future away, but I never actually realized it wasn't one you wanted. Why didn't you tell me that you played football for me?"

Did Reyna dump it all on him in those few minutes they were in the hall? My admiration for her grows, even as this is a conversation I'd really rather not have while I'm lying in a hospital bed, feeling more vulnerable than I care to admit. "I didn't see a point. I enjoyed it well enough, but I'd known for years it wasn't what I wanted to do with my life. Something I tried to tell you."

"But I believed the only reason you didn't want to go pro was because of Reyna."

"Yes, because you were too stubborn to listen to anything that was coming out of my mouth."

My father takes a deep, steadying breath. "I'm sorry, Michael. I'm so, so sorry. You have no idea how many times I wish I'd just died in that accident so that I didn't have to suffer the loss of you. After your incident overseas—" He pinches the bridge of his nose as his shoulders begin to shake.

Ma, completely taken aback by his display of emotions, gets up and walks over to him. She kneels beside him, but he shakes his head.

"I'm fine, Delilah," he says, then takes a deep breath. "I was so angry with myself that I wasn't paying attention. When I veered off the road and found myself barreling toward that tree, all I could think about was how much I was going to regret not getting to tell you how I felt. How sorry I was. And then I lived, but I was too stubborn. But I need you to know now, Michael. You and your sister are my biggest achievements. Knowing the man you've become makes me proud to be your father, and I am so incredibly sorry that I caused you so much pain."

Never in a million years did I think I would get an apology from my father. So to see him sitting there, tears streaming down his cheeks, as he says he's sorry, throws me completely off guard. "I—thank you."

My father nods, then turns to my mother. "And I've been terrible to you, my love. I've been angry, so angry at myself for letting my emotions get the better of me. I am so sorry for everything you've had to deal with, and even if it takes every moment of the rest of my life, I'm going to make it up to you."

My mother throws her arms around my father and crushes him in a hug, and the two of them remain there for long enough that I'm starting to feel like a third party in my own hospital room.

Finally, right on time, my sister pushes open the door, and she and Matty come in. She eyes our parents and then me before setting the bakery box in her hand down on my tray. "What's going on here?"

"I'm realizing just how awful I've been to you all over the years and am promising to do better."

"Dad." Margot tears up and wraps an arm around his shoulders, then looks at me with an expression that lets me know she'll be pumping me for information later. Which is fine. Except I'm not entirely sure what to tell her, since I'm not even certain what caused this drastic shift.

But as I look at my dad, I see the man who'd driven me to my first boxing match. Who'd taken me out for ice cream when I lost—horribly—and stood at my side as I learned to fish. And I know that while Reyna's words had a huge impact on the change I'm seeing here, there's only one thing that could have changed him this way.

Thank you, God. Thank you for bringing him back to us.

"WE'VE GOT NEWS FOR YOU," LANCE SAYS AS HE, ELIJAH, and Silas stroll into the hospital room. He offers me a folder, and I take it, then glance back out the window one final time before opening it. I'm finally back on my feet after Doc told me it would be better for my recovery if I were up and moving around as I could tolerate.

I flip the folder open and find myself staring at a surveillance picture of a familiar man in an expensive suit. Anger flashes to life inside me as I stare down at the man who questioned Reyna and me. "This is the man who ordered Reyna's abduction."

"I thought so." Lance crosses his arms. "It seems Carter just put a particularly nasty guy in prison. Drugs, people, information...the guy traffics it all."

"This guy wasn't in prison."

"That's because no one can get him on anything." Lance sighs. "The man you're looking at is Zeke Phillips. He's a lawyer out of Miami and represented Willy Carson, who Carter just put behind bars two months ago, shutting down a massive operation. Or so everyone thought when they'd believed Carson was at the head of it."

"What was a lawyer from Miami doing representing someone from Boston?"

"Carson's not from Boston," Elijah tells me. "He was visiting, and they picked him up for drugging some woman's drink at a bar. There was an undercover there and he saw the whole thing. They didn't even get Carson for anything else until Carter pulled some evidence that Phillips claims never existed in the first place. The whole thing smells."

"But we know who he is, and that he had us held against our will. Can we not turn that in?"

"We need proof," Lance replies. "This guy is as slippery as they come. We go at him and were inciting a war."

"He incited it when he came after Reyna." I hand him the folder. "Does the fact that I nearly died not go for anything? What about the guys you grabbed from the banquet?" They haven't confirmed that anyone was arrested, but given I'd knocked one guy unconscious, I'm assuming so.

"Claim they thought she was pretty and wanted to grab her," Elijah says.

"Which is a lie so no one will press any further after the confession." I shake my head.

"Exactly. And, word has it, Zeke Phillips himself is in Boston offering them legal aid."

I go completely rigid. "Then we go get him."

"You're in no condition to be going anywhere," Silas says, speaking up for the first time since they entered the room.

"Doc says I need to be on my feet."

"On your feet, not in a fight. Michael, you nearly died. Do you understand how serious that is?" Lance questions.

"I'm not an idiot," I snap. "But this guy came after

Reyna. He's the one who tried to kill me. If we stand a chance at getting him, we need to do it."

"We need proof," Lance says. "Even what we sent Carter isn't enough. All we'll do is let him know we're on to him. As of now, he doesn't know you and Reyna are back in Hope Springs. We plan to keep it like that."

"You sent Reyna home though. He'll have someone watching her house."

"She's at the Redding's place," Lance says. "The pastor and his wife agreed to host both of you until this passes, since if they're watching her house, they're going to be keeping an eye on your gym, the office, and our places." He uncrosses his arms. "I'm sorry, Michael, but we need to do this right or this guy is going to walk."

I know he's right. I hate that he's right. "You're sure he doesn't know we're here?"

"You've been completely off the books since we got you into town. It's possible that someone spotted you, but highly unlikely."

"My family visiting would look suspicious."

"Not since—according to hospital records and staff —they were here so your dad could get a checkup."

I stare out the window, then walk over and take a seat on the edge of the bed. "How could Carter do this to her? If he knew this guy was dangerous, how could he not warn us?"

"That was my first question." Based on Elijah's expression, he wasn't overly thrilled with Reyna's brother's explanation. "According to him, he never actually believed Carson would come after anyone. He'd believed that after he was put away, the entire operation was shut down. It wasn't until you went missing at the banquet that he even suspected it had anything to do with the case since no one had made a move on him or his family."

"Yet he had them under protection." I shake my head.

"That was my argument," Lance replies. "Carter behaved poorly. His reactions put you, Reyna, and their parents in jeopardy, and we can handle that later. Right now, we need to focus on getting you better and finding a way to get this guy for everything else."

"I felt so helpless. So absolutely useless." Since we've been back, I haven't had a chance to process everything the past few days held for Reyna and me. And there's *a lot* there. How broken I was. How I kept slipping in and out of consciousness, dreaming of war zones and all the times I let her down.

"What did you do? After you were shot. After the accident. When you were struggling...what did you do?" Lance asks.

"I prayed," I tell him. "A lot. It's all I could do."

Lance reaches out and rests a hand on my good shoulder. "Then you weren't helpless, brother."

CHAPTER 24
Reyna

"You do not have to do that." Kyra plucks a dirty cup from my hand and carries it into the kitchen.

"I don't mind cleaning up," I tell her with a laugh. "You both are doing so much for us."

"Please. It's the least we can do. You and Michael are practically family, you know that."

It's nearly eleven at night, and Michael is on his way here from the hospital. Kyra and Pastor Redding have made up both of their spare bedrooms so the two of us have somewhere to hide.

Hide.

It infuriates me that we aren't allowed to go home. My bed. My sheets. My clothes. Here's hoping it's only temporary.

Kyra's cell rings, and she answers it, then turns to face me. "It's for you."

"For me?" She nods and offers it to me. "Hello?"

"Reyna, it is so good to hear your voice."

Carter. "What do you want?" I snap. My tone is sharp, furious, and frankly—he deserves a lot worse.

"To check on you." He seems honestly taken aback by my anger, his tone shifting from joyful to cautious. "I've been so worried. When Lance called and said you were missing—"

"And Michael," I snap.

"Of course."

"He almost died. Do you know that? Do you know he was shot, then suffered fractured ribs, a collapsed lung, and still had to trek through the swamps after being beaten while we were held captive?" Carter is completely silent, and somehow, that only fuels my anger even more. "He had a massive infection by the time we got him to the hospital."

"Reyna. I really am sorry."

"You're sorry. You know, Carter, my entire life, I've looked up to you. You were my strong, protective older brother who could literally do no wrong. But you really messed up this time, and Michael almost paid for it with his life."

"I know. I just... How was I supposed to know they were connected?"

"How could you not?"

"Reyna. I didn't know. You have to believe that if I genuinely thought you could be in danger, I would have done something."

"Did you seriously not put two and two together after I was attacked *weeks* after you put a man in prison?"

"No. Because I hadn't heard anything about it. Reyna, I put bad people in prison every single day. How could I have known that this one would put you at risk?"

"You sure worried about your family, though, didn't you? They had protection. Which meant you were worried on some level. Yet, you didn't even take the time to say, 'Hey, Reyna, I just locked a bad guy up. Keep an eye on your surroundings.'"

He sighs into the phone. "My family lives with me. Every single day. They're here in Boston. In the media. Anytime I'm working on a high-profile case like this, I take extra precautions."

"Then you should have done it for us. He could have gotten to Mom, Carter. Dad. He got to me. I'm just grateful I wasn't alone." I consider how that might have been. I still would have tried to escape, sure, but even as I physically helped Michael to those swamps, I don't imagine I would have made it far if I'd been alone.

"I regret it, Reyna. You have no idea how much I regret it."

I pinch the bridge of my nose and take a deep breath, my attempt at expelling some of the anger searing my insides. "Look, I don't want to argue about this, Carter. I honestly don't even want to talk to you right now. It's been a long couple of days—weeks, really—and I want to get to bed."

"How is Michael?" He's trying to extend the conversation, but I have no interest in doing so. He wants to talk? He can wait until my life is no longer in danger. Until Michael can go back to his gym and I can resume my days. As of now, they're going to have to find someone to step up in my place at the school—at the job I love—because everyone in town has to think I'm still missing.

"He's alive. Goodbye, Carter." I end the call, then offer the cell back to her.

"You all right?" She sets the cell back down, and I plant both palms on the countertop as she moves farther into the kitchen and starts scooping leftover spaghetti onto a plate to heat for Michael.

"I'm struggling with anger," I admit.

"Toward Carter?"

"Yes."

"I can't say I blame you there. What he did must feel an awful lot like betrayal."

"It does. I mean, I can understand from his perspective. He really does put dangerous criminals away all the time. And I know that if he had suspected for even a second that my life could be at risk he would have told me."

"But he didn't, and Michael almost died."

"Exactly!"

She puts the plate into the microwave and starts it.

"Are you angry with Carter because of what happened to you? Or because of what nearly happened to Michael?"

I consider a moment. "I'm angry at this entire situation. At the fact that people do evil things and others like my brother get targeted for doing what's right. I'm furious that we can't go after this Zeke guy for what he did to us, all because we don't have proof, even though he nearly killed Michael and me." My eyes fill. "God has a plan. I believe that. But how am I supposed to cling to my faith when everything around me is falling apart?"

Kyra comes around the counter and takes my face in hers. She stares into my eyes like she's looking straight through to my soul. It's something she's always been able to do. The woman can make you open up and pour your heart out, then help you put it back together without so much as speaking a single word. "I won't stand here and tell you that you have to just put your faith in Him because you already know that. What I will remind you is that people choose to do horrific things because they are sinful. Because they themselves are prisoners of this world. God can take the horrific and make it beautiful, and something beautiful will come out of this. You just might not see it yet."

I take a deep breath as I let her words sink in.

It took me a long time to see the beauty that came from my heartbreak. Truly, it wasn't until Michael nearly died that I began to understand. Because he left me and joined the military, Michael saved countless lives.

He met Lance and Elijah, and they came here and opened up Knight Security.

And since then, Michael has dedicated his life to helping others.

I think of Sunny. Of the fact that he kept her and her baby safe when that man tried to rip the infant from her arms.

I think of Eliza, who was stalked and abducted.

I consider Andie, who was nearly murdered.

Each and every time, it was Michael and his team who stepped in.

Perhaps that's the beauty in my heartbreak. That the man who shattered me into pieces is the same one who has helped put so many others back together.

The door opens, and Michael walks in, Lance at his side.

My gaze locks on almond eyes that I have spent countless hours staring into, and I know—without a doubt—our story is not done.

He was my first love.

And, God willing, he'll be my last.

"HOW ARE YOU FEELING?" I TAKE A SEAT ON THE COUCH beside Michael.

He sets the folder he was reviewing down and

glances over at me. "Better now that I've showered and eaten a meal not prepared in a hospital kitchen."

I laugh and tug a blanket off the back of the couch. Since it's well past two in the morning, Pastor Redding and his wife have already turned in for the night. But even as I tried to lie in bed and get some sleep, I found myself unable to do anything but stare up at the ceiling fan as it whirred above me. "I can imagine."

"How are you doing? We've talked an awful lot about me, but not you."

"Well, you were the one who was shot and nearly died," I remind him.

"You could have died, too." He sits up a bit straighter and turns, propping one knee up on the couch so he can fully face me. His arm is in a sling, but the color in his cheeks is back, and although his movements are slow and stiff, he's moving. Which is a gift from God after everything he went through.

"I'm okay."

"Are you? I mean it, Reyna. You've been through the wringer."

I swallow hard as emotion wells in my throat. Truth is, I'm not okay. Far from it, even. But I am so incredibly tired of crying. Of feeling so helpless. "I'm managing."

"Reyna. You don't have to be strong with me. We're —friends." He hesitates before the last word. Before I can respond, he grins. "You told my dad off."

I cover my face with my hands and giggle. "I did."

"It felt good, didn't it?"

"You know, it really did. It probably shouldn't have, but being able to air it out felt nice." I narrow my gaze. Michael's father was never violent, but he had a mean tongue when he was worked up. "Did he take it out on you?"

"Actually—brace yourself—he apologized to me."

"He did what?" And because I can't fight the urge to touch him any longer, I scoot closer and drape my arm over the back of the couch so I can face him. My hand grips the hand that he has stretched out over the back too, and the moment our skin meets, I'm greeted with an overwhelming avalanche of butterflies in my stomach.

"He did," Michael replies with a smile. "It caught me off guard. My mother and sister, too."

"Michael, that's great."

"It felt a lot like healing," he says. "And that was nice."

"I'm really glad."

We fall into companionable silence, and I start to draw my hand back, worried that I've gone too far. Michael tugs my fingers, taking my hand in his. "I'm sorry that I wasn't more present once we got to Caleb's. I—"

"Michael, you took a beating. On top of being shot and being in an accident. Why are you apologizing? Honestly, I don't know how you stayed on your feet as long as you did. Doc was shocked, too. He said for all intents and purposes, you shouldn't be here today."

"Yeah, he told me that, too. It seems I have a habit of surviving when others think I'm grave-bound."

"Good. Keep it up."

"I'd rather stop being in situations where I have to maintain those odds." His gaze levels on my face. "I'm so glad you survived, Reyna. And I cannot thank you enough for bringing me out, too."

My cheeks heat. "You would have done the same."

"In a heartbeat."

"You took a bullet for me."

"I'd take a thousand of them if it meant you walked away alive."

"Michael—" I tear up, the emotion finally getting to be too much for me to hide anymore. I need space to think, to find a way to put into words all that I'm feeling. So I withdraw my hand and get to my feet. "I think I'm going to head to bed."

"Okay." Michael stands and retrieves his folder, then tucks it beneath his injured arm and follows me down the hall.

Our rooms are across from each other. He stops outside his door, and I pause outside of mine.

We turn toward each other.

"Goodnight," he says.

And I can't fight it anymore. I rush forward and cup his face, then yank his mouth down onto mine. The kiss is explosive.

Soul-igniting.

World-tilting.

And I deepen it, wondering how I went so long without Michael Anderson in my life.

He pulls away and rests his forehead against mine, his ragged breathing a perfect tempo for mine. "I can't breathe without you," he whispers. "The moments you aren't there, it feels like my lungs can't fill with air."

"I feel the same." I kiss him again, gently this time, savoring these quiet moments where we're together, our lives unthreatened. "I don't want you to move to Boston when this is over. Please don't leave."

His gaze levels on mine. "Are you sure?"

"Yes. I don't want distance. I want you. I want the life we should have had. I want you to keep promising to count the stars for me. I want a marriage. Children. A future. And we can't have that if you leave Hope Springs."

With his good hand, Michael cups my cheek, his thumb caressing my skin. "Then I'll count every last star for you, Reyna. And I will dedicate my life to making you happy."

He kisses me again, then pulls away, and I slip into my room, leaning back against the door.

A future with Michael felt impossible. But now, it's right in my grasp.

We just have to survive this first.

CHAPTER 25

Michael

Being unable to get to the gym has been one of the downsides of having to stay hidden. It's been a solid week of staying at the Redding's place, and although I can't even begin to describe the joy I feel at seeing Reyna every day, I'm desperate for my heavy bag. My weights. For something to work out all of this frustration at having to stay put.

Lance and Elijah are digging as best they can into Zeke's history, while Sheriff Vick and Carter attempt to get the guys who attacked us outside the banquet to crack. They're maintaining their story, though.

According to them, they don't work for anyone.

Apparently, going to prison on attempted kidnapping and assault charges is better than risking the wrath of Zeke Phillips.

Even with the skills Elijah possesses for getting his hands on information otherwise undiscoverable by the most talented investigators in the world, he's struggled to get anything on Zeke.

The guy is squeaky clean.

Reyna laughs, so I glance up from the laptop I'm using for my own research to watch her eat a ball of uncooked cookie dough. She and Kyra have spent a lot of time in the kitchen, 'baking their troubles away'—as the pastor's wife calls it.

When he's not at the church, Pastor's helping me rehab, and I'm beyond grateful for the help, given I'm finally able to remove the sling and start moving my arm around. The bullet went into my pectoral muscle and embedded itself, so the damage to the surrounding tissue was substantial.

Nothing that can't be healed with time and exercise, but it'll likely cause me aches for years to come—if my prior bullet holes are any indication, anyway.

Someone knocks.

"I'll grab it."

As we usually do, Reyna and I move out of sight— just in case. Kyra looks through the peephole, and the confused expression on her face has me drawing my firearm out from its holster, and lining up right behind the door.

It could just be that she's surprised to see who's on the other side, but when she meets my gaze and shakes her head, I know she has no idea who the knocker is.

"Do I answer it?" she whispers.

Another knock.

I nod, then remain just out of sight, but close enough that I can pull her out of danger if necessary.

She plasters a smile on her face, then pulls it open. "Hi, can I help you?"

"Yes, ma'am. I'm looking for Pastor Redding. Is he by chance here?"

"No," she replies. "I'm sorry, but he's not in right now. Can I ask what this is about?"

"He knows a good friend of mine—Michael Anderson? And I'm just trying to get a message to him."

"Oh, I'm afraid Michael is missing. But I can let my husband know you're looking for him. What's your name?"

"No need for names. I think this message will come through clear enough."

I rip her out of the way, throwing her behind me and rushing around the door as the man raises his gun.

There's no hesitation as I aim mine—and squeeze the trigger.

———

THE ECHOING BOOM OF A GUNSHOT IS NOT AN UNFAMILIAR sound for me.

But I'd hoped to never hear it in my hometown.

I stand on the lawn of Pastor Redding's house, watching as Sheriff Vick talks to the coroner. Pastor Redding is holding his wife, and they're lingering near the door where Reyna, Eliza, and Andie stand.

I'm by myself. Hating the fact that danger followed me here because some egotistical psycho wanted to send a message.

Well, message received.

But the response is not going to be what he hoped.

I start toward Lance's truck, which is parked just down the street a ways, as he speaks with one of the deputies.

"Michael!" Reyna calls after me, but I keep walking.

I can't look back. Because if I do, I might not want to leave.

"Wait!" Reyna catches up to me and grabs my uninjured arm, turning me to face her. "Where are you going?"

"To handle this."

"What are you going to do?"

"What I should have done in the first place. Confront him on his own turf."

"Michael, you can't do that. We still don't have any proof—"

"Proof?" I yell as I point back toward the front of Pastor Redding's house. "He nearly killed her, Reyna! We've been looking for a legal way to take this guy down, and we haven't found one. Well, I can solve that right now." Rage envelops me like a welcoming blanket, urging me to do its bidding.

"You can't do this, Michael," Reyna insists, reaching up to cup my face.

"She's right."

I glance over my shoulder, surprised that Lance, Silas, Elijah, and Jaxson have all formed a half circle at my back while my focus has been on Reyna. "We can't let this violence come here."

"No, but there is a better way. There has to be."

I shift my gaze to Lance. "Then tell me what it is, and I will happily go that route. But he *knew* Reyna and I were there. He knew we were alive, and instead of coming for us himself, he sent a hit man after Pastor Redding's wife." Fear mingles with the rage, churning my stomach. Why did I let her open the door?

If I'd been one heartbeat slower she would have been killed.

Kyra Redding would have died right in front of me. Her only crime? Being there for us.

I close my eyes and take a deep breath.

"Hey, I got here as soon as I could." Carter's voice has me opening my eyes again. He's wearing casual clothes—dark jeans and a black T-shirt—and when he comes to stand beside us, I have to fight the urge to slam my fist into his face.

More anger.

More temper.

The enemy is having a field day with me.

"Michael."

I turn and see Pastor Redding standing right behind me. His gaze is hard, his jaw set. "I'm sorry," is all I manage.

"You saved her."

"I put her in danger."

"*We* put her in danger," Reyna corrects.

But really, it's me. I did it. Because I let her open that door. I gave her the go-ahead, knowing that she didn't recognize who was on the other side. "I let her open it," I tell him. "I told her it was okay."

"Had you not, he would have come through anyway, and then my Kyra might have been in the way." He glances back at her, then reaches out and pulls me in for a hug. "You saved my wife, Michael."

"If I'd been one second later." I picture her falling back, blood pooling on her chest, while I watched her die just as I watched Private Andrews take his final breath.

"But you weren't, son," he says. "You saved her life because God put you exactly where you needed to be at the precise moment you needed to be there. Just as he did when Reyna was attacked in that parking lot."

"I keep being in the right place at the right time, yet nothing gets solved." I glance back at Lance and try to keep my tone level even though all I want to do is yell. "Let me go, and I'll solve this right now. He'll never hurt another person again."

"You can't go after Zeke, Michael. It's suicide. Or at the very least, a prison sentence. He's connected and well protected."

"Then I'll happily rot in a cell knowing everyone I love is safe."

"Vengeance is not yours, Michael," Pastor Redding

reminds me. "It's not mine. It's not anyone's, no matter how badly we want it to be." He clenches his hands into fists, and for the first time in my entire life, I see his anger. "Vengeance belongs to God. Do this the right way. Don't sacrifice your soul for it."

"I killed a man today, Pastor."

"You stopped a man who was bent on hurting innocent people."

"Is there a difference?"

"I believe so, yes." He reaches out and places a hand on my shoulder. "You reacted in the moment, but this—going after him this way—is not in the moment. It's planned."

Desperation takes many forms.

It can make us do foolish things.

It was desperation for a life that was my own, for the ability to prove myself to Reyna, that drove me out of Hope Springs.

And it was desperation for the love I walked away from that brought me back.

But allowing my desperation for justice to drive me to take vengeance into my own hands is not the way I'm supposed to handle things. I know that. Truly, I do. But I'm so afraid that every moment we do nothing is another inch he gains in getting closer to us and everyone we love.

It has to stop. One way or another. I turn to Carter. "You're going to get me in with the men who attacked us outside of that banquet."

"Michael, I—"

"No. No excuses. He knows we're alive now, so pretending otherwise is a foolish move. I want to see them. I want to look them in the eyes and get them to admit they weren't working alone."

"I've tried," he insists.

"You have," I agree. "But I haven't. And I can be quite persuasive if necessary."

CHAPTER 26
Reyna

Normally, the last week before school starts is one of my favorite times. The halls are still empty, but there are fresh decorations on the wall and an entire year of hopeful days ahead.

I'd been so ready to resume my normal life, but now that I'm here, I'm longing for a lazy morning, sitting on the Redding's couch with Michael as we watch cheesy movies and pretend the danger outside doesn't exist.

Now that they know we're alive, I'm back at the school, Jaxson and Silas at my side as Michael, Lance, and Elijah are headed to Boston with Carter. They're planning to let Michael sit down with the men who shot him, and the idea of him staring them down terrifies me.

Which is irrational, of course, since the men will be unarmed and handcuffed. Though, I guess if I'm being truly honest with myself, it's them I fear for, not

Michael. He's been silent since Kyra was nearly killed three days ago.

I've barely seen him since I'm staying at Lance and Eliza's—at their insistence—and he remained at the Redding's to protect them. I check my cell for the hundredth time, hoping he's sent a text letting me know he's all right, but there's nothing here. Nothing but radio silence. I finish sending off a mass email to all the teachers welcoming them to the new school year, with a schedule of special events we have planned attached. As soon as it's out of my outbox, I get to my feet and stretch.

My muscles are still sore, and I'm not sure they'll recover until I've spent at least a week in bed sleeping off the stress from the past few weeks.

There's a knock at the door, and after glancing through the glass pane, Jaxson pushes it open. "Lilly delivered lunch." He offers me a Styrofoam container, then sits across from me as I open the lid and stare down at a cheeseburger and fries.

The woman knows the way to my heart, that's for sure.

"Thank you, God, for this meal. Thank you for blessing our each and every day, Lord. Amen." After the quick grace, I open a ketchup packet and squeeze some onto the tray. "Is Silas not eating with us?"

"He's the silent type," Jaxson says. "He's eating out in the entry hall."

"He definitely seems quiet."

"Lance says he's always been that way."

"They knew each other first, right?"

"Yeah. Lance met him when they were in the VA hospital together for a time. Silas had been messed up pretty bad, though Lance has never said how it happened. They hit it off, as anyone who meets Lance does, and he introduced him to the rest of us. Elijah and Michael first and then me a few years later at a veteran's retreat we did in the woods."

"You were a Marine, right?"

"I am."

"I remember Margot telling me about Michael's Army buddies and their Marine tagalong."

Jaxson snorts. "They followed me around."

I laugh, appreciating the genuine comradery he shares with the others. It's refreshing to see men as close as brothers in a world where people have never been so distant from each other. "You met them in the hospital, too?"

"Yeah." Jaxson shakes his head. "I'd already been there for a time, but I'll never forget them being wheeled in. I'd already met Lance before, so seeing him on that stretcher, so many holes in his chest—I actually prayed. And I'd never been a praying man before that."

"Lance seems to have that effect on people. Michael grew up in the same church as me, but he'd always had some distance. Not sure why, though I assume some of it had to do with his dad. But Margot told me that he found Jesus when he'd almost died, and that his friend Lance was part of the reason."

"Lance Knight knows how to guide people. It's one of the things that made him such a great OIC."

"OIC?"

"Officer in Charge. Sorry."

I pluck a fry from the tray and stick it in my mouth. "It's fine," I say as soon as I've finished it. "You guys all seem to work really well together."

"As I said, we each have our own skill sets, and no one tries to overstep the other."

"You said Lance leads, Elijah is the computer skills, Michael is the bodyguard, and you called yourself a—what was it—spotter?"

"Yeah. I was a sniper." He takes a bite of his burger. "I do better from high vantage points, and Michael excels at hand-to-hand. Most of the time. Guy did get shot recently."

I snort, nearly choking on a fry. It's dark humor, but somehow given everything we've faced, I can appreciate it. "And Bianca? Did you know her before?"

"No. Not really. I'd heard of her, sure, I think most of us stationed overseas had, but I didn't meet her until Lance called her when Michael was in trouble."

"Thank you for coming for us, by the way. I know that Michael is your friend, and it's your job, but thank you."

"We didn't come just for Michael," he says. "We care

about you too, Reyna. You're our people just as much as Michael is."

My heart warms with joy, and I continue eating. Jaxson and I enjoy our burgers in comfortable silence. The beep of my phone increases my pulse, and I turn it over to check the notification.

Michael's name illuminates my screen next to a partial message. Quickly, I unlock my phone to read and respond.

Michael: Just got to Boston. Carter is getting us into the prison now. I miss you. Stay safe.

Me: I'm not the one currently in danger. I miss you, too. YOU stay safe. I need you to come back so we can finish our conversations about the future.

Michael: I'll be there.

Smiling, I set my phone aside and take another bite.

So much ugliness has happened, but in the midst of it, God delivered me a partner. True love. And I can't help but grin despite the fact that nothing is settled yet.

The door opens, and Liam steps in, a smile on his face. "Reyna, it's good to see you."

Jaxson sets his food aside and stands. "Where's Silas?"

"He's still at the front. I told him who I was, and he let me through." His gaze remains focused on me even as he addresses Jaxson.

Jaxson steps back toward me, slow movements that don't seem off until he completely blocks me with his body and his hand goes to his lower back, where his firearm is holstered. "I know Reyna appreciates you stopping by, but she's not up for company right now."

"I'm so glad you made it back safely," Liam says. "I was so worried about you."

"I appreciate that, Liam, but Jaxson is right. I'm really busy right now. Maybe we can set up a lunch or something later?" Alarm bells are ringing in my brain, a warning that might as well be flashing neon lights.

"I was so worried," he repeats. "But I knew you'd make it back. You're too strong."

"I'm not going to ask you again." Jaxson steps forward, and a gunshot echoes through my office. I don't even have time to react before Jaxson is stumbling back into my desk and falling to the floor, blood staining the front of his white T-shirt.

Liam removes his hand from his pocket and reveals the gun he's carrying. He aims it at Jaxson, and I throw myself over my bodyguard.

"No! Liam, stop!"

"I am tired of people getting in the way of us, Reyna. First Zeke, then Michael, and now these *men*."

"Zeke?" My blood ices as I press one hand to Jaxson's wound and try to slip the other beneath him. He groans and rolls just slightly enough that the movement won't be noticed by Liam.

Keep him talking.

Keep him focused on me.

Someone else will have heard the gunshot.

"I told him that you were not to be touched. That we

were wrong and you wouldn't have anything to do with Carter."

"How do you know Zeke?" My hand closes around the grip of Jaxson's firearm.

"He represented my brother when your brother put him away. This whole thing was his plan. I was supposed to come here and find out what you knew, get to know you, and then—" He trails off. "I couldn't do it because you and I are meant to be, Reyna. I never wanted anything to do with my brother's work, either. And now that I know you don't either…"

I slip the gun from the holster. "You hurt my friend, Liam."

"I set you free. You're a prisoner, just like I am. My brother's goons wouldn't let me free of them, either."

"Liam, put the gun down, please."

"I can't do that." He tilts his head to the side. "You're coming with me, and soon you'll see that we're meant to be."

"Liam, I cannot go with you." I pull the gun out, but before I can raise it, Liam aims his at Jaxson's head.

"If you don't put that gun down, Reyna, I'm going to kill him where he lies. Don't make me do it. Please. Don't make me kill for you. I will. But don't make me do it."

My heart plummets, and I swing the gun around where he can see it, then set it on the ground.

"Good girl. Now, let's go."

"My friend needs help. Please. Let me get him help."

"We have to leave before the other one wakes up," he snaps. A brief dose of relief floods my system because if he's expecting Silas to wake up, then it means he's still alive.

"Reyna. No." Jaxson reaches across his body and clings to my arm while he uses the arm draped behind me to slip his phone into my back pocket.

"I'll be fine," I tell him, then take his hands and press them to his injury. "Tell Michael I'll be okay."

"Let's go!"

I stand and reach for my phone, just for show, and Liam shakes his head. "Leave it. You won't need it. We'll get you a new one when you can be trusted to see the truth. Come on." He reaches forward and grabs my arm, then shoves me out the door, the gun pressed up against my side, hidden from view.

Blood coats my hands, so I fold my arms as we make our way out of the school. That way if anyone is passing by, they won't stop and try to help.

I can't risk Liam hurting anyone else.

Please, God, let Jaxson and Silas be all right, and send Michael to me. Please send me help. I need You.

CHAPTER 27
Michael

I haven't been to many prisons stateside, though I spent quite a lot of time guarding and delivering criminals to detainment facilities overseas. However, despite their surface differences, they are very much the same.

Criminals with furious expressions glare at us from the other side of a chain-link and razor-wire barrier as we make our way toward the interrogation building. Some throw insults our way; others offer to show us a good time if we'd just step on the other side of the barrier.

More than five make threats at Carter.

He maintains his focus, though, not letting it seem like anything's getting beneath his thick skin. Not even when they make vulgar threats about his family. I turn my head and glare at a bald man with black ink on the top of his head, and he grins back at me.

"Don't let it get to you," Carter says.

"How do you deal with it? How do you continue walking instead of losing your temper?"

"Losing my temper won't do anything but land me on the other side with them. Which is exactly what they want."

We step into the building, and a blast of AC hits me in the face. After turning in our weapons and signing in on the visitor's log, we're ushered back to a private room with a viewing window. Elijah and Lance step behind it, while Carter and I continue into the main room.

Carter sets his briefcase down and takes a seat at the table, while I remain standing in the corner. "Not planning to sit?"

"No."

"Michael, you have to be careful with these guys."

"I'm not worried, Carter."

"They tried to kill you. It would be natural to be a bit apprehensive."

"I'm angry," I retort. "Not apprehensive. And it wasn't just me they nearly killed."

"I already apologized for not being forthcoming about what I was dealing with. I honestly didn't realize the two could be linked. Can I not make a mistake?"

"You came to us to protect her. You honestly expect me to believe you had no idea the two situations could be connected?"

He remains silent, but I can see the answer written

all over his face. The guilt. "I had my suspicions, but I trusted you to keep her safe."

"Yet you didn't bother giving us all the information we needed in order to keep her safe."

"How could you have protected her differently?" he asks. "If you'd have known that I was dealing with death threats over putting Willy away, what would have changed?"

"We would have been looking for proof rather than searching for a needle in a haystack," I snap. "Elijah could have spent time digging into the threats you received, finding a link, and taking care of it before she even could have been abducted. And had we known it was a threat of this magnitude, we *never* would have allowed her to attend that gala in the first place."

He starts to respond, but the door opens, and two guards walk in, leading two inmates wearing bright orange jumpsuits. Since it was dark and I was focused on staying alive, I hadn't had the chance to get a solid visualization of the men who attacked us outside of the banquet.

But now, I study them.

One is a bit taller than the other, his hair longer and pulled out of his face with a hair tie. A thick scar cuts through his left eyebrow, and when he glares back at me, I note one eye is blue while the other is brown.

The second man is shorter, his blond hair cut close to his scalp. He stares back at me from beady eyes that hold absolutely no remorse.

"Thank you," Carter tells the guards once they've secured the men's hands to the table in front of them.

The guards leave, and Carter takes a seat across from them while I remain standing in the corner.

"Who's your boyfriend?" The one with the different-colored eyes sneers.

"You don't recognize me?" I move a bit farther into the room.

Realization dawns, and the men look at each other. "You survived, huh?"

"I did."

"Good. Then our murder charges will get dropped."

"To attempted murder, sure," Carter replies. "However, as I told you before, I can get those changed as well, lessen your sentence, for one simple name."

"Mr. Rogers." The one with the beady eyes scoffs. "There's a name for you."

Carter doesn't bite, but I see the frustration in the way he grinds his teeth together. "Who are you working for?"

"Man, are you deaf?" the multicolor-eyed one snaps. "We told you we don't work for anyone."

"Which is a lie," I say. "I know you work for Zeke Phillips."

The smallest twitch from beady eyes.

"I know he represents Willy Carson, who you both are known associates of." The last part is a lie—at least in the sense that I don't have any actual proof of it.

"You don't know nothing," the longer-haired man states as he shakes his head.

I move in closer and plant both hands on the table between us. "I know that if you don't tell me what I want to know, I'm going to have my lawyer here step out and I'll use the tactics I learned overseas, from men much scarier than your boss, to get the answers I seek."

Beady Eyes swallows hard.

"Carter—"

"No," Beady Eyes replies.

"Shut your mouth, Gil," Multicolored Eyes snaps.

"No, Gil. Speak. We can make a deal just for you if your buddy here wants to keep his mouth shut."

"All I'm going to say is that you don't know who you're up against," Gil replies. "You can torture us. Beat us. Whatever it is you think you can do? He's worse. And you'll never see him coming."

"We've managed so far."

They look at each other and laugh, then turn back to me. "You're missing a big part of the picture there, bodyguard. And by the time you figure it out, it'll be too late."

The door opens, and Zeke Phillips strolls in, his expression furious. Carter stands, and I start toward Zeke, only stopping when Carter puts a hand on my arm.

"I would love to know why you think it's appropriate to meet with my clients without their lawyer present." Zeke pays me no attention despite the fact that

I know he recognizes me. And somehow, the genuine lack of focus on me angers me even more.

"Don't you recognize me?" I ask. "Or do I look different without a bullet hole and my hands chained above my head?"

Zeke glances in my direction, then turns back to Carter. "Your associate here obviously has me confused for someone else. And you must be confused yourself about appropriate behavior as a public prosecutor. Otherwise, you would have realized that meeting with my clients without me present is highly inappropriate."

"They didn't complain." Carter crosses his arms. "And neither of them asked for representation."

He glares around Carter at the two men who are visibly shaken by his arrival. "We'll make sure we cover that." Zeke straightens. "Now, if you'll excuse me, this meeting is over."

"We're far from through," I growl, meeting his gaze.

Zeke smiles at me. "I assure you, this will be the final interaction I have with you." The way he says it alludes to more. His tone. The grin that follows. Separately, I'd believe them to be nothing more than the arrogance of a man who believes he's untouchable.

But together they make my skin crawl.

The door bursts open, and Lance moves inside. "We have to go," he tells me. "Now." His gaze lands on Phillips, and he crosses the room, putting himself nose to nose with the attorney. "I'm coming for you, Phillips. One way or another, you're going to know what it means to cross our team." He growls the words, fury dripping from each and every one of them, which only worries me further.

Lance never gets mad.

He's one of the most even-tempered men I've ever met.

So what happened?

"I look forward to the challenge," Zeke replies, then steps aside and gestures for us to leave the room.

Carter retrieves his briefcase, and we step out into the hall.

"What is it?" I ask, noting the worry on Elijah's face as well.

"Jaxson is in the ICU, and Silas is in the emergency room."

I can feel the blood drain from my body, leaving me cold. "And Reyna?"

Lance's gaze meets mine. "She's been taken."

CHAPTER 28

Reyna

My pulse has skyrocketed, and it's all I can do to keep the car on the road. Liam is in the passenger seat, his gun pointed directly at me. Palms sweaty, I grip the steering wheel, my thoughts running a million miles a minute.

Will Jaxson survive?

Silas?

What will Michael do when he discovers I'm gone?

"It was you, wasn't it? The one that called and breathed on the phone?" I ask.

"I had to hear your voice once more after our date. I needed it."

"Why are you doing this?"

"I've already told you. I'm saving your life."

"By kidnapping me?"

"You don't understand, Reyna. My brother is a killer. He ripped me out of my freshman year of college and forced me to join his business. He threatened me with the lives of my friends if I didn't cooperate. And when he was busted for drugging that girl's drink—" Liam trails off. "I thought I was finally free. That I could put the past behind me...but then Zeke came and he ruined everything!" He yells the words, the calm, sweet man I'd come to know no longer present.

It's like a switch flipped in his brain and suppressed the normalcy I'd seen. "You could do what's right, though. You could testify against Zeke and then go back to your life." I risk glancing over at him.

He's eyeing me with frustration, as though there are pieces of the puzzle I'm failing to put together. "You don't understand. You don't get it. How could you?"

"Then explain it to me. Make me understand."

"The things I've done would land me in prison for the rest of my life. There would be no second chance for me. There *is* no second chance for me."

"But there is. Everyone gets a second chance."

"I'm not religious, so you can save that particular speech."

"Liam—"

"That's not my name. You don't call me that anymore."

"Then what is your name?" *Keep him talking until you have a better plan.* I try to run through my options. I could crash the car, but the highway out of town is notoriously quiet. It could be thirty minutes before someone finds us, and by then—who knows if he'll let me live.

"Wesley," he replies. "My name is Wesley. That's what you'll call me from now on." He reaches over and strokes the side of my cheek. "You captivated me from the first time we met. So kind. So wholesome. You've never done anything bad in your life, have you?" Withdrawing his hand, he looks back out the window, though he keeps the firearm trained on me. "I was drawn to your goodness, Reyna. Because I think it might be able to hide my darkness."

I could almost feel bad for him. *Almost.* "You shot my friend."

"He was in the way."

"Is that what you're going to do to me? If I don't listen to you?"

"No," He appears genuinely horrified. "I would never hurt you, Reyna. You have to believe that."

"But you let the others hurt me," I tell him, my stomach churning. Bile rises in my throat as I consider all the things he could do to me if we arrive wherever we're headed. "You didn't warn me that they were coming."

"I tried to protect you! I told Zeke you didn't know anything! It would have been okay. We could have left sooner, but Michael got in the way." He shakes his head. "He put you in danger."

"Michael saved me."

"Michael kept you from me. Because of that, I couldn't warn you. Not without raising his suspicions."

"Liam—"

"Wesley!" he interrupts.

"Wesley. We can do the right thing. Please. Put the gun away, and let's go back to Hope Springs. We can meet with the sheriff, and you can tell him everything."

"No. It's too late."

"What do you mean?"

"Zeke is going to send people to Hope Springs to kill you and that team that's been protecting you."

Gone is the nausea, replaced with bone-chilling fear. Lance. Eliza. Elijah. Andie. Jaxson. Silas and his daughter. Michael... Are they truly all at risk? "Please let me go back." Tears blur my vision. "Please let me warn them."

"I'll let you make one call when we get to where we're going," he says. "If it's not too late, then you can give them a heads up."

A truck comes over the ridge overhead and hope burns inside of me. I could scream out the window. Wave. Do something that causes the driver to realize something is wrong. My gaze lands on the lever that turns on the high beams.

I glance over at Wesley, who's staring out the window.

I inch my hand closer to the lever and pull it. Multiple times. Over and over again. And then they get closer, passing by and giving me a view of the driver.

Michael.

It's only a heartbeat as he passes by me, but our gazes lock, and the moment he's passed, I glance up in the rearview mirror as the truck brakes hard and spins back toward us.

"What did you do?" Wesley turns to look behind us. "You're going to make me kill them. That's what you're going to do."

I have a heartbeat to make a choice.

And I decide that giving Wesley something else to focus on is worth the risk to my life.

I turn the wheel hard, veering off the road.

"Get back on the highway!" Wesley roars.

And then the car slams into a tree.

Pain shoots through me, coming from every possible inch of my body as it's battered by the crushing of metal. I'm smacked in the face by the deploying airbags, powder filling my lungs, and I cough.

"Stupid!" Wesley roars. He slams the gun into the side of my head. "What were you thinking?"

I look over at him, turning my face and smiling as I see Michael rip his door open and yank Wesley free. He pins him to the truck and knocks the gun from his hand.

"Hey, Reyna."

I shift my attention to my side as Lance pulls my door open. "He's coming for all of you," I choke out.

"Who?" he asks.

"Zeke. He's sending men to Hope Springs. Eliza. Andie. Jaxson. Silas. They're all at risk." Tears blur my vision.

"They're going to be fine," Lance says. "We need to get you looked at."

"Paramedics are on their way," Elijah tells me.

"Call Andie. Have her get Eliza and Silas's daughter up to the hospital. Sheriff Vick has deputies there with Jaxson and Silas, so they'll be safe."

Elijah doesn't ask for clarification, just taps on the screen of his phone again.

"Okay. Can you hear me okay?" Lance asks.

"Yes. But I can't move." I try to shift out of my seat, but the dash has accordioned over my lap, pinning my legs beneath the steering wheel.

"It's okay. We're going to get you out." He glances to his left, then moves out of the way, and Michael comes into view. He kneels beside me.

"Hey, baby. How are you doing?" His tone is soft, but his expression is all worry.

"I'm okay. Did you get him?" Exhaustion sneaks up on me, almost pushing the pain away from the forefront of my mind. I'm so tired. So worn out.

"I got him. That was smart. Dangerous. But smart."

I smile softly. "I knew you would save me."

"Always." He tries to tug the steering wheel, but it doesn't budge. "What hurts?"

"Nothing right now," I say honestly because my entire body seems to have gone numb.

"Reyna, I need you to stay awake. Can you do that?" He looks over at Elijah. "How long until the ambulance?"

"Should be any minute."

"Can you pray with me? I don't want to die, Michael. I want to stay with you."

"You're not going to die." Michael's voice is strangled, and I glance up as Lance and Elijah both move in closer and place their hands on Michael's shoulders. He touches what's exposed of my arm since my hands are pinned.

Lance clears his throat. "Dear Lord, we come to You now, begging You to give Reyna the strength to pull through this. God, we thank You for getting us to her when we did. Please, Lord. Bring her through this. Amen."

As Lance finishes the prayer, a car screeches to a stop. "Bianca is here." Elijah turns away.

"Bianca. I like her," I say.

Bianca's familiar face comes into view. "Reyna, you and these near-death experiences. You gotta stop, girl. We can't be friends if you die on me." She shines a light on my eyes. "We can't move her until they get here with the stretcher."

"How did you beat the ambulance?"

"I was already in my car when Elijah called. And I can drive faster."

"Michael, Liam is Willy's brother." I close my eyes for a moment, my breathing getting more and more difficult with every passing second. I try to move again, to alleviate at least some of the building pressure in my chest.

"Stay still," Bianca tells me.

"You can tell me everything later, okay, baby? Right now we need to get you out."

"I love you," I tell him, my eyelids drooping. "I love you, Michael."

"I love you, too," he says. "Hang on just a bit longer, okay? Don't give up on me, Reyna Acker. We're just getting started."

Sirens echo in the distance, and I lose the fight with consciousness, letting myself slip into blackness.

CHAPTER 29
Michael

For the second time in as many months, I'm sitting in an emergency room waiting for news on Reyna's condition. Only this time, she was in much worse shape when she arrived. They'd had to cut her out of the car, slicing through the metal in order to free her pinned body.

She'd hit the tree so hard—and on her side—that it's amazing she survived at all.

Liam—or rather Wesley—on the other hand, was relatively fine. At least upon impact. I certainly made a dent in him once I'd ripped him from the car.

Once he regained consciousness, he made a deal with Carter to testify that Zeke Phillips has been running Willy Carson's business and was behind the attacks on Reyna and me.

Even better news, they'd managed to catch Asher and the other two men Zeke sent to Hope Springs as they tried to get into Andie's house. Because of Reyna's warning, Sheriff Vick had stationed deputies at everyone's homes, and they'd gone to hers first.

They've been arrested and have also agreed to help put their boss in prison. Though my request to spend ten minutes alone in a room with Asher was denied, I'm grateful to know he'll be rotting in a cell alongside his boss.

He and Zeke Phillips will spend a lot of time in prison.

But that doesn't help me right now. Not when the woman I love is in surgery to repair a bleed in her abdomen.

Lance sits beside me, his silent presence calming some of my fear, but only because if the worst happens and she doesn't pull through, I won't have to fall apart alone.

God, please don't let that happen.

The doors slide open and I look up as my mother and father come in. My dad's expression is furious. "How is she? Did you get him? Tell me you got that—"

"Reggie," my mother interrupts.

"We got him," I tell my dad.

The former cop looks relieved, but he leans forward in his wheelchair and places a hand on my leg. "She's a tough one," he tells me. "She's going to be fine."

It means the world to me that he's here at all. That either of them is. Especially since before my abduction, the only time my parents left the house was for my dad's appointments or the brief moments my mom had to go run an errand. "I hope so."

"Lance," my father greets as he offers Lance a hand.

"Mr. Anderson," Lance replies, shaking his offered palm.

"You took care of my boy. You call me Reggie. We're family."

The sentiment makes Lance smile, and truth be told, I'm grateful for it, too. "Reggie," Lance replies. "Michael is tough as nails. I've no doubt he would have found a way to save himself."

I nearly snort, a half-smile gracing my face despite my inner turmoil. "Doubtful. Not unless Reyna had been able to carry me out herself."

"Knowing her, she would have," my mother replies. She smiles softly at me as she takes a seat on my other side. "How are you?"

"Scared." I don't sugar-coat it. Why would I? The woman I love is fighting for her life.

"Any news?" Margot rushes in with Matty at her side. The teen looks tormented and for good reason. He was the one who found Jaxson bleeding out on the floor of Reyna's office when he'd gone to drop off some cookies my sister made.

He's the only reason Jaxson is alive. Silas had been tranquilized, the gun discarded since it had only contained one more dart. Which is why Wesley used a .45 on Jaxson instead of just knocking him out as well.

I shake my head, tears burning in my throat. "I feel so helpless. It's been hours."

"She'll pull through, Uncle Michael. She's tough." Matty takes a seat across from me.

"She is," Margot agrees. "I'm going to run back and check on Jaxson, okay? Matty, do you want to come?"

"No. I'm going to wait here. If that's okay."

She smiles softly. "Okay. I'll be right back."

"Wait, I want to go. I'd like to meet this former detective," my mother says as she strands. "If you'll be okay?" She hesitates beside my father.

"I'm fine, Delilah. Go." He smiles, and she kisses him quickly, then follows my sister down the hall. If I wasn't so broken inside, I might have fallen out of my chair at the sight of their affection.

I haven't seen an actual show of affection between them since before high school.

"What? Can't kiss your mother?" he asks, noting my shock.

"Just happy to see you both happy," I reply truthfully.

He smiles like a teen in love. "I missed my Del. It's been far too long since I was myself. I owe Reyna for that. She verbally smacked me so hard it made me see the past in a whole new light."

The lump in my throat is suffocating. "You were brave today," I tell my nephew. "You should be proud."

He shrugs. "I didn't do anything."

"But you did. Doc said you applying pressure as you

called 9-1-1 is the only reason Jaxson is alive. Thank you. You saved my friend."

He shrugs again.

"You're a hero, kid," my dad says. "Just like your uncle."

"And his grandfather from the stories I hear," Lance offers. "You're a legend with the Sheriff's department."

My dad snorts. "I don't know about that."

"It's true." Lance crosses his arms. "Just ask Sheriff Vick the next time you see him."

As they talk, I lean back and close my eyes, trying to keep my mind steady. For hours now, people have been coming and going. Pastor Redding and his wife. Lilly and Alex. Felix. Mrs. McGinley. They've been popping in, looking for updates, but I have none.

Leaning forward again, I stare down at my bruised knuckles. I'd slammed my fist into Wesley more times than I could count, stopping only because keeping him alive means answers. But I'd wanted to kill him.

I'd wanted so badly to deal that final blow.

And the entire ambulance ride back to the hospital, I'd been apologizing to God for allowing such violent thoughts to take root in my mind.

I'd begged for Him to heal Reyna.

And now, I have to wait.

I hate waiting.

The doors slide open, and Andie walks in alongside a little girl who appears to be no older than five.

"Any word?"

"No," I tell her. "Is that—"

"Silas's niece, yeah. Eloise, this is Lance and Michael. They're some of your uncle's friends. Lance, Michael, this is Ela."

"Hi," I greet, offering the girl the gentlest smile I can manage when inside, my emotions are a war zone. "This is my nephew, Matty. And my dad, Mr. Anderson."

"Hello," she greets, her cheeks turning a deep pink.

My dad and Matty both offer her similar smiles and nods.

"We went out for ice cream, but I'm bringing her back to her uncle now. Do you need anything?" Andie asks.

"No. Thanks."

"I'll be back in a few if you change your mind. Come on, sweetie." They disappear down the hall, going the same direction Margot and my mother went.

The trauma doors slide open, and Reyna's mother comes out.

I stand, trying to maintain my composure as she crosses toward me, bottom lip quivering, eyes full of tears. *Please, God, no. Please no.* "She's out of surgery," she tells me.

The relief I feel is immeasurable. "She's alive?"

"Yes. Doc said that she lacerated her pancreas, collapsed one of her lungs, broke three ribs, shattered bones in both of her legs, and had a tear in her stomach. But she's alive." She covers her mouth with a hand and chokes on a sob, so I wrap my arms around her and hold her against me, doing my best to keep my own tears at bay.

She's alive.

That's all that matters.

"She's not out of the woods yet, but he's hopeful that she'll pull through."

"Can I see her?" I ask, pulling away.

"Yes. Of course. She's not awake yet, but come on." She turns away and heads toward the doors.

I look back at Matty, my dad, and Lance.

"Go. I'll be fine." He takes the seat I just vacated, and my dad offers me a nod, letting me know he'll watch out for him. Lance does the same.

As I follow Reyna's mother down the hall and onto the recovery floor, it's all I can do to keep putting one foot in front of the other. My legs might as well be as heavy as lead, and I'm terrified.

What if she never wakes up?

She gestures toward a door. "Go. I'm going to call Carter and Henry so I can let them know her status."

I stare at the door a moment then take a deep, steadying breath, and push into the room.

It's mostly dark, with just a light over her bed casting a dim glow across her battered body, the machines beeping in the distance. An oxygen mask is perched on her face, and both of her legs are in casts.

My stomach plummets, and I lose the fight with tears.

The sobs come in rapid succession as I make my way

over to the bed and kneel beside her. I take one of her slender hands in mine, gripping it like a lifeline.

"I am so sorry, Reyna. I let you down again." I suck in a breath. "I failed you, and I am so, so, so, sorry."

My shoulders shake uncontrollably as I let out all of the fear and grief I've been holding in. Every single moment since I saw her in that car.

Since I watched her crash into that tree.

Heard the metal crunching.

And the screams ripped from her throat.

I let it all out, and then her hand tightens on mine. I look up and meet her gaze. "Hey, hey, baby." Using my free hand, I wipe my tears and get up so I can get closer to her.

She reaches up and tries to remove the oxygen mask, but I shake my head.

"You have to leave it on."

"Are you okay?" The words are barely audible as she speaks them.

But just hearing her voice makes me smile. "I am now."

CHAPTER 30

Reyna

Wearing a green dress and date night heels for the first time since my accident six months ago, I make my way into the school. I have maybe fifteen minutes to deal with the vandalism before I need to be out the door and waiting for Michael to pick me up for our date.

Date.

Michael and I have seen each other every single day since the accident, with him bringing me food or helping with stuff around my house. Our dates recently have consisted of flats and leggings, while going to the diner or vegging out on my couch. They've been amazing, but the opportunity to see Michael in a suit has me desperate to get the night going.

I am beyond giddy with excitement as I turn a corner and hear soft music coming from the gymnasium, which is what Sheriff Vick said had been vandalized.

Someone actually broke into the school. And according to him, he's never seen the gym look like it does now.

But music? Why would there be music?

I'm prepared for the worst, but then I step inside and find myself immersed in a memory.

A disco ball spins slowly overhead, casting lights all around the gymnasium. Silver and gold streamers hang from the ceiling, and white linen cloths cover five tables that have been placed around the edges of the gym.

And then Michael steps into view, wearing a tuxedo and a smile brighter than anything I've ever seen. Tears spring into my vision and my heart soars.

"Michael."

"Do you recognize this?" he asks, holding his arms out.

"Our senior prom," I admit. "I'll never forget it." It was the night he'd asked me to marry him. We were lying out in my backyard after dancing the night away, and he'd asked me to run away with him.

I hadn't known then that he was struggling with his life at home, and if I had I might've taken him up on the offer and fled together the moment we graduated. Then again, if I had, we wouldn't be here right now.

Michael crosses over to me, and I reach out to take his offered hand. "Every single moment I was away, I thought about this night. About how beautiful you'd looked in your gown, and how absolutely lucky I was to have captivated the attention of someone like you." He pulls me against him, one hand going to my lower back, the other taking mine in his.

We begin to sway, and I rest my head against his chest, letting myself be fully lost in the movement of his body against mine. Every moment we spent together over the years, every memory—bad and good—surfaces in a stunning reel of emotion playing through my heart.

I love this man. With everything that I am.

"We've been through a lot together," Michael says.

"Yes, we have."

"Even with the years apart, I feel like I've been with you forever."

I tilt my face up to his, and he leans down, capturing my lips. The kiss is tender. Loving. A gentle caress.

But it ignites a fire in my soul.

Michael pulls away. "I asked you to marry me the night of our senior prom."

"And I said yes."

"And then I left you." His expression darkens. "I don't know that I will ever forgive myself for leaving you."

"But you came back." I reach up and cup his face.

"I don't deserve you."

"You do, though. Michael Anderson, you deserve so many blessings."

"You're the greatest of them." He rests his forehead against mine. "Which is why—" He trails off and pulls away, then drops down on one knee and withdraws a velvet box. "I want to marry you, Reyna Acker. I want to spend every single moment of my life with you, so that we're never apart again. I will love you. Cherish you. Show you just how important you are to me each and every single day of our lives."

My eyes fill, emotion warming my chest as I stare down at the man I love on one knee. "I already answered you," I tell him.

"But I needed to ask again. I blew it the last time, Reyna. I won't this time. I'll marry you here and now if you'll let me. Or we can plan something. I don't care as long as you'll spend the rest of your life with me. Please say you will."

"Yes. Yes, I will marry you." Tears stream down my cheeks as he reaches down and lifts me, spinning me in a light circle before setting me back down and sliding the ring onto my finger. The diamonds dance beneath the disco ball above, and all at once, my family and friends come rushing out onto the dance floor, all of them dressed to impress in beautiful gowns and tuxedos.

My parents are dressed up. My mother in a glittery gold gown while my father's tie is a near match to the color. They're both smiling widely, looking happier than I can remember seeing them in recent years.

Michael's parents are wearing date night attire.

Even Eliza, as pregnant as she is, stuns in a violet gown, Lance at her side.

They rush forward, offering us congratulations and taking a closer look at my ring.

Someone clears his throat behind me, so I turn and see an older man standing behind me, clean-shaven and wearing a grey suit. I start to introduce myself, and then I see his eyes. Recognition slams into me. "Caleb!"

He laughs and accepts my hug.

"You're here!"

"I am. And I'm glad you recognized me." He runs his hands down the front of his suit.

"I'm so glad you're here! How are you here?"

"You said to visit," he replies. "And after you left, I realized that I missed people."

Hope floods me. "Are you here permanently?"

He nods. "If it's okay."

"Of course it is." Michael wraps an arm around my shoulders. "We wouldn't be standing here if it weren't for you, Caleb. We owe you our lives."

"Nah. You owe me nothing." His cheeks turn pink. "But I am happy to be here. I thought I'd miss my solitude."

I smile so hard my cheeks hurt, and I wrap my arms around him again. "Thank you for saving us. And thank you for coming."

"Caleb, I would like a dance." Mrs. McGinley reaches out and offers her hand.

Caleb's face flushes again, but he takes her outstretched hand. They're nearly the same age, and watching him draw her out onto the dance floor makes my heart soar. It's adorable.

"Reyna!"

I turn just in time to catch Emily as she wraps her arms around me. "Hey! What are you doing all the way out here?"

She pulls back, holding me at arm's length. "Um, girl, you disappeared from the banquet. Nearly died. Went missing for two weeks. Showed back up. And were abducted before nearly dying again. Be surprised it took me this long to get out here." She pulls me in again. "How are you feeling?"

I laugh. "I told you on the phone last night that I was fine." Ever since the accident, she calls me at least three times a week to check in.

"Still okay?"

I glance up at Michael. "Better than."

"Aww, love. Man, I want love." Emily glances around the room. "Any single men here interested in dating a fiery personality?"

Laughing, I shake my head. "Talk to them. Find out yourself."

"You're no fun." She pulls Michael down and kisses him on the cheek. "Thank you for making my friend happy."

"It's my mission in life," he replies, pressing a kiss to the top of my head. "And now, I'm afraid I want to steal her away for a dance."

I turn and face Michael. "If you think you can keep up."

"Always." He smiles and pulls me against him.

"Caleb showed up a week ago, but I asked him to keep it a secret for tonight."

"You always manage to surprise me."

"I'll do my best to never stop surprising you."

Tilting my face up, I stare into the eyes of my future. My Michael.

"Thank you for giving me a second chance," he says, then kisses me softly.

"I wish it hadn't taken me so long. We lost so much time."

"We'll make up for it."

He spins me in a circle, then dips me and kisses my lips. The ceiling opens the moment he pulls away, dumping thousands and thousands of silver stars on top of us. "There are one hundred thousand stars." He grins at me.

I tip my face up to look at him. Silver stars land in his hair, sparkling beneath the light. "You counted them?"

"I told you I would," he replies with a grin, then leans in and presses his lips to mine.

I just LOVE a swoony second-chance romance! If you loved Michael and Reyna's story, please consider leaving an honest review!

The series continues with Jaxson in TACTICAL

REVIVAL! Keep reading for the first three chapters, and if you'd like more sneak peeks, including episodes of Day at the Diner, an ongoing story told from Lilly and Alex's perspective, and a free digital copy of an upcoming novella featuring Caleb, then click here to sign up for my newsletter, or go to: https://geni.us/DayattheDiner.

CHAPTER 31

Tactical Revival: 1

JAXSON

PLEASE NOTE THAT THESE ARE UNEDITED AND SUBJECT TO CHANGE IN THE FINAL PUBLISHED VERSION.

Sweat beads along my skin despite the brisk March morning, but I continue pushing myself, pumping my arms faster as I sprint down the beach, the fast-paced tune of Brandon Lake's *I Need A Ghost* blasting through my headphones.

The sand is soft beneath my bare feet, making it well worth the risk of accidentally stepping on a shell. There's just something about running the beach barefoot that makes the start of a day perfect. I drop down and knock out thirty push-ups, then jump back up to my feet, wipe the sand from my hands and start running again.

In another mile, I'll repeat, just as I have every single

mile since I started running forty-minutes ago. It's a morning routine I've maintained—even in the rain—since I got clearance from Doc to be active after being shot and nearly bleeding out on the floor of the Hope Springs high school almost a year ago.

I've been at full functionality for seven months now, but even still, I still don't feel strong enough. Fast enough. I'm a Marine. A man who has seen more combat than I care to focus on. And after that, I'd been a detective at the LAPD for a decade. Ten years of chasing down bad guys and solving murders.

But a few months in the small, coastal town of Hope Springs, Maine, working private security with a group of other Veterans I've come to see as brothers, and I nearly died. The sound of a gun going off haunts my nightmares, as does the look on Reyna Acker's face as the man abducting her forced her out of my sight.

I hadn't been able to protect her then.

But I'm going to make sure I don't fail on my next job.

I pump my arms faster, as though picking up speed will force the memories from my mind. The nightmares that still wake me from a dead sleep.

A beep in my ear signifies another mile down, so I drop down and knock out another thirty push-ups, then push up and take off running again. My muscles burn with exertion, but I know that it's these last miles that truly make me strong. When I feel like I can't go anymore, that's when I find my strength.

I've made it another half mile when I see a familiar brunette standing at the edge of the ocean, her bare feet in the sand. The sight of her steals my breath and I come to a stop, heart beating heavily for a whole new reason.

The breeze toys with her dark hair, gently caressing the strands that have come loose from her loose bun. Her jaw is strong, her features elegant as she stares out at the crashing waves. She's wearing bright pink shorts and a white t-shirt beneath a pale pink cardigan.

She's beautiful. Breathtaking. And not for me.

I start to turn around, head back up the beach, but then she glances my way and I note the troubled expression on her face even as she offers me a wave and a soft smile.

So instead of bolting the other way, I head toward her. Stopping at her side, I remove my headphones and shove them into my pocket. "Surprised to see you out here this early."

Margot O'Connell—or rather Margot Anderson, as she's officially divorced now—sighs and brushes some of the strands of her thick, dark hair behind her ear. She's the younger sister of Michael, one of my closest friends and co-workers. She also happens to own the B&B I've been staying in for the past year. "I wanted to see the sunrise. Matty stayed with Michael last night, so I'm flying solo."

I turn to stare out at the sunrise alongside her, enjoying the way the world wakes up. It's my favorite time of day because it's the only point where everything is starting fresh. The day is a blank canvas, so many different opportunities awaiting.

I steal a look at her out of the corner of my eye. Her jaw is set, her shoulders stuff. It seems that for Margot, the day is going to be anything but a fresh beginning. "Everything okay?"

She sighs and runs a hand over the back of her neck. "I'm tired."

"Margot." I know her well enough to see that something is truly bothering her.

"Chad called."

Anger surges through my system. In fact, the amount of fury I feel for a man I've never met should probably concern me.

But Chad O'Connell left his wife. Abandoned his son. And even if I didn't know what it feels like to be left by the people who are supposed to love you most, I'd still see the man as absolutely useless. "What did he want?"

"According to him?" She scoffs. "A relationship with Matty."

"You don't think that's what he wants?" I may have been a homicide detective with the LAPD before moving here to Hope Springs to work at a security firm, but it doesn't take a cop to hear the skepticism in her voice.

"No. I think he wants money. Or more of my dignity. Who knows, really. I just— I wish he would stay gone."

A tear rolls down her cheek and she quickly wipes it away.

Seeing her pain guts me.

I wish I could drive to whatever hole her ex crawled into, drag him out by the collar of his shirt, and tell him he'd better back off or I'd throw him in a cell and toss the key. Unfortunately, that would be assault no matter which way you spin it.

Margot is a good person. Her son is a good kid. Chad will bring nothing but problems back into their lives.

So, unable to do anything other than be here for her, I cross my arms and continue staring straight ahead. Getting involved in personal business—especially the personal business of my best friend's sister—might be a mistake, but I can't keep myself from trying to help where I can.

Margot has been more than kind to me. She's allowed me to stay in the maintenance apartment of the B&B for such low rent it should be criminal, and she cooks me dinner most nights even though I tell her it's truly not necessary since I'm just as happy to occupy a booth in the diner.

Truth is, I prefer her company. Which, is dangerous. Because the more time I spend with her, the more I want to be around her. The beat of her broken heart haunts me because all I want to do is be the one to put it back together.

If only mine weren't in pieces, too.

Clearing my throat, I face her. "What can I do to help?"

"Oh, nothing." She waves her hand as though she's dismissing me away. "I'll get it figured out. I just really thought I was done dealing with him when the divorce was final and he took off for good."

I have no idea what really happened between them, though according to Michael, Chad skipped town one night and never came back. I have my suspicions that there's more to it, and Margot likely doesn't want to give her older brother any reason to let his temper loose.

The former boxer has a reputation for a reason.

Given that I have my own divorce I try to avoid talking about, I haven't pressed and have no intentions of doing so. Sometimes, bitter business is best left buried.

"Do you have a busy day?" she asks me, then turns and starts walking back toward the path that will lead to the B&B.

I follow, even though I wanted to get another few miles in. I sense she needs the company, and since she's been a friend when I needed one, it seems only fair to return the favor. Then there's the whole, I love her company piece of it.

"Michael and I are headed to Smith Harbor for an install." The town is about a twenty-minute drive from Hope Springs, and while we didn't have any business there before, we just picked up a handful of clients after some teens broke into a bunch of neighborhood vehicles.

"You guys have been out there a lot lately."

"Yeah. We've done a couple installs a week for the past two months."

"Good for business." She heads up the stairs, then drops her sandals at the top and slips back into them, her coral-colored toenails peeking out of the top.

"What about you?" I ask.

"The Butlers are checking out today, so I'll be getting that room ready for the Greys, who will be arriving sometime this evening."

Her tone is already exhausted. She'd had to let her cleaning lady go last week, so she's been doing it all. The books. The cleaning. At least Lilly, the local diner owner, and Kyra, our town's baker and the wife of Pastor Redding, have stepped in to help with providing breakfast until Margot can get someone else hired.

She's drowning, though, and too proud to ask for a rescue.

"Well, if you need help—"

"You've done far enough for me already," she interrupts.

"Doesn't feel that way," I reply. "Changing out a lightbulb here and there hardly seems fair in exchange for room and board."

"Trust me, it's fair to me." We reach the B&B, so I rush around and pull the door open. Breakfast is in full swing already, with muffins, donuts, and fresh coffee out and set up in the dining room.

After waving at a few of the guests, I follow Margot back into the kitchen where she pours us each a cup of coffee. She pours a bit of creamer, some honey, and a splash of cinnamon into her cup, then turns and leans back against the counter.

"When Chad and I bought this place, he was supposed to handle the maintenance while I ran the rest of it. It was my dream, so when he started to skip certain tasks, I just let it go. I'd felt so guilty for asking for help." She shakes her head, and my contempt for her ex-husband grows. "Anyways, thank you for your help. And I'm sorry to lay it all on you first thing this morning."

"Don't apologize. I hear venting is what friends do for each other."

She grins at my joke. "I'm worried about how Matty will take it if Chad decides to come around and really does want to start trying to have a relationship with him. Truthfully, they didn't get along even before Chad bailed. Matty isn't into football or baseball. He likes to box, but only occasionally when he can get in the ring with Michael. Really, Matty loves to play chess. It's one of his favorite things to do, and Chad just couldn't understand why. He told him it was the hobby of a weak man." She shakes her head angrily. "Who tells their son that?"

"Someone who has a small brain and doesn't understand the game."

Margot laughs, the happiest sound I've heard from her all morning and it brings me a dose of joy I hadn't been expecting. "You know what? He most certainly does have a small brain." She takes a drink of her coffee.

He'd have to if he left you both behind. I run a hand over the back of my neck, uncomfortable at the track my thoughts have jumped onto. "I like to play chess, and I'm pretty good, too. So let me know if Matty ever wants a run for his money."

Her expression completely lights up, and for a moment, it steals the air from my lungs. Margot is my friend. My best friend's sister, so there can be no romance between us. But I can certainly appreciate the beauty she absolutely radiates. Especially when a smile from her brightens every aspect of my day. "Matty would love that so much. I'll have him get with you about setting up a game."

"Great." I finish my coffee, then rinse the cup and stick it in the dishwasher before turning to Margot. "I'll see you later. Let me know if you have a to-do list for me once the Butlers check out. I really can help if you need me."

As I head upstairs, I mentally tally everything I need to accomplish today. From grabbing breakfast at the diner to updating my paperwork, the installation, and one final follow-up with Doc. It's been nearly eight months since I was shot, but because of the fact that my back has already been broken once and is pieced together with a rod and pins thanks to an IED that nearly killed me overseas, he's been monitoring my recovery a bit closer than he would have anyone else.

According to him, if the bullet had been a centimeter to the left, it would have blown out the rod and likely paralyzed me permanently given there wouldn't have been enough bone left to stabilize me. Thank God it wasn't.

I'm just getting out of the shower when I hear my phone ding. Wrapping a towel around my waist, I cross over and note the name on my screen. My heart drops, and my stomach twists into knots.

Not again.

Rosalie: Hey, I'm just checking in again. It's been a few weeks since we talked, and I would love an update on your care. Talk soon, honey.

I cringe at the message. I'd accidentally answered *one* phone call because I hadn't been paying attention to the caller, and it opened a door I closed a *long* time ago.

Still, I suppose there is some irony in the fact that both Margot's ex-husband and my ex-wife decided to try and make contact on the same day.

My phone rings again and I half expect it to be her calling, but thankfully it's my brother's name on the screen. I have a moment of hesitation, but shove it aside to put the phone on speaker. "Hey, Tyler, what's up?"

"How you feeling, bro?"

"Back to normal. How are things with you?"

He sighs into the phone, Tyler Payne's code for bad news delivery. *Great.* "Not too bad. Sherry is about ready to pop any day now." His wife of two years is pregnant with their first child, a little boy due next month.

"I bet." But I don't buy into the good news. It's his typical delivery method. Hit me with the good news, then slam a right hook of bad right into my jaw when I'm not looking.

"So listen—" He trails off a moment. "Dad called."

"Not interested."

"Jaxson."

"Not interested," I repeat. "You want a relationship with him? Good for you. I, however, want nothing to do with the man."

"You can't hate him forever. He's all we've got."

"No. He's all you've got. I have you, and I don't need him." Our dad left us when we'd been young. Bailed on our mom who was already struggling with being a parent as it was. She wanted nothing to do with us, so she dropped us off at a shelter and never came back. I was sixteen, and my brother was nine.

It's why I have no tolerance for Chad. My father abandoned me, too.

Typer and I barely scraped by, living on the streets until I turned eighteen and could legally adopt him. And that was a fight in and of itself. Two years of stealing food, sleeping in alleys or shelters, and hiding from the authorities who would have thrown us in different group homes and we likely never would have seen each other again.

"What happened to forgiveness?" he asks me, knowing I've been on a journey to grow my faith for the past few years.

"I can forgive him and want nothing to do with him," I reply. "Is that all you had to say?"

He sighs again. "He wants to talk to you. To air things out."

"There's nothing to air out." The familiar anger climbs up the back of my neck and I have to force it down and remind myself that it's not Tyler's fault. He'd been young then, younger when our dad bailed.

He doesn't remember all the fighting.

Or the fists.

But I do.

And while I am working to forgive, forgetting is not something I can do.

"Jaxson, he's our dad."

"I have a Father," I tell him. "And He will never leave me. I don't need Bradley Payne."

"You've got to let the past go or it's going to drag you down," he argues.

"I'm not being dragged down by it," I tell him truthfully. "I just don't have the same interest to share a meal with the man who bailed on us." My phone beeps, so I glance at the screen and note Lance's name flashing. "I have to go. Work is calling."

"We're not done with this."

"We are. Love you, Ty, tell Sherry I said hi." Without waiting for a response, I swap lines. "What's up?" I ask, phone still on speaker so I can pull on my boots.

"How soon can you get into the office?"

"I'm just getting dressed now, so fifteen minutes? Why?"

He sighs into the phone, which tells me whatever news he has is not good. "We've got a missing person," Lance says. "And Sheriff Vick is requesting our help."

CHAPTER 32
Tactical Revival: 2

MARGOT

"**Y**ou are more than welcome, Mrs. Fry." I smile despite being in my office alone, so happy that I could accommodate a date change for her and her husband's sixtieth wedding anniversary trip.

Sixty years.

What is that like? I couldn't make it thirteen.

"You are a darling, Margot. We are looking forward to seeing you again. It's been far too long!"

"It really has. Two years, right?"

"Oh my! It really has been that long, hasn't it?" They'd had to cancel their annual trip last year because of their great grandson being born. But she'd made sure to call and tell me that the little boy and his mother are doing great, and I'd even sent a bouquet of flowers to the new mother.

And now this time they're having to move their trip out because her husband came down with something.

Chad never understood my desire to connect with those who stay here. My need to make them feel cared for. He saw people as dollar signs while I see them as family. Close friends. People who trust me to make their trips special and stress free.

Even as I'd given him credit for supporting my dream of opening this place, I know he only quit his job because he'd hated it and thought this place was going to be an instant money maker. When it hadn't been, and we'd started struggling, he'd gotten angry and resentful.

"I can't wait to show you pictures of little Bobbie! He has gotten so big!" she exclaims, pulling me out of the darkness of my thoughts.

"I am looking forward to it. I'll see you next month, Mrs. Fry, I hope Mr. Fry starts feeling better soon. Let me know if there's anything I can do between now and then."

"Thank you, dear. We will see you and your sweet boy next month. Goodbye!" She ends the call cheerfully and I set the receiver down, then lean back in my chair and close my eyes.

Sweet boy. Matty hasn't behaved like a sweet boy since Chad left. He just keeps getting more and more volitile. Honestly, the closest I've seen him to his true personality is when he'd jumped to action saving Jaxson's life.

He'd applied pressure to the gunshot wound the

former detective sustained, then called 9-1-1 before calling me. I'd arrived right as the ambulance was bringing Jaxson and Silas Williamson, a former Navy Seal they'd brought in to find my brother when he'd been missing, out on stretchers.

Seeing Jaxson Payne looking so weak was far more difficult than I could have anticipated. While I don't know the former Marine well, he's a powerful force to be reckoned with. Anyone who spends more than ten seconds in a room with him can sense it.

My thoughts drift back to the beach this morning. To seeing him standing in the sand, barefoot, muscles slick with sweat, the light breeze toying with his dark hair. Attraction swirls in my gut but I shove it back down.

He's one of my brother's best friends and one of his business partners.

And I have a thirteen-year-old son to worry about. The last thing I need is a romance that will likely fizzle and burn out just like the marriage that was supposed to last me a lifetime did.

My gaze lands on the worn bible sitting on the edge of my desk. Tears fill my eyes because I look immediately to the right of it, and take in the stack of bills piling up. Some of them are pink.

Final notices.

And I have no idea how I am supposed to pay.

As it so often does when this happens, my mind fills with intrusive thoughts.

I'm not smart enough to run a business.

I'm not capable of keeping this place afloat.

I might as well quit now, before I lose what little savings I've managed to put away for Matty's college fund.

God, please help me. I can't do this without You. I know I can't and I know You are here for me. Please keep me strong. Amen.

The bell above my front door dings, so I push to my feet and slip out into the front, a smile plastered on my face. That is, until I see the bane of my existence standing on the other side of my counter.

Seems the devil is working overtime to drive me out of the peace I fight so hard to maintain.

The last year hasn't changed Chad at all. He still looks every bit the jock he'd been when we were in high school, with the years only adding a few more lines to his otherwise youthful face. When he sees me, he shoves his hands into his pockets. "Margot."

I cross my arms. "What do you want, Chad?"

"You won't answer my calls."

"Because I have nothing to say to you."

His cheeks turn red. "You don't get to decide that."

I try to make myself look busy by rearranging the stacks of Post-It's on my front standing desk. That way, maybe, he won't sense the nerves. Being alone with Chad is something I never wanted again. Not after I'd finally had it with his violent outbursts. It started with screaming and throwing things...and then he slapped me.

It was the first and last time he ever put hands on me.

"I do get to decide that thanks to the divorce decree. Now, leave. This is my home and my place of business." My gaze drifts to the entryway security camera and I try to breathe. I know Knight Security monitors it, so even as it's just Chad and me, I know I'm not truly alone.

"I'm not going anywhere until you let me see Matty." His tone picks up that all-too familiar flash of anger.

"*Matthew* doesn't want to see you." Hearing him call our son by his nickname makes me nauseated. He lost that right when he chose to throw everything we'd worked for away.

"Because you have poisoned him against me." He tightens his hands into fists at his sides, and my gaze flicks to the letter opener on the check-in desk to my right. It might be the only thing I can use to defend myself.

"I didn't do anything. That was all you, Chad."

He places both hands on the desk between us and I stiffen. Surely he wouldn't do anything here. Not in the middle of the day when anyone could walk in...but I still can't put my nerves at ease. All the guests have checked out.

No one is due to check in for another two hours.

What if—the door opens again and Silas strolls in. Standing just as tall as Jaxson, the man is six-foot-three of solid muscle. And while the former Navy Seal is a man of few words, his expression speaks volumes. He's pissed that Chad is here, and I send up a thank you to God for my brother pushing to install the security cameras.

"You are not welcome on this property," Silas says, crossing his arms.

Chad doesn't even give Silas a glance. "This is none of your business. Margot is my wife and we are discussing personal matters."

"Margot is your *ex*-wife," Silas corrects. "And she, her son, and her property are all under the protection of Knight Security, which makes it my business."

Chad looks from me to Silas, then back to me, his expression even more furious—if that's possible. "You hired your brother's toy security company to keep me from my son?"

"Toy security company?" I let out a humorless laugh. "I'll be sure to tell Michael that. He'll get a kick out of your appreciation of his company. Either way. What I do and who I hire is none of your business. Get out."

His expression softens and he runs both hands over his face. "Fine. But can we please talk, Margot? I'll meet you at the diner. I really just have some things I want to discuss."

"I don't—"

"Please," he says again, his tone a bit more anguished than before. "I really messed up with our son and I want to make it right."

The part of me not completely obliterated by his

betrayal understands his need to make things right with Matty. And even as I know our son cannot stand his father, I also know there's a part of him that wishes things were different. "I will hear you out," I tell him. "But I won't make Matty do anything he doesn't want to. And that includes seeing you."

Chad smiles, flashing that boyish grin that once had me weak at the knees. "Done. Diner tonight? Seven?"

"Fine."

Chad turns and leaves, completely ignoring Silas. When the door closes behind him, the newest addition to Knight Security, moves closer to my desk. "Are you okay?"

"Annoyed. Angry. Grateful you showed up."

"Elijah called. He's on monitor duty since Michael, Jaxson, and Lance are with Sheriff Vick right now."

A bite of panic pushes past my anger at Chad. "Is everything okay?"

"I haven't gotten the update yet," he replies. The man is all business every time I see him. Except when he's out with his four-year-old niece. A little girl he's been raising ever since her parents passed. "You good, though? I can hang out a little longer if you're worried he will come back."

"No, it's okay." I wave him off. "Thanks, though. Chad got what he wanted, he won't be coming back."

Silas offers me a single nod, then turns and leaves the B&B. The little bell over the door jingles as it closes behind him. Taking a deep breath, I lean my head forward and try to steady my nerves.

Surely Chad is not coming after me for partial custody. Not after he already gave up his rights. Can he do that? Can he come after me now that our agreement is finalized? Anxiety fuels my panic, so I head into the kitchen for a glass of water.

No. Chad cannot have Matty. I told myself that I would never stand in the way if Matty wanted a relationship with his father, but I will fight tooth and nail to keep my son from being forced to share a space with his cheating, abusive father.

Not that anyone knows about the abuse. I never told a soul—especially not Micheal. My brother would have killed him.

The former Army Ranger would have made my ex-husband disappear, staining his soul with the blood of a man undeserving to even breathe the same air as him.

It was not a risk I could take, so I kept it to myself.

The bell dings and a stab of panic shoots through me. Is he back?

"Mom?" a familiar voice calls out.

I press a hand to my heart and take a deep breath. "Back here!" After setting the water down, I head out of the kitchen and meet Matty near the front desk. Anthony Bell, Matty's best friend since kindergarten, is with him. "Hey, boys. You got here early." I glance at the clock, surprised that it's not actually that early.

"We ran." As evidenced by his red cheeks and

breathless smile. "Mom, can I stay the night at Ant's? We've got a science fair project due in a month and we both really want to get working on it."

I study him closely, looking for any tells that it's a lie, but get none. Anthony is a good kid. One of the only boys Matty hangs out with who is an actual good influence on him. Is it possible my son is finally getting back to normalcy? Back to the study-loving, happy boy he was before his world imploded?

A wave of hope flushes through me.

And then the remnants of Chad's desire to get close to him seeps in. What if Chad ruins it? What if seeing him, reverts Matty to the troublemaker he was right after Chad left? Tagging police cars and stealing candy from the corner store?

"Your parents are home?" I ask Anthony.

"My dad will be. Mom is working the night shift at the hospital. I can have him call you if you'd like, Mrs. O'Connell."

I try not to wince at him calling me by Chad's last name.

"Anderson," Matty corrects, elbowing his friend lightly.

His cheeks turn red. "Mrs. Anderson. Sorry."

"No worries, hun. It's a hard habit to break, trust me." I smile. "If you could have your dad call me, that would be great. You guys will just be working on the project then? Not going anywhere?" I hate that he won't be home tonight—that I'll be alone, but Matty behaving like a typical thirteen-year-old is balm to that wound.

"Yes, mom." Matty rolls his eyes. "I'll call you right after dinner and before I go to bed, too."

"And you better not be late for school tomorrow. If you are—"

"I know, I know, trouble city." He laughs.

"You got it." I open my arms and he steps in closer, wrapping his around and hugging me. I breathe him in, enjoying every second of this moment before he pulls away. "You guys have fun. I love you, Matty."

My boy grins at me. A sideways smile that reminds me of his father at that age. Before he became the womanizer he is now. *God, please let my boy stay kind.*

"Love you, too, mom."

CHAPTER 33
Tactical Revival: 3

JAXSON

"You said your daughter is home visiting?" I ask, jotting down a few impressions on my notepad. The way the parents are behaving, the feel of the home we're standing in. This one is nice and tidy, though well-lived in.

These people love their daughter, and it's clear from the photographs adorning the mantle that she loves them too. Which means she didn't just leave in the middle of the night, or walk out without saying goodbye.

Dread coils in my stomach, but I shove it down to focus on the facts.

"Yes," the mother—Mrs. Finch—replies. "She got back home Thursday night since she has no classes on Friday." She sniffles, her grey eyes red and glassy. "She's getting her masters in physical education." Her voice breaks. "I never should have let her go out for that run this morning." She cries. "It was still dark. I should have made her stay."

Her husband pulls her in closer and Sheriff Vick, who is dressed casual in jeans and a t-shirt today, reaches out to take her hand. "Millie, we'll find her. I'm sure she just got turned around. Besides, she's an adult. You couldn't have made her stay."

"I could have tried. She's never been gone this long. Normally, she's back an hour after leaving. She's been gone eight hours now. Eight hours, Ray!" Mrs. Finch covers her face with shaking hands.

I leave Lance to ask the rest of our questions and turn my attention to the photographs. The cute blonde staring back at me has something familiar about her, though I can't quite place what it is. She has the same grey eyes as her mother, her features soft yet refined.

She's slender, a runner, and every photograph has her genuinely smiling. Occasionally in cases I've been called in on, you can tell that home life is little more than a façade put on for social media's benefit. But this family truly love each other.

That familiar sense of dread is back, so I beat it back down again. I spent too many years on the force. Too much time identifying the dead and breaking the news to family members all while promising to hunt down the killer who stole their loved one.

God, please don't let this be another one of those cases.

Please, God, help me find her. Alive.

"Was anything amiss when she left this morning?" Michael questions.

"No," her mother replies. "She got up, drank her smoothie, grabbed her bottle of water and left."

"Without a cell phone?"

"Kleo doesn't carry her phone often," Millie replies, her voice shaky. "And never on runs. She doesn't like to be tied to anything when she's out. Our girl is all about living in the moment," she cries.

"I get that," I reply, offering them a kind smile. Unfortunately, even though I do understand it, it makes it even more difficult to find her. "Did she carry any form of protection? Pepper spray? A knife? A firearm?"

"She carries a knife," her father replies. "After her twenty-first birthday I tried to get her to start carrying a firearm, but she said it weighs her down. She carries most of the time, but on her runs she sticks with the knife."

I nod, then close my notepad and stick it back into my pocket. "I'm going to go walk the area. See if I can't trace her steps."

"We did that this morning," her father insists.

"Sometimes a fresh pair of eyes helps," I say, then offer Michael and Lance a nod, before slipping outside. They both know I do better with facts than people. Not that I can't handle an interview, God knows I've done enough of them to be decent at it. But once I have the base facts, I do much better from a distance. Where I can be in the quiet of my own mind, re-tracing the final moments of a victim in order to discern what happened to them.

It's a bright day, the temperature perfect for a t-shirt given our spring weather. I move down the front steps, then head out onto the sidewalk into the direction her father said she runs in. I don't move much faster than a walk, though, because I want to make sure I don't miss anything.

Even the slightest of details can lead to a break in the case.

Once, a single hair clip abandoned on the sidewalk led us to a woman who'd been missing for three days. And we would likely never have found her if not for the fingerprints on it.

So, as I walk, I look for Kleo Finch's 'hair clip'.

The sidewalk is relatively trim as I keep walking, the grass clipped short on either side of it. The road isn't super busy, though enough so that if she were attacked in broad daylight, the likelihood of someone driving by and seeing the attack is high.

However, it wasn't broad daylight when she attacked. It was five in the morning and I doubt there were many people out on the road then. No one to witness an abduction. That familiar dread coils in my belly.

I monitor the sidewalk for any scuff marks or anything that might allude to a struggle, while also keeping an eye on the houses. If anyone had been out this morning, maybe they saw something.

Definitely worth knocking on doors as I make my way back to the Finch's home.

My phone rings, so I dig it out of my pocket and check the read out. I don't recognize the number, but it could be Lance or Michael calling me from the Finch's for whatever reason, so I press it to my ear. "Payne," I answer.

"It's about time."

Every muscle in my body goes rigid and my stomach churns at the mere sound of her voice. "Rosalie."

"So you do remember me. Here I thought that time in the hospital gave you amnesia."

"What do you want?" I pinch the bridge of my nose and stop walking, knowing that if I continue, I won't be paying near the attention I need to be.

"I want to talk to you. It's all I've been trying to do for weeks now."

"And I told you the last time we spoke that I had nothing else to say."

"Jax," she starts.

"No. Rosalie. I am working and this is hardly the time."

"Listen—" She sighs into the phone. "I want to see you so we can clear the air. I know you're in Maine now, and I'm actually headed to New York in a couple of days for a conference. Can we meet up? I can come to you. See where you're—"

"No. There's nothing to clear."

"There is for me."

"There's not for me," I repeat. "Goodbye Rosalie." I end the call and take a deep breath. The phone rings again and I'm prepared to answer it and tell her just how tired I am of her constant phone calls, but the B&B's number appears on my screen. "Hey, everything okay?"

"Hey, yeah, it is now. Silas came and handled it."

Unease climbs up my spine. "Handled what?"

"Nothing important. Caleb showed up, Elijah sent Silas. Caleb is gone."

"Are you okay?"

"Yeah, thanks." She hesitates a moment, as though she wants to say something else about it, but changes her mind. "Anyway, you know how you offered to help earlier?"

I smile. "Vaguely."

She laughs. "I was wondering if you wouldn't mind grabbing a paint can from Felix's on your way back? I need to do some touch up paint later, but won't have time to get it before the hardware store closes. If not, it's okay, I can figure—"

"I don't mind." I can't help the stupid grin that adorns my face yet again, or the way I can picture her twirling the cord her office phone around her finger because she refuses to go cordless at the B&B.

"Really?"

"Really. We're nearly done taking statements and I can pick it up for you later. If you show me what you need painted, I can take care of that, too."

"Jaxson, you don't need to do that."

"I don't mind. Seriously. Will Felix know what color you need?"

"He will. It'll be waiting at the front counter. Thank you so much. Seriously, Jaxson. You are a lifesaver."

"It is my job. See you later, Margot."

"Bye."

The call ends and I shove the phone back into my pocket. I'm just about to start walking again when I glance to my right and note a path of slightly bent tall grass. It's still standing, but not nearly as high as the surrounding area.

All the distractions melt away and my hand goes to the firearm at my hip. I inch closer to the path, careful where I am stepping so I don't disturb any possible evidence if there is something here.

The hairs on the back of my neck stand on end as a prickling awareness that I'm being watched settles over me. I glance around, trying to see if there's anyone there, but I spot nothing but houses.

No one is on the street. No one looking out the windows.

Still, I can't beat back the feeling as I return my attention to the tall grass. Everything in my gut screams danger, but I press forward, not wanting to spare the moments I would need to make a phone call until I know exactly why it is I'm making one.

A few feet into the tall grass, hidden away just out of sight, a young woman is lying on the ground, wearing shorts, a tank top, and running shoes. Her blonde hair is streaked with sweat and matted with grass. But I see no blood. I rush forward and kneel at her side.

"Kleo, can you hear me?" I ask, checking to feel her pulse.

Her grey eyes flutter open. "I don't—" She trails off, eyes rolling back into her head.

I monitor her pulse, noting that it's far slower than it should be, then use the tactical flashlight I always carry to check the reaction of her pupils. She appears drugged, though uninjured. I pull out my phone and call 9-1-1. "This is Jaxson Payne, I found a barely conscious twenty-one-year-old female and need an ambulance." After rattling off my location, I end the call and tap Lance's contact. "You're going to be okay," I tell her as I wait for him to answer.

"Knight."

"I've got her. About two miles up the road from her house. Ambulance has been called."

"We're on our way."

After ending the call, I shove my phone back into my pocket. Kleo tries to sit up, but she falls right back down, so I offer her assistance while monitoring the way she reacts to movement.

"Do you know what happened?" I ask her, propping

her up with my bent leg at her back, the other knee down to hold us both upright.

"No. I—" She rests her chin to her chest and takes a deep breath. "I was running and—I'm so dizzy. Why am I dizzy?"

Sirens wail in the distance. "Can you remember anything?"

"No. I'm so tired." She starts to fall back, so I steady her as the ambulance pulls up right at the same time Lance's truck and her parents small SUV stop at the curb.

"You're going to be just fine," I tell her, so thankful that it's the truth. *Thank you, God. Thank you for guiding me to this girl so she can get home to her family.*

***

"Hypoglycemia?"

"That's the one," Michael says over my Bluetooth speaker. Since Margot needed me back at the B&B, I cut out as soon as I knew Kleo was going to be okay.

Once they got her stabilized, she was able to tell them everything she remembered, which wasn't much. Apparently, she'd stopped to tie her shoe, and as she was kneeling got dizzy. Sherrif Vick believes she must have wandered into the brush and fallen over. It's lucky I found her when I did.

While it's the more likely version of the story, especially given that there were no signs of assault, there's something about it that is still bugging me. Then again, it could just be my own case history sneaking into the recesses of my mind.

Unfortunately, there weren't many cases in L.A. where the pretty missing girl was found unscathed.

"Is that something that happens to her often?" I ask.

"They were all surprised," Michael replies. "So I'd say no. Doctor said it's not uncommon, though. Especially for runners. And Kleo has apparently been preparing for a full marathon, and has been really careful of what she's eating. Her mom thinks she wasn't eating enough."

"Man, well, I'm glad she's okay."

"Same. So, listen, Chad was at the B&B today."

"Margot told me."

"Oh?" His tone leaves little to no room for accusation, but it makes me uneasy anyway. The last thing I want is for him to think I'm moving in on his younger sister. "She called me earlier to ask if I could pick up some paint for the B&B. She mentioned that Elijah sent Silas over when he caught Chad on the camera."

"So glad we got that facial recognition update to the cameras. Not that Elijah wouldn't have recognized him anyway. I put his face up like a BOLO."

I laugh. Mainly because Michael showed Chad's picture to each of us when the guy left town. "Same. She okay?" She'd sounded fine when I spoke to her earlier, but it's possible she was just trying to put my mind at ease. Would she have told her brother if she'd been left shaken by the visit of her ex?

"You should know, you clearly talk to her more than I do." He laughs. "Just kidding, yeah, she's good. Anyway, Reyna and I are headed to Boston for the weekend, you need anything before we head out?"

"Nope. You two have fun."

"Great. See you Monday morning."

"See you."

The call ends just as I'm pulling in front of Felix's hardware store. Climbing out, I take a moment to stretch and breathe in the salty sea air. Living in L.A., I was near the ocean, but it was never like this. The air was never quite as crisp, the weather as perfect.

Here, the ocean feels like the center of this town, whereas in L.A., the ocean is merely a small part of the big city. You can feel completely alone even as you're in the center of a crowd. Not in Hope Springs, though. Everyone knows everyone here, and you never feel alone.

"Hey, Mr. Payne!" Lanetti Ester, the newest waitress at Hope Diner now that Lilly is on bed rest, jogs up the sidewalk toward me. Her smile is bright, her blue eyes shining with interest.

I'm at least ten years older than her, but the age gap clearly doesn't sway her from the interest she seems to have taken in me.

I plaster a friendly smile on my face—but not too

friendly—and offer her a wave. "Hey, Lanetti. On your way to work?"

"I am. You coming in for dinner tonight?"

I wish I had other plans. But as of now, I've got nothing. And the last thing I want to do is assume I'll be eating dinner with Margot and Matty. "I am."

"Great." She grins and begins to toy with a silver cherry blossom on a chain around her neck. "Well, I'll see you later then?"

"Sure thing."

She offers me another smile, then starts back down the sidewalk, looking back over her shoulder as she does.

I wish I could find a way to kindly tell her I'm not interested. That even if we were closer in age, I'm still dealing with drama from my ex-wife, and a relationship is just not in the cards for me. But I have no clue how to do that and not completely crush her, so I sigh and head into the hardware store.

Felix glances up from some papers he's reading behind the counter, and a smile graces his aging face. "Hey, Jaxson, how's it going?"

"Not too bad. Margot said you have some paint for her?"

"I do." He sets the papers behind and reaches down to lift a gallon of paint from the floor. He sets it on the counter, along with a wooden paint stick and two brushes. "She doing okay?"

"Why do you ask?"

"I saw Chad earlier. He was headed into the diner."

"He there now?"

Felix shakes his head. "Alex said he left a few hours ago." Alex is married to Felix's daughter, Lilly, and the two of them own the diner. "I just want to make sure she's okay. Chad was always a troublemaker, but him leaving she and Matthew like that—I wish we could ban him from town all together."

Chuckling, I lift the can of paint. "Maybe someday," I tell him. "Thanks for this."

"So, listen—" Felix trails off, so I set the paint can down again. He runs a hand through his grey hair. "If you're interested in Margot like that, you should know that we're all really protective of her."

I've been expecting a talk like this ever since I accepted her invitation to move into the maintenance apartment at the B&B, though to be honest, I expected it to come from Michael rather than the hardware store owner. "I'm not moving in on Margot," I tell him. "I'm not looking for a relationship. Fleeting or otherwise."

Felix runs a hand over the back of his head this time. "Sorry, I didn't mean to assume, I just—I don't want to see her hurt again."

"I get it." I smile so he knows I take no offense, then lift the paint, stick, and brushes. "Thanks again. See you around."

As I set the paint and supplies down in my truck, I stop and stare out at the ocean again. I wish I could have told him that I had no feelings for her. That my not moving in on her is because I only see her as a friend rather than my own fear of commitment after the divorce that stole nearly everything from me.

The truth is, I feel a lot more for Margot than I should.

And it's getting a lot harder to bury those feelings.

Maybe it's time to find a new place to live.

TACTICAL REVIVAL IS COMING SOON! PREORDER YOUR copy today!

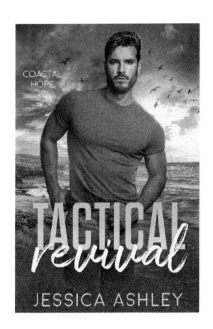

A DETECTIVE STRUGGLING TO PUT DOWN ROOTS. A single mother fighting to make ends meet.

Former homicide detective Jaxson Payne knows a thing or two about starting over. His marriage imploded after he broke his back serving as a Marine overseas. He was told he'd never walk again. However, he was back on his feet within months, proving his resilience is only outmatched by his faith.

After moving to Hope Springs for a fresh start, he's hoping to finally close the door on his past. But it seems the ghosts that still haunt Jaxson have followed him here, bringing danger to his front door.

Margot Anderson had her entire life planned out. Then her husband left her and their thirteen-year-old son. She's spent the last year holding their lives together with prayers and a positive outlook, and then a former Marine moves into her B&B.

Jaxson Payne is everything she should avoid. He's handsome. Strong. And her older brother's best friend. But as danger sets its sights on her, Jaxson is her shield, making it clear that there is nothing he won't sacrifice for her and her son.

If you are looking for a sizzling (but not spicy!) romantic suspense, with a protective Christian hero, a small town that protects its own, and a team of wounded veterans turned private security officers, then Tactical Revival is for you!

Get your copy today!

. . .

THIS CHRISTIAN ROMANTIC SUSPENSE DEALS WITH:

  -*Coping with trauma*

  -*Discovering your worth*

  -*Seeking God in everything*

  -*Healing from your past*

THE COASTAL HOPE SERIES CAN BE ENJOYED IN ANY ORDER!

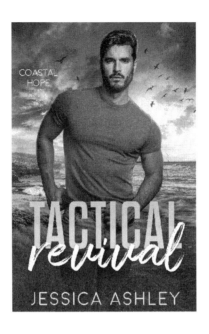

A detective struggling to put down roots. A single mother fighting to make ends meet.

Former homicide detective Jaxson Payne knows a thing or two about starting over. His marriage imploded after he broke his back serving as a Marine overseas. He was told he'd never walk again. However, he was back on his feet within months, proving his resilience is only outmatched by his faith.

After moving to Hope Springs for a fresh start, he's hoping to finally close the door on his past. But it seems the ghosts that still haunt Jaxson have followed him here, bringing danger to his front door.

Margot Anderson had her entire life planned out. Then her husband left her and their thirteen-year-old son. She's spent the last year holding their lives together with prayers and a positive outlook, and then a former Marine moves into her B&B.

Jaxson Payne is everything she should avoid. He's handsome. Strong. And her older brother's best friend. But as danger sets its sights on her, Jaxson is her shield, making it clear that there is nothing he won't sacrifice for her and her son.

If you are looking for a sizzling (but not spicy!) romantic suspense, with a protective Christian hero, a small town that protects its own, and a team of wounded veterans turned private security officers, then Tactical Revival is for you!

Scan the code below with your phone's camera to download your copy of Tactical Revival! Or, go to https://geni.us/TacticalRevival .

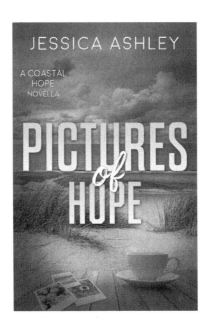

Get your hands on Alex and Lilly's story for free today!

As a travel photographer, my life has been one adventure after the next.

Every location I visit a far cry from the small town I grew up in.

A place I'd been desperate to escape after my ex broke off our engagement and joined the military.

However, home has a way of calling you back.

Three years after my mother's death, I find myself returning to Hope Springs.

But I'm not the only one who came home.

The man who practically left me at the alter is here, too.

And he's determined to heal what he shattered all those years ago: me.

Scan this with your phone's camera to download your freebie! Or, go to www.authorjessicaashley.com/free-novella

About the Author

Jessica Ashley started her career writing spicy romance novels, and had written over sixty before deciding she wanted to use her love of storytelling to help bring people closer to God.

Now, she writes inspirational romance and hopes that each book will draw people closer to seeking His word.

She is an Army veteran, who resides in Texas with her husband and their three children (whom she home-schools).

You can find out more about her and her books by scanning the QR code with your phone's camera, visiting her website: www.authorjessicaashley.com or by joining her Facebook group, Coastal Hope Book Corner.

Scan the QR code below with your phone's camera to connect with her!

Also by Jessica Ashley

Coastal Hope Series

Pages of Promise: Lance Knight

Searching for Peace: Elijah Pierce

Second Chance Serenity: Michael Anderson

Tactical Revival: Jaxson Payne

Perilous Healing: Silas Williamson

———

COMING SOON:

The Hunt Brothers Search & Rescue

Bravo

Made in the USA
Columbia, SC
24 February 2025

54373376R00217